THE WAYWARD
ASTRONOMER

THE WAYWARD
ASTRONOMER

GEOFFREY THOMAS

ILLUSTRATIONS BY DAVID LILLIE

This book is published by Corvus Publishing LLC, in association with Vivid Independent Publishing, LLC. The Dreamkeepers universe is copyright of Vivid Independent Publishing, used under license.

ISBN-13: 978-0-9978235-0-9
LCCN: 2016914391

Distributed by Itasca Books

Cover Design by David Lillie
Illustrations by David Lillie

Printed in the United States of America

This book is dedicated to my grandfather, Kenneth Baskin.
Thank you for giving me a world filled with wonder, a heart full of
love, and a soul strong enough to smile at each new day.

WELCOME TO ANDURUNA

The Dreamworld. It is a reality that exists parallel to our own. Every human on earth has a counterpart, a being that lives in this fantastical realm. These creatures take on all shapes and sizes, they carry our hopes and fears, and they all have tremendous hidden powers, just waiting for the right moment to be unlocked. These other selves are known as Dreamkeepers.

The city of Anduruna is a place that many Dreamkeepers call home. On the surface, it is a peaceful and prosperous place. Most are content to call life within the city walls good enough. But as with many things, a deeper truth lies hidden beneath the surface. Here, all citizens are prohibited from unleashing their inner abilities by a strong-willed and heavy-handed government. Those few that choose to defy the wishes of City Central Authority live on the brink, risking banishment or worse if they are ever discovered. The peaceful veneer of civilization is cracking at the seams, as if fate is waiting for the right hero or villain to come along and light the fuse.

Who is your Dreamkeeper? What would it look like? What would it fight for? For family? For freedom? For love? If destiny rose up and threatened to swallow you whole, would you be brave enough to step forward to meet it?

Welcome to Anduruna. Your journey begins here.

Anduruna

Dune
Sea

Alchera
Ocean

Star Fall Mountains

Galypsa

Ruskol

Talocan

Margate

Norvondire

Sabbaton

Theophanies

Kojiki

Eridan River

Sky Road

Kittim

Diony
Desert

Eridu
Delta

There really is no such thing as true darkness, Halcyon Adhil mused to himself as he stared up at the nighttime sky, marveling at the sheer explosion of color pouring down from the heavens. He could see the gamma-ray bursts from supernovas, the fiery ultraviolet from a young main sequence, the smoldering infrared from an ancient red giant in the final stages of existence. He was looking into the past as he looked up at the stars, a silent witness to events that had transpired eons ago.

Hal blinked his orange reptilian eyes and squinted as a fierce gust of wind pelted his body with stinging glittering flecks of snow and rock. His tail turned away from the wind, coiling up tightly to conserve body heat. Hal was a feathered reptile; a raptor. Neither dinosaur nor bird, he found himself on the terminus between two eras of evolution. His scaly skin was colored a dark jet black, save for patches of green around his eyes and along his limbs. A crown of gray feathers atop his predator-shaped head buffeted and billowed in the blustery air. All Dreamkeepers had distinct appearances as varied as the stars in the sky, so it was no surprise that he hadn't met many others with physical similarities to himself.

What many people had a difficult time getting used to was his tail. The chimera-like appendage had a snake head at the end, with a quartet of blood-red eyes. He looked down at it, tightly coiled into a compact bundle on the stone platform, eyes shut against the wind. Slow awareness of just how cold it was outside on the Starfall Mountains caused Hal to pull the collar of his jacket more tightly about his neck. His tail operated semi-independently from his own conscious will, but was not intelligent or sentient in its own right. It was a sometimes useful, often annoying, broadcaster of his emotional state and subconscious thought. It had no name, as it was just another part of himself. He would no sooner start naming each hand or foot; they were all just parts of his body.

Hal's tail looked up and blinked as a wedge of yellow light poured onto the platform from the now-open door behind him.

"Hal!"

The voice was loud, accusatory, and female. In an instant, the faint halo above his head disappeared as he returned his eyes to the normal visible spectrum, but it was too late to conceal what he had been doing. He turned, looking over his shoulder at the angry purple and gray fox behind him. As she marched towards him, his tail recoiled from her defensively, head lowered. "You were using your power again, weren't you!" Her words were partially swept away by the stinging wind, but they resonated with the clarity of truth.

Hal raised his hands in a gesture of surrender. "Relax, Miri. The mountains aren't going to turn me over to the troopers. We're the only living beings within a dozen miles of here." His voice was deep but raspy, a poor defense against the fury of his research partner.

"That's not the point!" She jabbed a finger into his chest and looked up at him defiantly. "If you keep pushing your luck, one of these days someone *will* see you, and then you'll find yourself in far more trouble than you can handle. The observatory isn't your own personal playground. You're lucky I don't turn you in myself!"

Miri was clearly upset, but Hal knew that she was only acting this way out of concern for his safety. Power violations were not tolerated in Anduruna, even for more benign powers such as his own.

"Yeah, yeah, I know. Sorry." The apology was one Hal had issued many times before. Miri was one of the few people who knew that he had discovered his power to see other ranges of the EM spectrum, and mercifully, she had been a good enough friend to keep it to herself through the years. The wind pelted the two of them with another stinging gust, causing Hal's tail to hiss in dissatisfaction.

"Come on." Miri grabbed his arm and started to lead him away from the edge of the railing back towards the door. "If you stay out here too much longer you'll turn into an ice cube."

She led Hal back into the small observatory, which was considerably warmer and far less windy than the snow-covered mountains outside. The main room consisted of a large hemispherical chamber, housing at its center a sophisticated and expensive telescope. The complicated array of mirrors and lenses was mounted onto a mechanical platform that could be precisely controlled via data scroll to observe any celestial object. This remote facility became Hal's sanctuary, at least for a couple days at a time, whenever the conditions were optimal for conducting astronomical research. Buried among the many peaks of the Starfall Mountains, the observatory sat miles away from Anduruna, comfortably forgotten by all except the brave academics who called it home. For Hal, it was one of the few places he could feel safe using his power to see the world with different eyes.

Crackling flames in the fireplace off to one side helped breathe some life into the mostly open room. A cast-iron kettle hung over the flame, as simmering stew bubbled a rejuvenating aroma into the atmosphere. Hal's tail tasted the air eagerly, angling closer to the fire.

"What's cooking? It smells good." Hal reached for a chair at one of the work tables covered with scattered pages of his own handwritten notes.

"I don't know why you always ask." Miri sighed, walking over to the pot and stirring the contents with a long-handled spoon. "It's always the same thing. Bander meat and vegetable stew." The steam from the simmering cauldron quickly fogged up her glasses, which she removed to wipe clean with the cloth of her heavy lab coat.

Miri, like Hal, was a fellow astronomer and assistant teacher at Calypsa District University, pursuing a doctorate underneath their mutual mentor, Doctor Kincaid. They had known each other for years, constantly competing against one another as they rose through the ranks of academia. She was smart, ambitious, and highly attractive by most opinions. The rumor mill often whispered about all the time they spent "doing research" together out in the mountains, but so far, that's all they *had* been doing. Research. They had settled into an often rivalrous but close friendship over the years, and things had never progressed anywhere further than that.

"I'm hoping one of these days you'll surprise me," Hal answered, pulling the chair out from the table. "Perhaps you'll finally snap, murder one of your annoying students, and cook him into a delicious meal for me."

Miri chuckled, flicking her tail as she placed her eyeglasses back on her face. "You shouldn't joke about—oh, Hal!" The warning was a split second too late. As he started to sit down in his seat, Hal was jolted with an electric shock, sending himself and the chair clattering to the ground. Miri's pet, a spark ryuu-neko named Tesla, had been napping in Hal's chair until the raptor tried to sit on him. The skittish yellow thing darted away in a flash, leaping up into Miri's lab coat with his charged haywire fur crackling in surprise.

"Ugh, damn it, Tesla! Why can't you pick a safer place to sleep?" Hal's tail snapped at the ryuu-neko in agitation as he pulled himself back onto his feet, righting the fallen chair before carefully slipping into his seat. The yellow critter shied away, clinging onto Miri and looking to her for protection as she folded him into her arms.

"Maybe you should look where you're sitting next time. Poor Tesla." She smoothed the statically charged fur of her pet, which was staring worriedly at Hal's agitated snake-tail.

"I don't think that critter ever liked me," Hal grumbled, reaching out with scaly arms to congregate the notepaper littering the table into a single neat stack.

"It's your tail. You know it bothers him." She gave Tesla a small kiss on the back of the head and placed him on the floor. The furtive pet quickly scampered off to places unseen, no doubt to choose another inconvenient hiding place for Hal to discover later on. Miri turned back to the stew and began to ladle the contents into a pair of bowls. She walked over to the table and sat down opposite Hal, sliding his dinner across to him with a wry smile.

"Hey, you know I can't do anything about that." Hal's tail rested on the edge of his bowl of soup, tasting the steam billowing out from it. "Anyway, the weather is really starting to get nasty out there. I think we should head back to Calypsa tomorrow morning first thing before a snowdrift blocks off the main pass back to the city. As charming as the present company is, we don't have the supplies to last us more than a few days should we get stuck up here in the mountains. Remember what happened last year?" Hal offered an amused grunt, shaking his head. "I'm not shoveling that much snow ever again."

"Yeah, you're right." Miri sounded disappointed as she swallowed a mouthful of the piping hot stew, her ears lowering. "I was just hoping to get some more observation data while the moon was full. I don't want to wait another lunar cycle. At least I managed to gather some good rock and mineral samples for the geology lab earlier today."

Hal listened silently as he ate his stew. Though the taste was very familiar, the warmth it gave him was more delicious than the flavor of the ingredients themselves. Hal had always despised the cold, but through his occupation he had been forced to get used to it. There was no better place to observe the stars than from the tops of the Starfall Mountains, save perhaps the top of the Sabbaton Tower itself at the heart of Anduruna. "I think the geology department should send some of their own . . ." Hal trailed off suddenly, his tail now upright and alert, head swiveling around and tongue tasting the air as if looking for something.

"What?" Miri gave Hal a concerned look, but soon it became clear that something wasn't right. "Wait, do you hear that? Sounds almost like an eruption." Her fur started to stand on end, ears swiveling towards the door. Soon the entire building was vibrating from the tremors, as if the whole mountain range were caught in the throes of a mild earthquake.

Hal grabbed his bowl of soup and downed the rest in a single inelegant gulp, standing as he did so. Better to get the food into his stomach before the earthquake spilled it on the floor. He wiped at the few droplets that escaped his mouth and ran for the door. As he flung it open and stepped out into the chilled mountain air, the source of the rumbling became apparent.

Up in the sky, a massive fireball was tearing its way through the atmosphere, shedding smaller short-lived flashes as it descended. It was a meteorite, and a rather large one, too, if they could hear its descent. This rare phenomenon was also alarmingly close to their present location. There was hardly any time to speak before it impacted the ground, slamming into a gully not more than two miles away. The meteor disappeared from sight, silently kicking up a smoky cloud of sparkling dust and pulverized rock to mark the point of impact. A few seconds later, the delayed shockwave reached them, shaking the entire observatory with one last tremor before the ground once more became still. After the vibration settled, the sound of the wind was all that remained.

"A meteor impact this close! Amazing!" Hal was instantly excited, his tail thrashing around eagerly as if trying to get a better view. "To think that something that large would land so close to the observatory! This is an incredible opportunity!" It was rare to hear Hal's voice so animated. The development had clearly riled up the normally calm raptor.

He turned to run back into the observatory to grab his expedition gear, but was quickly stopped by Miri, who planted both hands on his shoulders. "Hal, take it easy. We're not going out there at night in this weather. We'd freeze to death for sure."

"But th—" Hal started to protest but was quickly cut off.

"No." Miri put her foot down, literally, stomping a paw in emphasis. "Freezing to death, bad. We can go search for the meteor tomorrow when the sun is out and snag it on the way back to the city. It's not going anywhere."

Hal blinked his orange eyes at his companion, vertical pupils narrowing, wondering if he should protest further, but she was right. Freezing to death for the sake of science was not exactly plan A. "Fine." His tail kept looking behind him towards the impact site, even as she pulled him inside, nearly shutting the door on it.

Hal let out a vexed sigh and walked back to the table to retrieve his bowl and help himself to a second serving of stew. His tail thrashed restlessly as he ladled the soup; Tesla watched it warily from the top of the telescope, having climbed atop the device during all the excitement. The hapless ryuu-neko was far beyond Hal's attention at this point; he was focused on only one thing: tomorrow he would find that meteor. He only hoped that in a remote place like this, there wouldn't be anyone else showing up to claim it first.

Hal and Miri left the observatory early in the morning and began the long hike towards the meteorite impact site. Even though his face didn't show it, Hal was clearly excited about the find, and his tail energetically bobbed and weaved as they walked, taking in the glittering splendor of the Starfall Mountains. As the sun rose, the rays of light reflected on millions of tiny particles in the snow, showering the landscape with flashes of blue, purple, and white. Even in the bitter cold, Hal felt warmed by the natural beauty of his surroundings.

Miri was slightly less enthusiastic about their early-morning trek. The sharp fox was not a morning person, and though she enjoyed scientific discovery and the occasional adventure, she was the sort of researcher that preferred working comfortably in a lab to climbing sheer rock faces in the morning cold. Tesla, also present for the expedition, sat wrapped around her neck like some sort of living yellow scarf. Like Miri, the creature was not yet ready for adventure, and remained wrapped around her slender frame, dozing in the sunlight and contentedly sharing body heat.

"We have to be getting close now," Hal reported. Staring out into the snow, a faint halo appeared over his head while he used his power to see other ranges of light. An elbow to the ribs quickly snapped him out of it. Looking over, he was greeted with the disapproving glare of his companion.

"I hope so." Miri sighed. "You know I don't like being cold and forced to march when the sun is barely even up yet."

Hal chuckled, his tail resting its head on top of Miri's. "Well, well, please excuse the inconvenience, your majesty. I promise I won't make a habit of doing this every day." His tail flicked its forked tongue and blinked its quartet of crimson eyes.

"You wiseass." Miri chuckled at Hal's sarcasm. After giving him a light jab in retaliation she wrapped her arm around his and pulled herself closer to his side. This caused a slight hitch in Hal's step as he matched stride with the shorter fox, but he thankfully avoided falling face-first into the snow.

"I'm cold," Miri explained, her ears twitching briefly. "Does this bother you?"

"No, not at all." Hal shook his head but said nothing more, content to continue the hike as things were. They walked in silence for several more minutes, the time punctuated only by the occasional howl of wind and the crunching of snow beneath their boots.

"Hey Hal?" Miri eventually spoke up, breaking the quiet.

"Yes, Miri?"

"Do you think we each have a destiny?"

The profoundness of the question caught Hal off guard. "What? Why do you ask?"

"Well, I don't know," Miri started. "I'm just thinking, do we have some sort of unique purpose for being here? For being alive?" She kicked at the snow, sending a sparkling cloud of powder up into the wind. "Am I meant for something special, or am I just another snowflake among millions of snowflakes, blowing around in the wind without direction or control?"

Hal frowned, wind ruffling the dark feathers on top of his head. His tail flicked its tongue at Miri as it hovered alongside her. He wasn't sure if something was deeply troubling his friend, but the question had him pondering his own beliefs. "What do you think, Miri?"

"I think I do have a destiny. We all do. I have to believe that." She rested her head on his shoulder as they slowly marched on. "The world can feel like such a cold and terrible place sometimes, but I don't want to believe that it is. I guess, in the end, I just want to know that my life matters somehow."

Hal was quiet for a long time before speaking his mind. "It's not so cold when you stand in the sunlight." He stopped their close march and turned to face Miri. His voice was quiet, but there was a fire behind his orange reptilian eyes. "I think we can each make our own destinies, Miri. I have no idea where our paths will lead, but maybe someday we will discover if we are worthy of the time have in this world."

"Do you think our lives will be worth it?"

Hal laughed. "I don't know, Miri. But one day we will find out." He gave Miri a warm, reassuring hug before breaking the embrace with a clap on the shoulder. "But enough with the heavy questions already; we've got work to do. The impact site should be down the next drop."

At the cliff's edge they could see the crater. The meteorite had landed along the banks of a river. At the center of a small depression lay an unassuming black hunk of rock that was presumably their fallen star. Hal reached for his climbing gear and began to set up for rappelling down the steep cliff.

"Sorry, Hal. I guess I always have a lot on my mind. It gets lonely up here in the mountains, and you're one of the few people I can talk to." She made an apologetic face as she likewise readied her climbing gear.

"Don't worry about it. I think about those things sometimes too. Besides, we're friends. You know you can talk to me about anything that's on your mind."

"Yeah. I know."

Once the ropes and harnesses were secure, Hal started down the mountainside using short, experienced hops to lower himself bit by bit. As he carefully climbed down the slope of cold and wet stone, Hal could see Anduruna far off in the distance. The massive tower in the center of the city looked no larger than a toothpick. Barely even a memory of greatness. A mere whisper of authority. Out here in the mountains, Mother Nature was the only ruler Hal had to obey.

Miri followed soon after, likewise working down the cliff wall with a practiced and deliberate pace. Tesla, who was used to their excursions by now, simply buried himself in Miri's pack to ride out the descent.

When he reached the floor of the ravine, Hal started towards the meteorite. He activated his power to see the wayward star with his true eyes. He could hear Miri's verbal objection from somewhere behind, but her words were scarcely acknowledged before a blinding light from the meteor overwhelmed his senses. Hal dropped to one knee and blinked his eyes, trying to shake away the spots he was now seeing.

"Hal! Are you all right? What happened?" Miri's footsteps rushed up behind him, and he could feel her hand on one shoulder.

"I . . . I don't know." Hal stood and shook his head. "That falling star, it's emitting so much light in so many spectrums. It was like staring straight into the sun!"

Miri looked over at the offending chunk of rock. Its lumpy, malformed surface sat quietly, half buried in the snow. "It just looks like an ordinary rock to me."

"You don't see the world as I see it, Miri. There is more to this falling star than what appears." Hal slowly started towards the meteor, a faint halo shimmering over his head as he squinted to glimpse at other ranges of light.

The illumination was dazzling, awe-inspiring, and with each step closer he could almost feel the light piercing his mind. A weight formed in the pit of his stomach, growing more massive with every movement closer. Miri watched warily from a distance, arms crossed across her chest, her face drawn into a worrisome frown.

Hal was so close now, standing only a foot away from the fallen star. His eyes burned with searing pain. The weight grew heavier in his chest, forcing him to one knee. He slowly reached out one taloned hand towards the fallen fragment. The closer he came, the louder the silence grew in his ears; suffocating, deafening, and momentous. One scaled finger crossed the gulf of time and space between them, and touched the surface of the glowing light.

Cold. A tremendous, soul-shivering chill. This burning star was colder than any ice Hal had ever felt, and it cut through him in an instant, chilling him to the core.

The silence was unbearably loud, his body so heavy, the light so blinding. He wanted to look away, to move, but he couldn't. An eternity passed in that brief second, as Hal was held captive by the piece of heaven.

"Hal!" Miri's voice was screaming in his ears, and Hal felt himself pulled backwards. Suddenly, Hal's senses returned with a sharp, disorienting flash. It took a few heartbeats for Hal to realize that he was on his back in the snow, looking up at the morning sky and the distressed face of his research partner. The halo disappeared from over his head as he blinked in surprise.

"Hal! Were you even listening to me? I've been screaming at you this whole time, and you just kept walking towards that meteorite!" Miri pinned him to the ground, practically sobbing, her fur standing on end. "What the hell is wrong with you? What happened?"

Hal blinked again. His tail moved groggily as if awakening from some deep sleep. He looked over at the meteorite: it was just a black rock sitting atop a mound of snow. "I . . . I'm sorry. I don't know what came over me. That stone. That star. It was blinding. Captivating. I didn't know what I was doing."

"I don't like this, Hal. I think we should leave this damn thing and pretend we never even saw it. It was almost like it was controlling you!" Miri got off of him and helped Hal up out of the snow.

Hal dusted himself off and looked over at the meteor again. In normal light it appeared to be a harmless lump of ore. It was dull, quiet, and lifeless. He frowned with concentration. "There is definitely something wrong with that thing, but we can't just leave it for someone else to find. We need to study it."

"What? No! Are you crazy? I've got a really bad feeling about that thing. It's not worth it." Miri looked terrified of the meteor, and her unsteady emotions caused Tesla to retreat into her backpack for safety.

Hal held up his hands and sighed. "Look, I'll just take a small sample for study and leave the rest. We might be able to learn something valuable from this thing. I mean, seriously, Miri, we could be looking at an entirely new type of energy source! This could change our world as we know it."

"Yeah, but change it for the better, or for worse?" Miri countered, crossing her arms. "Remember what you said about making the right choices, Hal? Well, I get a really bad feeling this one is going to bite us in the ass. I just know it."

"Maybe you're right, but I can't just ignore an opportunity like this. We can't ever learn and grow and evolve by sticking our heads in the sand, Miri. You of all people should know that." Hal hissed in response and turned away, walking back to the meteor. He used his hammer to chip away a palm-sized sliver and placed it in one of his front pockets for safekeeping. Even a fragment of the fallen star was heavy, and Hal doubted the two of them could carry away the entire meteorite by themselves, even if they wanted to.

Miri frowned, but didn't try to stop him from taking the artifact. "I hope you know what you're doing, Hal."

"In all truth, I don't," Hal admitted, "but we'll learn more about this mystery star soon enough." He stood, dusting off his hands. "Come on, let's get out of here."

"You're not going anywhere!" A gruff voice emerged from behind them, and Hal heard Miri gasp in surprise. "Hands up! Turn around! Slowly!"

The cold weight of fear settled over Hal's body, and as he turned, he found himself staring down the barrel of a springer rifle.

Hal grimaced as he stared down the business end of a springer carbine. The deadly weapon was carried by a rather tough-looking wolf wearing heavy winter clothing. Several tick marks were etched into the wooden stock—seven, to be exact—and underneath the kill tally was carved a single word: *Jessie*. Apparently, this springer had seen some action, and Hal was not feeling all that enthusiastic about becoming the eighth notch.

The wolf grumbled in a deep and commanding voice, "I said hands up!" His breath sent a dense cloud of water vapor floating into the sky, thick like smoke in the cold morning air. Hal slowly rose his arms in surrender as his tail stared unblinking at his captor. Hal wasn't sure who this person was, whether he was a trooper or a thug or a merce-nary, but whoever he was, the wolf was not alone. Behind him were three other armed individuals, all wearing civilian winter clothes but packing firepower that suggested that this entourage was more than just some hikers out for a stroll.

Hal glanced over at Miri as he heard her whimper at the springer barrel pointed in her face. She was fighting hard to keep her composure, and for a moment Hal regretted his insistence on recovering that meteor. Miri was a scientist; she wasn't expecting mortal peril in her day-to-day duties. Had they remained at the observatory, this morning would have been a lot less complicated. A dark-furred female with blood-red eyes regarded Miri with a sneer as she pointed her springer threateningly. The other two armed guards stood back a few paces, springers at the ready but not aimed at anyone in particular.

Everyone stood in silence as the wind sent occasional sprays of glittering powder between them. Finally, Hal cleared his throat, breaking the strained peace. "Um, can we help you?"

The response to Hal's question was swift. His mouth was still finishing the question when a rifle butt smashed into his jaw with a jarring, sickening *thwack*. The unfortunate astronomer tumbled gracelessly down into the snow. Hal coughed and blinked away the spots from his vision, and a warm metallic taste began to flood his mouth. He spat, and into the snow fell two of his teeth, punctuated by a deep crimson spatter of blood. As the stain seeped into the snow, it was renewed by a steady drip of more blood.

The wolf shouted down at Hal: "I did not give you permission to talk!"

Miri let out a cry of alarm but quickly silenced herself, not wanting to suffer the same fate. Another voice emerged from behind the gunmen. It was silky smooth, refined, and yet almost haunting in the way certain words trailed off. "Calm yourself, Brother Miles. These two won't be offering any resistance, will they?"

Hal swallowed some more blood and turned his head to look up at the new voice. Stepping forward from behind the thugs was a woman clad in heavy white robes. Her clothing seemed more ceremonial than purposeful, and when she spoke, everyone, even Brother Miles, paid close attention. Her footsteps in the snow made little sound, almost as if she were a ghost floating over the surface of the icy terrain.

Hal couldn't see her face very clearly. Her features, for the most part, were obscured by the large hood draped over her head and the billowing clouds of fog from each breath exhaled. Yet, through the fog, a pair of bright, glowing, ice-blue eyes regarded Hal with sinister calm.

"These two are fortunate," the hooded woman continued. "They are witness to Celestia's blessing. They do not comprehend the gift she has sent to us, but even nonbelievers can be touched by her presence."

Zealots . . . great, Hal thought to himself as he slowly rose to one knee, wiping away the blood from his face. Hal wasn't a religious man, but he had heard of these people before. The Order of Celestia was a relatively new religious group that worshiped their eponymous goddess, whose eventual return from heaven was foretold to bring everlasting peace, justice, and order. They said that Celestia lived up in the heavens, looking down on the mortals of the Dreamworld, but in all of Hal's time studying the heavens, he had never seen any evidence of their claims. Not that it mattered. Here they were, all the same, pointing weapons in his face and making unsettlingly vague statements about gifts and blessings.

"What do you want from us?" Miri spoke up hesitantly, fear and worry dripping from every syllable as if she were trying to bite back each sound as it escaped her mouth. After Hal had been brutalized for speaking up, it was doubtful she wanted to receive the same treatment. As each second passed, Hal was starting to believe that they may not survive the morning.

"Want?" The hooded woman chuckled to herself, sending an involuntary shiver down Hal's spine. "This isn't a matter of wants, my dear. This is a matter of what is necessary. The goddess sent her gift to this world, but you were not supposed to be the first to witness it. No one outside the Order can know of what she has bestowed upon us." Her voice dropped in pitch slightly, becoming as icy cold as the wind blowing around them. "So what are we to do with you two wayward souls, hmm?"

"Evil bitch," as Hal was now mentally referring to her, walked closer to Miri, emitting a low chuckle. She extended one arm towards Miri's face, revealing a black-furred hand with slender fingers as the sleeve of her robe fell back a few inches. "My, my. You are a pretty one, aren't you?"

Miri recoiled from her touch, offering an uncomfortable but defiant grimace.

"And such fire in your eyes too. It would be a shame to waste the life of such a lovely young lady."

Miri let out a small grunt of disgust as the hooded woman turned away and focused her attention on Hal. He was still kneeling on one knee in the snow, blood continuing to slowly drip from his wounded lips. He experimentally ran his tongue over the shattered portion of his teeth, feeling the gap created by his missing fangs and the sharp crags of a third chipped tooth.

"And you, Mister Hero? What shall we do with you?"

Hal grunted, reaching down to scoop up his missing teeth. "You can start by not adding to the dental bill I'll have to pay now." His deep voice was dry with sarcasm, and he let out a half-amused, half-pained grumble as he slipped his teeth into a coat pocket.

"Oh? Are you sure you want to take that attitude with us, when your life hangs in the balance, young man?" The hooded woman stepped closer to Hal, folding her arms together and hiding her hands in the folds of her robes.

"Hmph." Hal rose to his feet and regarded this mystery woman with a critical eye. He was tempted to use his power to get expanded visual information of her, but he didn't want to give them *more* reason to shoot him than he already had. "Look, just tell us what you want. You already seem to have some issue with us getting to the meteor before you, and I can't magically go back in time and change that. I know

I'm not as pretty as Miri, so why don't you tell me what I need to do to not get shot today?"

The hooded woman laughed again, this time loud and heartily. The echoes of her bone-chilling amusement reflected off the walls of the ravine, returning to the listener in unsettling stereo. "Your boldness is refreshing, young one, but I will not tolerate any further insolence, and even less so will Brother Miles."

Miles grunted in agreement and offered Hal an unfriendly sneer.

The woman continued. "Answer me this, Hero: Did you touch Celestia's gift?"

Hal froze. *Oh shit.* He was pretty sure that touching the holy meteor of these lunatics was something he shouldn't have done. Remembering how it had held him captive renewed his concern that there really was something special about that fallen star. If these zealots got their paws on it, he was fairly certain they wouldn't be using it to bring all people together to hold hands and sing songs of happiness and peace. Unsure of how to respond, Hal set his mouth into a firm line and swallowed some blood, answering the question with stony silence. His tail hovered over his left shoulder, blinking each eye sequentially at the woman.

"Oh? Not feeling very talkative anymore?" Miles grunted in amusement. "The lady asked you a question, boy. Did you touch the bloody rock or didn't you?" He cocked his weapon, and a tightly coiled spring-propelled round settled itself in the firing chamber with a distinctly tangible *clack.*

"Leave him alone! We haven't done anything to you. Please, just let us go!" Miri cried out, her voice pleading for sanity and calm. "We promise we won't tell anyone about—"

"Shut it!" Miles fired his springer into the ground at Miri's feet, sending a short-lived splash of glittering powder flying up at her knees. The spring and empty casing from the now-spent round fell silently into the snow at his side. "You're next, missy, so if I hear you make another sound, the next one goes through your throat!"

The robed woman continued to stare at Hal, those haunting cerulean eyes peering out from beneath her hood. "I haven't heard your response yet, Hero. Answer me now or we will shoot the girl."

Despite the calm in her voice, Hal knew this was not an empty threat. He begrudgingly offered an answer, hands clenching into fists. "Yes, I touched the bloody rock, all right? Leave Miri out of this. She didn't touch it."

"Is that so?" The robed woman sighed and shrugged her shoulders, turning towards the four armed guards. "Very well. Seize the girl. We will bring her back to Anduruna and the Archbishop. I'm sure he can find some use for her." She turned her glowing blue eyes towards Hal one final time. "As for the raptor . . . kill him."

"What? No!" Miri cried out in desperation. "Please stop this!"

"Get on your knees!" Miles commanded Hal, leveling the weapon at his chest.

"Like hell I will!"

Miles fired his springer again, this time sending a round straight through Hal's right knee. The joint shattered as the metal slug buried itself in his flesh, and Hal screamed in pain as he fell. His sound was the primal cry of a doomed man. His anger and his pain rebounded off the walls of the gully before escaping out into the cold morning sky.

"No!" Miri lunged at the nearest soldier, attacking the other woman tooth and nail, her voice filled with desperation. She was quickly overwhelmed, however, as two others joined the fray and physically wrestled Miri down into the snow. She fell kicking and screaming, continuing to struggle.

Adrenaline coursing through his veins, his heart racing, Hal reached for his climbing pick and struggled to bring himself back to his feet in spite of his shattered knee. Miles smiled and aimed his gun at Hal's skull, gloved finger tightening on the trigger.

"Agh!" One of the soldiers wrestling with Miri cried out in pain and fell into the snow, convulsing heavily as smoke rose from his singed clothing. Tesla, who had been hiding in Miri's pack the whole time, had emerged in defense of his master and delivered a high-voltage electric shock to one of the soldiers. The little yellow furball darted around between the legs of his opponents, sending them into momentary chaos.

"What the—?" Miles turned towards the commotion and the valiant ryuu-neko. He was distracted for only a moment, but Hal was fighting for his life, ready to do anything in the name of self-preservation. Roaring in anger, Hal pulled himself up on one leg and swung his climbing pick at Brother Miles with all of his strength.

Miles realized his danger at the last moment, but it was too late to react. The sharp end of the pick hit him square in the throat and didn't have the courtesy to stop there. Designed to punch through ice and stone, the pick had a far easier time with skin and bone. It slid effortlessly through flesh, stopping only when the blade was buried all the way up to the wooden shaft. As Hal finished his swing, a dark spray showered his face with a fine mist of gore, quickly followed by a hideous gasping and gurgling sound. Miles collapsed into the cold snow, coughing up heavy globules of blood, grasping weakly at the large pick still buried in his throat.

Hal fell alongside him, unable to keep his balance. He immediately scrambled for the fallen springer, his only hope for survival.

The hooded woman, who had initially left the dirty work to her cronies, quickly drew a springer pistol from her robes, turning it on Hal.

Time seemed to slow to a crawl.

Hal's hands closed around the snow-covered rifle.

The pistol turned towards his chest.

He lifted the barrel and swiveled it towards the woman.

Her finger tightened on the trigger.

His finger tightened on the trigger.

Hal lost the duel. The pistol slug hit first, slamming into his chest with the force of a sledgehammer. A sharp splintering sensation shot through his body as his torso was rocked sideways from the impact. His own shot flew wide, taking out a small notch in the woman's hood but failing to hit the face inside.

The young astronomer had no time to even scream before she fired again.

And again.

And again.

Each round was a fireball of murderous intent that sent his limp body jerking backwards.

Oh god, Hal thought to himself. *I'm dying. I don't want to die!*

The woman calmly paced forward, stopping only a few feet away from Hal as she aimed her pistol one final time at Hal's chest. "Goodbye, Hero."

Hal thought he saw a smile cross her lips before she fired again. The last round slammed Hal's body backwards into the snow, where he lay in an expanding pool of his own blood. He could hear Miri cry out in sorrow and rage, but he couldn't see her. Already the corners of his vision were beginning to black out, as if he were descending down some long, dark tunnel.

He felt something kick his body, and he started to slide backwards through the snow, carried by gravity down the shallow slope.

"Hal! Hal!" Miri's voice grew fainter as a suffocating silence settled over his senses and the world faded away.

I'm sorry, Miri.

Hal's last thoughts were of her as his body slid into the water, where eager currents dragged him down into a frigid embrace. Somber and silent, the aquatic procession stole him away, carrying his body off to destinations unknown.

4

I*f I had known what would await me the day I first stepped onto that boat, surely I would have been too afraid to even begin the journey.*

Hal stirred. He could hear a voice, faded and muffled, reciting a story with slow deliberation. The voice continued:

But my ignorance was my strength in that moment. As the crew cast off the bowlines and our frigate slipped free from harbor, the captain said to me with a smile, "Pity them, son. Those poor souls we leave behind will never understand."

"Understand what, Captain?"

"That the heart of the tempest is the only place we belong."

Hal's tail was the first to open its eyes, and in his mind he could feel the sensation of shape, light, and movement. Hal struggled mightily to open his true eyes, and when he finally did, he was greeted with a warm light and a blurred world that was slow to come into focus.

"Hey Grampa, lookit! Mister Tail is waking up!" The second voice was that of a young girl, squealing with joy.

"Ah, very good, Sasha. Be a good girl and get a cup of water for our guest. We will finish story time later," the first voice replied, cracked with age, sounding like a squeaky floorboard mixed with a rusted hinge.

Hal blinked, and through the haze he could make out an ancient-looking owl sitting at his bedside, closing a large leather-bound book into his lap. The little one was scampering away through the doorway, eagerly fulfilling the task asked of her.

The owl placed the book on a small nightstand next to the bed, and Hal could see now that he was lying in a cozy little bedroom of what appeared to be a rustic cottage. His clothes were gone, and much of his body was wrapped with thick white bandages. Though Hal tried to move, his body felt like it had been turned to lead, and even the smallest twitch of a finger consumed all of his strength and effort, leaving him exhausted.

"Let me help you." The old man reached forward and gently helped Hal pull himself up to an upright seating position, adding an extra pillow to support his head. The owl gazed into Hal's eyes, welcoming him back into the land of the living with a gentle but somewhat sad-looking smile. "It is not often that we get visitors out here in the Eridu delta. Even less often do we get visitors who have traveled to the land of the dead and returned to speak of it."

Hal struggled to speak. "I . . ." His voice cracked and halted, and he only then became aware of a desperate thirst that tightened his throat. As if on cue, the little girl returned, clutching with two hands a crude ceramic mug filled with water. Perhaps it had been filled a bit too much, as it splashed and sloshed with each eager step, spattering the wooden floor.

"Here's your water, Mister Tail!" She held the cup aloft above her head with a smile. As Hal's vision continued to come into focus, he could see that she was a small raccoon with large green eyes, not much more than four or five years old. She stood on her toes to raise the glass higher, expecting Hal to take it from her.

Due to Hal's difficulty moving, the owl accepted the water in his stead, patting the young girl on the head. "Thank you, Sasha." Gingerly, the old bird raised the cup to Hal's lips and tilted it forward. "Slowly now."

The water tasted cold and sweet on his tongue, though the chill of it caused Hal to cough violently on the first attempt to swallow. The owl patiently waited for him to recover, and eventually Hal was able to manage a few gulps between coughs. Even though he was gasping for air, the water had provided a small token of rejuvenation, enough to attempt to speak. "Who—?" Hal winced as a sharp pain jabbed from within his chest, reminding his lungs that they should not do too much. "Where . . . am . . ."

"Easy, traveler. Easy." The owl placed a hand on Hal's shoulder, gently pushing the wounded raptor back into the pillows. "You must not push yourself too hard. You are still in very bad shape." The caretaker placed his hand on his chest, introducing himself once Hal was resting comfortably. "I am Mordecai. This little one is my granddaughter, Sasha."

The girl smiled, fidgeting out of shyness. She seemed more interested in the head on Hal's tail than in Hal himself, and she reached out to pet his tail with a smile. "Hi, Mister Tail." His tail blinked its eyes slowly, but remained resting without complaint on the edge of the bed.

Mordecai continued, "You are in my home. A simple farm on the banks of the delta." He reached out one arm and wrapped a wing around Sasha. "It was little Sasha here who found you, quite by accident, while fishing for our supper. We pulled your body from the water and brought you ashore, believing you to be dead. That was four days ago." His demeanor grew more serious as he gazed with concern at Hal's bandaged body. "You can imagine our surprise that you were still alive. You had very severe injuries. Very severe, indeed. In all likelihood, we should not be having this conversation right now."

29

Mordecai shook his head, a grim expression forming over his face. "I had nearly finished digging you a grave when my wife, Illyana, noticed that your heartbeat had returned."

Blinking his eyes, Hal saw even more of the room and noticed an older woman, a raccoon with similar coloring to Sasha, leaning against the door frame. Her eyes were closed and her head was turned to have her ears towards the conversation, listening quietly from the background.

"The fact that you are now awake and alive is nothing short of a miracle."

Hal took a few deep breaths, trying to get his head around his new situation. The last thing he remembered was the pain of being shot. The dull sensation of falling. Cold. He did not dream. He did not see his life flash before him. There had been only emptiness, and suddenly he was here in a bed with an unfamiliar man telling him how he was lucky to be alive . . . again.

"What is your name, traveler?"

Hal blinked again and tried to focus. It was almost like he was learning to speak again, and his muscles were slow to respond to what his brain asked of them. "Hal. My name is Halcyon Adhil."

"That's a funny name!" The little girl hopped on her toes, giggling to herself.

"Sasha!" Mordecai scolded her with an admonishing frown. "That is not polite. Go with Grandma and get ready for bed. I need to speak with Mister Adhil alone for a while."

Sasha reluctantly obeyed and scampered out of the room, grabbing her grandmother by the hand and leading her away out of sight. Once they were gone, Mordecai sighed and shook his head. "I apologize for my granddaughter. She is quite eager."

"No, it's ok." Hal took another deep breath, finding it difficult to get rid of the tightness he felt in his chest. As his nerves came back to life, he was gradually being overtaken by a throbbing pain that started in his knee but moved up his leg to spread throughout the edges of his chest. The pain threatened to spider inward towards his heart, but it seemed to fade before reaching the center. He looked at Mordecai and tried to swallow before speaking. His mouth once again felt terribly dry. "Are you a doctor?"

"I was, once. And lucky for you I still keep some of my equipment here." Mordecai seemed to understand Hal's thirst and once more helped him sit up, holding the water to his mouth. As he did this, he continued his explanation, growing far more serious and clinical in his description now that they were alone. "You had multiple springer wounds from two different-caliber weapons. Your knee was shot by a rifle; those rounds are designed for penetration. It shattered the bone and passed through, but did not destroy much surrounding tissue. With sufficient time to heal, you should be able to walk with maybe only a minor limp."

Hal grimaced as he finished his water, some droplets falling from his lips down onto his bandaged torso. That wasn't the worst news in the world, but it wasn't that great, either.

"As for your chest wounds," Mordecai continued, "they were quite significant. They would have been irreparably fatal under normal circumstances, but as I was removing the shrapnel from your body, I discovered something." He hesitated, almost unsure which words to use. "Something I have never seen before."

He reached over and produced a data scroll, which appeared to be some sort of x-ray image of Hal's body. In his chest there were several irregularly shaped fragments highlighted in red. Hal instinctively put a hand over his heart when he saw the image, and wondered why he could feel no pain, no sensation, no anything other than that clamping tightness in the center of his chest.

Mordecai cleared his throat. "These points are all fragments of some sort of rock that you had in your front pocket. It looks like a bullet struck the rock and embedded several slivers of it into your flesh.

I was going to attempt to remove the shrapnel, but I found that your body had . . . merged with the foreign debris." Mordecai nodded to himself, as if agreeing that "merged" was the proper word to use. "The cells around these fragments are integrating the shrapnel into themselves, changing their cellular structure, almost as if they were feeding on it and evolving from it. It may be this mutation that has kept you clinging to life when you should have died."

Hal looked down at his chest and allowed himself to use his power. Somewhere buried under the bandages and the skin he could see several blue points of light. From each of those points, small tendrils had begun to snake out like fluorescent veins or arteries. Mordecai seemed surprised to see a halo form over Hal's head, but he didn't raise any objections. "I can see them." Hal swallowed and looked back up at Mordecai. "What does this mean?"

"It is hard to say," Mordecai reluctantly responded. "What it *looks* like is a new form of cancer. Your cells are mutating, and the mutated cells appear to be expanding. Unfortunately, most cancers are fatal once they've spread too far. I do not know if this . . . evolution . . . will ultimately destroy you or save you. Only time will tell."

Hal was silent for a long time. Mordecai placed one hand on his leg and gave him a sad smile. "Take comfort in the fact that you have been given a second chance at existence. Perhaps a chance to make different choices, no? Say the things you never had the courage to say? Do the things you never had the opportunity to do?" The owl patted his leg.

"Maybe." Hal gave a noncommittal answer, deep in thought, a troubled look twisting his face into a grimace. The throbbing in his leg was distracting, and it was still quite difficult to speak through the pain. His thoughts drifted to Miri, and every time he closed his eyes he could hear her voice in the back of his head. Sometimes it was the sound of her screaming. Other times it was quiet conversations and simple moments they had shared together.

Was she even alive? Even if she was, she must think that Hal had been killed. He didn't realize until now how much he had taken her friendship for granted. Miri was pretty much his only friend, given the isolated life he lived. Maybe they could have been something more . . . but he had never allowed himself to acknowledge that possibility. Why? Hal wasn't sure why. The reasons all seemed so petty, so distant. They didn't matter anymore. How much time did he have left to make things right?

"I am sorry to burden you with heavy truths so soon after you have woken." Mordecai made an apologetic face. "But I believed it best to tell you now so you do not live the rest of your days under false pretenses."

As difficult as it was to hear, Hal was grateful to learn the cold, hard facts now rather than later. "How fast is it spreading? Can you tell?"

Mordecai shook his head. "I have only been able to observe you for a couple days, and mutagenics are not my area of expertise. The best I can tell is you have maybe a few months before the majority of your biological structure has changed. It is impossible for me to predict anything more precise without more data."

"I see." Hal was silent once more, clutching one hand over his heart as he stared up at the rough wooden ceiling. A few months? That wasn't much time at all. He wasn't even sure if he would be able to walk in a few months.

"I think I've given you enough to think about for tonight." Mordecai placed the glass of water on the end table next to Hal's bed with the weighty *thunk* of ceramic on wood. "Rest up, young Halcyon. If you need anything, just call out and one of us will help you."

Hal nodded without looking over, though his tail managed to lift itself to watch Mordecai move towards the door.

"I will check on you in the morning. Sleep well, traveler." With that, Mordecai extinguished the light and shuffled out of the room, leaving Hal alone with his thoughts.

Hal wasn't sure how long he lay there in bed awake, an agile mind racing inside a broken body. At some point it began to rain, and loud, heavy raindrops splashed onto the roof of the cottage. The intensity quickly increased from scattered thumps to a cacophony of sound and nature. He looked up at the ceiling and could see nothing but the dark shadows of a lightless room, blind to the rain beyond.

Closing his eyes, Hal thought about many things. He thought about home, about family, about the stars in the nighttime sky and the chill of the mountains. He thought about the joy of discovery, the comfort of a friend, the contentment of deep conversation. He thought about the rain and the power of nature and the nature of power. But most of all, he thought about the dreams he never spoke of. The love he never shared.

When he opened his eyes again, he looked through the ceiling and through the clouds to the burning points of light beyond, taking in a sight that he and he alone could ever see. He asked the stars no questions and begged them no wishes, and they responded in turn with only majesty and silence. It was not just a beautiful sight: it was beauty itself. The very concept distilled into its most eternal and basic truth. Even the most wretched and hopeless souls would be moved to tears, if only they could ever see it. This lonely glory was something Hal had to carry alone.

I will find you, Miri, Hal promised, *and we will watch the stars together again at least one more time.*

With the universe as his mute companion, Hal eventually drifted off to sleep, and in his final thoughts of the evening, he thought about only one person.

5

Hal was bedridden for the next few weeks as his body continued to heal. Though he was eager to get back on his feet and back to Anduruna, he found Mordecai's small family to be very good company and capable caretakers. Each day they would share their meals with him, all crammed into the same small room to provide him company and conversation. It was through these conversations that he came to know each of them very well.

Hal learned that Mordecai had been a traveling doctor for several decades, satisfying both his wanderlust and his desire to help others as he ventured from region to region treating anyone who needed his skills. Be it rich or poor, citizen or bandit, Mordecai always helped anyone who crossed his path, and espoused the idea that all life was worth the effort to save.

It was during Mordecai's travels that he met Illyana, who was in fact completely blind. She suffered from a degenerative disease that destroyed her optic nerves, and had lost her sight quite young. Originally just another patient for the wandering doctor, she eventually became his love, and the two came to find happiness and fulfillment together. Their pairing was unusual, but it had survived the test of time.

Sasha was four. Four and a *half* actually, as the young girl would often insist. She loved helping her grandparents with tasks around the cottage and declared with pride that she was going to be a sailor when she grew up. And a princess. She always called Hal "Mister Tail," and loved to poke and play with his unusual four-eyed appendage just to see how it would react.

Every evening, Sasha and Mordecai would have story time in Hal's room, and it had quickly become his favorite part of the day. Hal would read a story to Sasha, and then she would attempt to read a story back to Hal, usually from a much simpler children's book. She was young, but bright, and full of life. A stark contrast to Hal's own crippled state. Over the days that followed, Hal shared the story of his fateful morning and the events that had brought him to Mordecai, and his caretaker was merciful in not prying too deep into the all-too-fresh and painful experience.

It took a handful of weeks, but eventually Hal had healed enough to where he could take his first hesitant steps out of bed. His knee was still wrapped in a sturdy brace, and he couldn't walk so much as hobble along with the help of some crutches. Each step sent a spike of pain jolting through his leg, but it felt so good to finally get out of bed that Hal barely even noticed it. Reclaiming some small measure of mobility was an important first step, and gave Hal hope that maybe he could reclaim his life as well. In fact, both he and Mordecai were surprised just how quickly his body was repairing itself. Perhaps it had something to do with the meteor shard, or pure strength of will, but Hal was just happy to be alive and moving again, regardless of the reasons.

The morning that Hal finally emerged from bed, Sasha had already gone outside to fish and play, and he found Mordecai and Illyana out in the garden, enjoying the warm sunlight and gentle breeze of the Eridu delta. Mordecai sat alone on a stone bench, watching Sasha off in the distance, as Illyana tended to the flowers in her garden.

"Ah, so you've finally managed to stand on your own!" Mordecai's croaking and aged voice greeted Hal with delight. "How are you feeling?"

"All things considered, I feel pretty good. Better than dead, at least." Hal inhaled a deep breath of the sweet-smelling garden air as his tail blinked up at the sun. "For a long time, I wasn't sure if I'd ever manage to crawl out of bed. Everything hurts, but I've gotten used to the pain."

"Good, good. Despite your injuries you are a healthy young man. I have high hopes for your ability to make a full recovery." Mordecai patted a space on the stone bench next to him. "Come. Sit. Illyana and I will be happy to have your company."

Gingerly, Hal lowered himself into a sitting position, trying to keep as much weight as possible off of his wounded leg. The process was difficult, but once he was seated he could take another deep breath and wait for the pain to subside. He took a moment to simply enjoy the outdoors and the fresh air. "You know, this is the first time I've been to the delta. It's beautiful." Hal's tail coiled itself up on the edge of the bench, happily basking in the sunlight.

"Yes." Illyana spoke up, not bothering to take her hands away from her task. She spoke with a mild accent, as if Anduruna was not her original home. "It is peaceful here. A far better place to raise a child than the busy districts of the city. Sasha can simply be a child, full of life, without a care in the world."

Hal watched Sasha out in the distance, splashing around on the shallow banks of the river. "Yes, she certainly seems happy." Hal hesitated before asking a question that had been on his mind. "You said that Sasha is your granddaughter, so, uh, where are her parents? Do you raise her yourselves?"

"Ah." Mordecai's voice lost its earlier cheer. "Her parents disappeared a few years back. They were sailors, and after departing on a journey one day, they simply never returned." The old bird sighed heavily, shaking his head at the ground. "There was never any wreckage, so no one knows for sure, but the ocean is as dangerous as it is beautiful. Sometimes . . . it simply swallows people whole." Mordecai shook his head again. "I am sorry for not telling you earlier, but they are sad memories, and not something I enjoy thinking about."

"No, no, it's all right. I didn't mean to . . . I'm sorry." Hal fell silent. A chill shot through his chest, and he rested one hand there, wincing away the pain as he took a few deliberate deep breaths. It would happen, every now and then, the sudden shock of pain and cold, and he did his best to cope. When it didn't feel like icicles stabbing through his heart, his chest was numb and tight. The new sensations were a reminder that he was still recovering from near-fatal injuries, and that the rock that perhaps had saved his life still had cold, stony shards embedded underneath the scar tissue.

"You don't need to apologize," Illyana responded in a calm voice. "Life challenges all of us, and rarely waits for us to be old and wise before it begins. Sasha is so young; she has only a few memories of her parents, and she is not growing up without family. Mordecai and I are here for her, and she is becoming such an eager and adventurous little girl." Illyana smiled and raised her head up into the warm sunlight. "We are blessed to have her."

"Yes, I can see that." Hal nodded and looked out at the river in the distance, wondering how his life would have been different if he had grown up out in the delta, removed from the city, surrounded by relative peace and tranquility.

"Hey, Mister Tail!" Sasha bounded up to Hal with a smile. In her tiny arms, she proudly clutched a bander-fish: a proud prize from a morning spent playing along the shore. The iridescent stripes that gave the fish its common title shimmered in the morning light, reflecting into the air alongside Sasha's peals of laughter. "I brought your tail some breakfast!"

Without waiting for Hal's response, Sasha hefted the fish into the air, trying determinedly to feed it to Hal's unusual appendage. It bobbed and weaved just out of the way of her clumsy attempts, eliciting a fresh cry of joyous laughter. Hal smiled at her raw, innocent energy, deciding to forgo the lengthy explanation on how his tail didn't have a digestive tract. Instead he offered a more suitable explanation. "I don't think it's hungry, Sasha. Maybe later."

"Awww!" Sasha hopped up and down, nearly losing her grip on the slimy catch. "Ok! I'm gonna catch another one for later!" The little girl wasted little time, scampering off to brighten another corner of her undiscovered world.

Hal laughed as he watched her run off, admiring her zeal for being a child. For being alive. Miri would love her.

Miri.

Hal's smile darkened and disappeared. Miri wasn't here alongside him, enjoying a peaceful country life. She was back in the city, taken away to who knows where, deep within the walls of Anduruna.

Mordecai seemed to notice Hal's change in expression, taking the opportunity to broach the subject. "I am wondering, young Halcyon, who do you call family? You have not spoken of any of your own in all this time." The old bird rested both hands on the top of his cane, looking over at Hal with large curious eyes.

The wounded raptor sighed and shook his head. "If you really want to know, I'll tell you about my family. But it's not something I usually talk about." Mordecai nodded, but said nothing. Illyana continued to work in her garden but kept one ear turned to hear his story.

"I don't know how familiar you are with the district of Calypsa, but it can be a dangerous place. Order is a delicate balance of power between different organized criminal families, city officials, and cutthroat street gangs. My family, well, my father, was a high-ranking boss in the Cordova mafia."

Hal shook his head, realizing that he had to finish the story now that he had started. "They did the usual stuff: smuggling drugs and weapons, illegal gambling rings, extorting local businesses, and bribing public servants to turn a blind eye. I actually ran a few jobs myself, once I got older. Both me and my twin brother, Marcus. Nothing too serious, just courier work mostly, delivering messages, money, those sorts of things." Hal laughed a little to himself, while his tail seemed to watch his head with confusion. "Man, I thought I was such a hotshot back then. So did Marcus. We were such idiots."

Hal's tail curled back up in the sunlight and stared at the ground. Mordecai was watching him with a thoughtful expression that seemed a little sad, but after a moment of silence came and went, the story continued, seemingly of its own will. "Our mother never approved of any of it, of course. She loved us with all her heart, but she saw the path we were walking and what lay at the end. Not many professional mobsters have a story that ends happily ever after. Dad kept us from ever getting involved with the real dirty work, but we knew that we would be made men if we stuck with it long enough.

"The problem with organized crime is, well, I guess the name says it all. You make enemies with rival families. You compete for money, resources, and territory, and to secure those resources, violence becomes the means to the end. Dad was a big shot, maybe doing a little too well, disrupting the balance, and because of that, a hit squad was sent to remove him from the equation."

Hal winced, fighting back another sharp lance of pain through his heart, and took a few deep breaths. Mordecai's expression had grown grave and sad, the lines on his face morphing from creases to deep craggy valleys. "We don't know who exactly was behind the attack, but the end result is all that mattered. They burst into our house around dinnertime, opened fire on anything that moved, then ran off into the night. Marcus and I were out making a drop, but Dad, Mom, and Katya, our little sister, were home.

"We returned from our job only to find that our family had been massacred. I don't think I can use words to describe what that felt like. I've spent years trying to bury that memory." Hal bunched his hands into fists, clenching them so tight he nearly pierced his own scales with his talons. Slowly he relaxed them after a long while.

"I'm sorry." Mordecai offered the only words anyone could offer. Illyana remained silent, having stopped tending to her garden once Hal had begun speaking.

"Look, you wanted to know about my family, so now you know: I don't *have* a family anymore." Hal's voice had grown angry and sharp, and he nearly spat each word as if trying to rid his mouth of some foul taste. It took Hal a moment to settle his electrified nerves before continuing. "My brother and I parted ways after that. We each dealt with our grief differently. I went legit, studied astronomy at the university, and removed myself from the world. Those memories seem so far away when you stand alone at the top of the mountains and look up at the sky."

Illyana seemed to be considering Hal's statements carefully, no doubt measuring the weight of his words against his tone of voice to dig deeper for the truth only she could see. "Where did your brother go? Surely you would have supported each other through those difficult times."

"Marcus? Well, I haven't spoken to him in over five years." Hal felt a twinge of shame as he admitted that tragic fact. "Whereas I left the city behind and lost myself in the snow and the stars, Marcus ventured further into the chaos and lost himself among the din of the city. He bounced between jobs, lovers, ideals, religions. He was always looking for some answer but never found one. He was filled with so much rage, so much restlessness." Hal sighed. "We didn't see eye to eye on where to go after it all happened. We had some arguments, those arguments led to some fights . . ." Hal shook his head, staring at the ground. "We lost touch and went our own ways. I have no idea where he is now."

"How sad." Illyana walked over to Hal, taking a seat next to him on the edge of the bench. She reached out and found his tail, which remained coiled in the sun, staring vacantly into the distance. "Do you not think that you should find him again? Your brother?" She gently pet his tail, her voice low and filled with concern. "All of us have only so much time to call our own. Spending it alone is not the way to live a happy life."

"Marcus and I followed the same path before, and it brought us nothing good. I think it's better that we each follow our own roads now." Hal lifted his head, looking over at his blind caretaker. "But you are right, Illyana. No one should have to life their life alone and afraid. That's why I need to get back to Anduruna as soon as possible and find Miri."

"Miri. The girl who was with you when you were attacked?" Mordecai nodded. "You speak often of her. She must be important to you."

"You could say that." With great difficulty, Hal stood up, willing his shattered knee into compliance despite sharp protests of agony. "Up until I met you, she was the only friend I really truly had in my life. And now she's been dragged into who knows what: some cultist-operated mineral-hoarding conspiracy thing. Ugh, it sounds like a badly written story hook from some fantasy tale."

Hal grabbed his crutch and released a small sigh of relief from his tight and broken chest. The numb pain guided him back to reality. It was almost like he needed to remind himself to breathe after getting so caught up in his own meandering monologue. "Sorry for the whole life story," Hal apologized. "Honestly, I haven't talked about my past in, well, a long time. It's making me think."

"Thinking is good." Mordecai nodded in agreement and stood as well, resting one wing on Hal's shoulder. "I am grateful that you chose to share your story with us. I know it is difficult to tell. Remember, young one, you have a new lease on life. Today is a new day. Enjoy it for what it is."

"Yeah." Hal adjusted his weight on the crutch and his one good leg. "I'm going to try going for a little walk, stretch out. Get a little fresh air and more time to think about everything." A cooler gust of wind slipped through the air, and Hal noticed some darker clouds moving in from the sea. "I better make it quick. It looks like a storm is on the horizon."

"Yes, so it would seem." Mordecai took a step back and offered a craggy but warm smile. "Just be careful not to push your body too much. At my age it will be difficult for me to drag you in from the rain."

Hal smirked, then limped away from the cottage out into the open field, wandering nowhere in particular. Behind him he could hear Mordecai and Illyana conversing with one another, though his mind was so busy he paid no attention to the words exchanged.

"That poor boy is lost, I'm afraid," Mordecai lamented.

"No," Illyana disagreed. "His path has a destination. He simply does not know what it is yet."

6

As the days passed, Hal's condition continued to improve, and faster than anyone expected. Though Hal still required a cane to walk around, he could do so with less difficulty as time passed by. Soon it was time for Hal to insist that he was healthy enough to return to Anduruna and resume his search for Miri and the people who had turned his life upside down. Though Mordecai and his family were saddened to see Hal go, they knew the day had to come eventually.

And so, it came to pass that early one morning the family loaded up their groundcar and hitched up their old manekale to take produce to market in Anduruna; Hal joined in as a passenger with a one-way ticket. They loaded up early in the morning, just as dawn was beginning to settle over the delta and dispel the morning chill. Out here in the countryside, groundcars pulled by beasts of burden were the most convenient method of transportation, especially for farmers like Mordecai who sold produce to the hungry citizens of Anduruna. There were no telepads. No ferry boats. None of the conveniences of city life. But today, still on the edge of recovery, Hal didn't seem to mind the slow going.

It was a several-hour journey from the verdant and tranquil Eridu delta to the Theophanies district of Anduruna. Hal rode in the back of the groundcar, sitting next to Illyana, while Mordecai and Sasha sat up front. The four of them shared the space in silence for some time, as the rising sun lent warming rays to burn off the morning dew. The morning was blanketed by a beautiful sky of yellow-orange that only Hal could truly understand the depth of.

"The sunrise is beautiful this morning," Hal finally said, eager for some conversation to pass the time.

"Yes, it truly is," Illyana answered, smiling, eyes closed, basking in the sun's glow as she leaned against the door.

"How do you know?" Hal turned to look at Illyana, his raspy voice betraying a spark of curiosity. "You can't see the sunrise at all."

Illyana seemed to chuckle to herself for a moment. "My boy, one does not need to see the sunrise to understand that it is beautiful. I can feel its warmth, its radiance. Just because I am blind does not mean that I cannot appreciate it."

Hal pondered her response. "I hope that should the worst happen to me, I can share your positive attitude. I don't know what I would do if I couldn't see anymore."

"And is going blind the worst thing that could happen to you?" Illyana countered with a sly smile. "You know what some people say, about the spirits being excellent listeners. I think you should be careful with your words, lest you tempt fate."

Hal snorted and shook his head. "Good point." He sobered up a little as his tail continued to lounge comfortably in the sun, all eyes closed. "Though, it had to have been difficult for you, going blind. How did you cope with that?"

"It was very hard." Illyana's smile disappeared, though she didn't seem reluctant to share her story. "I was filled with fear and despair as my world shrank in around me, until eventually it disappeared completely. The best doctors in Anduruna could do nothing to help me."

The older woman rested one hand over her heart, clutching at the old memories. "In truth, I felt very powerless in those darkest days. I had even at one point considered taking my own life."

Hal frowned at that unsettling truth. "What stopped you?"

"A silly little thing called pride." Illyana laughed, sounding cheerful despite the grim topic. "If I had killed myself, I would have given in, and proved that my life was worthless. But my life wasn't worthless. No life is without value, even the lives of the wretched and the miserable.

"It was a good thing I didn't follow through. I met Mordecai, fell in love, and learned to experience the world anew. I have a loving family now, and a comfortable and quiet life that helps me cherish each day here in my later years."

Hal put one hand on his chest, idly rubbing at his fresh scars and the buried shards of fallen star hidden within. "But you must miss your vision sometimes, still. I mean, the entire world is out there. The sun. The stars. Everything."

"Yes, there are times when I wish I still had my eyesight. I have never seen the face of my husband, or my grandchild. Sometimes the world seems very small when you are blind." Illyana fell silent. "But, every time I feel like that, I tell myself to stop and listen."

"Listen to what?" Hal asked.

"The world." Illyana laughed at Hal's untempered curiosity. "You see, my boy, when you open your heart to life, even the small moments can be quite large. You will learn that the world is always singing to us, even when all is quiet." She turned her face towards the morning light, offering her surroundings a contented smile. "The day is singing to us, even now."

Hal shifted his weight and looked out the window at the verdant scenery beyond. The creaking and rocking of the old wooden wagon wheels offered a calming soundtrack to his moment of reflection. He heard Sasha giggle from the front of the cart, followed by the muffled but amused mumblings of Mordecai. Hal couldn't help but shake his head and laugh. "I guess you're right about that. Both you and Mordecai seem to be very happy, and very wise. I can't thank you enough for saving my life."

Illyana placed one hand on Hal's arm and gave it a comforting pat. "You're very welcome, young man. Tell me, what do you intend to do when we reach Anduruna?" Her expression hardened slightly as the topic turned towards current events.

"That's a good question." Hal frowned, staring at his feet. "I've been trying to figure that out ever since you pulled me from the river." He turned his head to look at his tail, which looked back in turn, flicking its tongue. "Miri has to be alive, and those—I don't know what to call them—zealots? cultists? They're the ones who started all this madness. I guess I'll try to get more information about them and go from there. Find some answers and get to the bottom of everything."

"And what if the answers you find are not what you expect?"

"I'll play it by ear. I don't know." Hal felt his mood slip into frustration. "I just need to find Miri. Make things right again."

"Were things always so right to begin with?" Illyana countered, challenging Hal's thinking.

"What?" He hissed in irritation at her question. "I don't know. Yeah, things were fine. I had a good life, a good job. I had privacy, peace and quiet, a comfortable routine. Things were good, you know? Normal."

Illyana nodded, though her expression was dubious. "So is that what you want? Your old life back?"

Hal felt an impotent anger swell up inside him as the questions continued, even though Illyana was being polite. "What do you want me to say, Illyana? *Yes?*"

Hal let out a frustrated sigh, feeling his emotions take control of his words. "I should be dead right now, but instead I'm alive but dying from cancer slash space radiation poisoning. It's like I was given a second chance to live, but this? This is no gift." He spat the last word with disgust. "You know, every waking moment all I can think about is how I'm going to *die* and how terrifying and lonely that feels. When I go to sleep, all I see is the face of the one person in this world who I actually cared about, who I dragged into this nightmare without even trying to. And I never actually had the courage to say how I felt!"

Hal felt his lips curl into an angry sneer as he balled his hands into fists. "So damn right I want my old life back, because all I have now is a bloody death sentence and a pile of regrets to keep me company!"

The echo of Hal's shouting bounced back at him like a slap in the face from inside the confines of the carriage. Illyana recoiled from the volume, her expression becoming profoundly sad. Hal realized that all the sounds of light conversation from outside had stopped; he had been shouting at the top of his lungs. The anger faded as quickly as it came, leaving in its place a heavy, oppressive silence.

"I'm sorry. I shouldn't be raising my voice at you." Hal felt terrible about the outburst. He sheepishly sat back in his seat, wondering why he had resorted to practically screaming at the blind old woman who had saved his life.

Illyana's hand returned to find his, and she gave it a gentle squeeze without offering any words. She was afraid, perhaps, of inciting more anger from the raptor. Hal's tail gingerly found its way over to her lap where it rested and closed its eyes.

"I'm sorry. I just . . . I guess I'm feeling a little overwhelmed with the whole situation. I didn't mean to get angry at you."

She patted his arm and nodded. "Let us enjoy the journey and rest while we can. Things will get busier when we reach the city."

Hal took a deep breath and looked back out the window. "Yeah."

***

It was early afternoon by the time Mordecai's groundcar finally approached the arches of the great aqueduct that formed the perimeter of the city of Anduruna. As they drew nearer, Hal could see the monumental shadow cast over the countryside by the Sabbaton tower that stood at the city center. The massive structure stood at the very heart of Anduruna, and while still many miles away, its sheer height dominated the landscape. The tower was home to the Viscount, City Central Authority, and all the bureaucrats that presided over the seven distinct districts that composed the city at large.

Their carriage passed through the great walls of the aqueduct and emerged into the grand and opulent Theophanies district. Occupying the southwestern wedge of Anduruna, Theophanies was home to the oldest architecture in the city and the largest collection of Sacrare cathedrals and religious fervor. It all felt quite overdone, with an aesthetic and energy that overwhelmed the senses, which is exactly why Hal tended to avoid the place when he could help it. It was a stark contrast to Calypsa, where he called home. Every street they passed through was positively teeming with people and activity. Merchants and missionaries alike competed for the attention of passersby, hoping to sell their wares or their faith to whomever could be made to listen. Tall, elaborate cathedrals dotted the streets, casting long shadows of majesty over each avenue. Here, all other districts became nothing but a memory.

Hal pulled his jacket closer around him like a cloak to ward off the rest of the world as Mordecai pulled the carriage to a stop at their destination. Some workers, apparently familiar to Mordecai's family, immediately set to work unloading the produce and unhitching the manekale from the cart. Hal gingerly stepped out of the vehicle onto the edge of the street and squinted away the dazzling reflections from stained glass windows and towering fountains.

Mordecai shuffled over to Hal and wrapped one wing around him with a warm smile. "So, young Halcyon, is this where you would like to part ways? You know that you are welcome to stay with us for as long as you like."

"I know." Hal shook his head and planted his cane in the ground, steadying his weight. "All of you have done so much for me. I really am grateful for everything, but I need to find some answers without wasting any time. A lot of time has already passed by."

Mordecai clapped Hal on the shoulder with an understanding nod.

"Hey, Mister Tail?" The voice of Sasha emerged from behind Mordecai's robes. The little girl shyly poked her head out from behind her grandfather.

Hal tried to crouch down to be at her eye level, but the shooting pain in his knee quickly made him think better of the plan. "Yes, Sasha?" He tried not to wince at the girl and offered a smile to cover up his discomfort.

"When you're all better and you find your friend, will you come back and play with me again?" She sounded more than a little sad that Hal would be leaving.

"Of course, Sasha. I hope to see all of you again soon." Hal feigned levity, even though in the back of his mind he was unsure if he would ever see Mordecai's family again. "Just remember to be a good girl for your grandma and grandpa while I'm gone."

"Okaaaaay." She smiled shyly and watched Hal's tail with a smile as it swiveled back and forth trying to cope with the busyness of Hal's new surroundings.

"Safe travels, Hal. I hope you find what you're looking for." Illyana reached out to touch his hand and offered a sad smile.

"Thank you, Illyana. Thank you to all of you for caring for me." Hal felt a bittersweet loneliness settle over him as they all said their goodbyes.

Mordecai took Sasha to go look after their manekale, leaving Hal and Illyana briefly alone amidst the din of the street. She reached out to brush Hal's face with a gentle and comforting touch. "You carry a large burden, young man, but do not let it define who you are."

"I'll try not to."

Illyana chuckled and turned away. "Until we meet again, Hal. Take care of yourself." She offered one last touch and shuffled away with Mordecai's guidance. He gave Hal a warm smile and a knowing nod before walking away to tend to his duties.

Like a slow rain, the noise and chaos of the city street trickled into Hal's perception. It began like a room full of whispers that grew louder and more urgent into a whirlwind of indecipherable syllables and sounds. As the volume of a thousand voices rose around him, he rested one hand on his chest and took a full deep breath, staring at the ground at his feet. He gripped his cane firmly and stepped forward, raising his head to look through the crowds.

"All right," he muttered, blinking through the glare. "Let's get started."

7

"**S**o, you were attacked by religious gunmen, left for dead, and your friend was kidnapped. Do I have that right?"

"Yeah, that's right."

Hal sat in a sparsely furnished "interview room" at one of the Theophanies police precincts, sitting across from a skeptical detective. Stereotypically enough, the detective was sipping from a mug filled with some form of hot stimulating beverage, jotting some notes into his file as he took Hal's statement. The veteran canine officer looked tired and largely disinterested with what Hal had to say, as if he was going through the motions until the questioning was complete. The sterile, harshly lit room was equally unwelcoming to Hal's senses. Neither one of them seemed to be happy, as if merely tolerating the conversation was the best outcome to be expected.

"Uh-huh." The detective took another sip of his drink and shuffled through some papers in front of him. Like a rational person, Hal had decided to go straight to the police. A part of him had hoped that maybe Miri had already been found, but no such luck. The missing-persons case was still open, and from the looks of it, little progress had been made towards a happy resolution. Hal was wanted as a "person of interest" behind their mutual disappearance, and though not under arrest, he certainly hadn't been given a warm reception at the police station. If anything, he felt like he was regarded as a prime suspect.

The detective continued his questioning with a frown. "And they followed you up into the mountains because they wanted the meteorite you found?"

"Well, that's what they said they were after, and they shot me to get their hands on it. I don't think they were following me; I just happened to get there before them." Hal sighed impatiently and shifted his weight in the uncomfortable metal chair. It didn't feel like the detective cared much at all about Hal's situation.

"Do you know anything about the meteorite? Why it would be valuable to them?" One eyebrow arched up on the other side of the cloud of steam rising from the mug.

Hal hesitated for a moment. He wasn't sure how to explain the sensations he felt when he touched the meteor, and he certainly couldn't tell them that he used his Dreamkeeper power to perceive the energy it was emitting. He also doubted they would let him go free if he explained how fragments of the meteor had somehow fused with his body, and that they may have been the reason he did not completely die from his injuries. There would be far too many questions, with far too few answers, and he didn't have enough time to play that game.

The lie came easier than expected. "No, I can't think of any reason, other than it's a relatively rare geological curiosity. But geologists don't usually murder people for mineral samples."

"Huh." Another sip from the mug. "Can you describe the person who shot you?"

"Well, two people shot me. The guy who shot my knee was a wolf named Miles and I killed him. The woman, I don't know who she is; I didn't see her face very clearly. She was wearing a hooded robe."

"Wait, wait, wait. You killed someone?" The detective's voice suddenly seemed a lot more serious.

"With a climbing axe, yeah." Hal poked at the front of his neck, right below his vocal cords. "Right here, in the throat. It was a lucky off-balance swing, but I was fighting for my life. Didn't have enough time to run back to the city to call the cops first."

The police officer narrowed his eyes at Hal, setting his cup off to the side of the table. "You realize what you just said could put you in jail?"

"You did hear me when I said that he shot me, right?" Hal's tone was bright and defiant; he was hardly willing to back down. "In my knee? You know, this one with the *bullet hole* in it?" He used his cane to tap at his shin, just beneath where he got shot. "It was self-defense all the way. I didn't have any other choice. They were going to execute me."

The detective frowned and made a few notes on one of his sheets. "So who was this woman, then, the one who also allegedly shot you?"

"Like I said, I never saw her face, but she had a foreign accent and glowing blue eyes." Hal's tail hovered over the table, peering down at the police officer's notes and flicking its tongue repeatedly. "She said she was from the Order of Celestia, that new religious group that started kicking around recently. Apparently their Archbishop wanted the meteorite, so he sent her group to retrieve it."

"The Celestials?" The detective recognized the name, and seemed rather surprised to hear them mentioned. "They've never caused any trouble before. In fact, quite the opposite."

Now it was Hal's turn to narrow his eyes. "Why do you sound so surprised?"

"Well," the detective hesitantly offered, "they've been more cooperative than most with supporting local law enforcement here in Theophanies. They started a program awhile back for rehabilitating released convicts: the Second Life initiative. Prisoners selected for special parole go to work for the church for a while, find faith and all that stuff." The officer shrugged. "As far as we can tell, so far, so good. None of the prisoners released to the church have been repeat offenders. A 100 percent success rate, though it's still a relatively new program. It has a lot of local political support."

"Well, maybe there's more going on over there than you realize."

"Maybe, but I think it's unlikely. The people who were after you were probably with a different outfit, using the Celestials as a scapegoat. I'll open an official inquiry, but I don't know if it will turn up anything solid. Honestly, this case should be transferred to Calypsa PD." The officer gathered up his papers into one neat stack.

"Whoa. Wait. Hold up a second." Hal was starting to get angry with the officer of the law. "I tell you the truth, and all of a sudden you think I'm full of shit because I drop the name of this one church?"

"Hey! Relax, kid," the detective fired back with the weight of anger behind his voice. "I'm telling you the historical data says the Celestials support *reducing* crime in this city, not increasing it. On top of all their programs, they also provide significant financial donations to local law enforcement agencies. They've nearly doubled the revenue we brought in from this year's community fund. Funds that go to keeping Anduruna safe. Keeping citizens safe."

Hal shook his head and snorted. "I thought my generous taxes paid for that. What, is your pension not fat enough already?" Hal's tail bobbed a little, emitting a hiss that almost sounded like a laugh. "'Community fund' sounds an awful lot like an officially sanctioned bribe to me."

"Are you *trying* to give me a reason to throw you into a holding cell?" The detective stood up from his chair, slamming his palms on the brushed metal table between them. "According to my files, you've been arrested twice before. Let's see here." He grabbed one of the papers and held it aloft. "Arrested under suspicion of being an accessory to racketeering and extortion. Arrested under suspicion of being an accessory to armed robbery." The detective sneered. "You have a criminal record, Adhil. No one would think twice if I decided to keep you here for further questioning."

Hal likewise stood from his chair, staring the other man straight in the face. "Maybe if you learned how to read the whole report, you'd see that I was *released*, with no official charges pressed on either of the two counts. I was never convicted of any crime. I'm a free and innocent man." His voice was low and cold. His tail bared its fangs and didn't blink.

"I know all about the crime families and their history over in Calypsa. You're only free because your daddy was a crime lord with a high-priced lawyer and enough resources to cheat the system."

"My father was a great man and the victim of a triple homicide! A murder that to this day the police of Anduruna have done nothing to solve. A murder that even City Central Authority has failed to solve! Zero arrests, zero progress. Go ahead and tell me that you're good at your job, because I could really use another laugh."

The detective slammed one palm on the table. The other hand gripped the case file, waving it angrily in the air to clear away Hal's disrespect. "That's it, you little punk!" Spittle showered Hal's face as the livid police officer continued to berate him. "I'm holding you for temporary observation in the investigation of the disappearance of Miriel Rodgers!" The detective grinned. "Duffy!" A junior officer opened the door to the interrogation room and popped his head in. "Take Mister Adhil here and throw him into an empty cell. Let him cool his heels while he thinks about being more cooperative."

"Right, boss."

The detective folded his arms across his chest and smiled smugly at Hal, confident in his superior position of power and authority. "Maybe tomorrow morning you'll have a more conducive attitude towards this investigation, and we can try having this conversation again."

Hal snarled. "You little shit! I did the right thing and came to you for help because my friend is missing! Just because I hit a nerve you're going to put me in a cell?" Duffy and another officer each grabbed one of his arms and started to pull him from the room by force. "You cops are all hypocrites! Just armed thugs with a government-issued badge!" Hal struggled and shouted as he was forced from the interrogation room. "Assholes! Pigs! I don't have time for your bullshit!"

Hal was unceremoniously thrown into a small holding cell on the other end of the building. The heavy iron door slammed shut with a decisive clang, leaving the raptor alone with his frustration and rage. After continuing to shout profanities for a few minutes, Hal ran out of energy, and he collapsed into an exhausted heap of scales and feathers onto the simple fabric cot.

It took some time for his emotions to settle. As the adrenaline high started to subside, Hal took a deep breath and let it out slowly. Just a few hours had passed since he had made it back to the city, and now he could do nothing but feel disappointed in where he had ended up. Hal glanced over his shoulder to see his tail's four blood-red eyes staring at him calmly. It flicked its tongue at him and cocked its head to the side, as if asking, "What now?"

Hal didn't have the answer to that question. He could do nothing but shake his head, emitting a sad sort of laugh before looking up at the ceiling.

"Well, shit."

T he following day was one of immense frustration for Hal, as he was kept overnight at the police station and questioned by several officers regarding Miri's disappearance, all asking the same questions in different ways. It was a relentless grind, and after repeating himself for the sixth or seventh time, Hal had had about enough. None of this was getting anybody anywhere.

Eventually, though, the police were legally bound to either officially charge Hal with a crime or release him. While they were reluctant to let him go, there was no evidence suggesting Hal was the mastermind behind his own lethal assault. Thus, after great trouble, he was finally released back into the wild to continue his search alone.

"Assholes," Hal muttered as he limped back out into the Theophanies city streets, letting out a heavy sigh. The sun was already well on its way down towards the horizon as late afternoon started to give way to evening. From the deep aching in his knee and the chill air that was whipping through the alleyways, it was likely that more bad weather would be rolling through soon. *How metaphorical*, Hal mused.

Looking around at the moving sea of people in the streets, Hal felt nothing but the urge to get away to somewhere less crowded. It dawned on Hal that he actually hadn't been back home to his apartment in well over a month; that was as good a place as any to go, since he lacked any concrete information on Miri.

The wounded reptile limped his way over towards the waterway to catch a ferry back to Calypsa. If he was lucky, he could make it back home before it got dark. This was the first time he'd had to do any prolonged walking on his shot-up knee, and much to his surprise, it didn't seem to hurt more than normal. Stairs, however, proved to be a much greater challenge, as any elevation change slowed him to a crawl and shot spikes of red-hot fire all through his right leg. Despite the discomfort, Hal did his best to fight through the pain and to hide the extent of his injury. If he wasn't careful, some less upright citizens might notice his weakness and attempt to take advantage.

Hal paid express fare on a ferry heading towards Calypsa, using up the last cash he had on hand. The hour-long ride through Norvondire into Calypsa gave Hal time to reflect on all that had transpired. It was likely that Miri was still being held by the Celestials, which meant he would need to eventually head back into Theophanies and stake out their church/cathedral/secret evil lair and get some information. As much as he wanted to do that right away, the rational side of his brain urged caution. Hal's injuries were a liability, and he needed to be smart about how he went about things, lest he end up getting shot in the chest and dumped into a river. He already knew the police were being bribed to look the other way, so there was no help there. There were alternatives outside the law, but in all honesty he didn't want to involve any of his family's old crime associates either.

As the ferry moved through Norvondire, Hal watched the crenelated architecture slowly pass by. The buildings seemed so strong, so certain. The invincible-looking fortresses stood proud and tall amidst the skyline, as if daring the world to topple them. Hal looked down, his tail still gazing at the scenery. Just a few months ago he had felt so strong and certain about where his life was heading, and now, well, now he wasn't sure just how much of his life still lay ahead of him. Despair loomed in the back of his mind like a shadow, like a heavy fog, threatening to descend upon him and envelop him wholly. But, if nothing else, Hal was stubborn, and perhaps that alone kept his heart from sinking completely into darkness. He was still alive. He still had some time left. He couldn't waste it.

The ferry reached its stop in Calypsa just as the sky was beginning to change shades. Thankfully, it was only a couple of blocks to his apartment from there. He limped off, taking in the familiar sights and sounds of his home district. Calypsa wasn't necessarily a peaceful place to live; it had a den of underground activity that could get the right person into a lot of trouble. Trooper raids weren't entirely uncommon, and poking your head into other people's business was a bad idea more often than not. Still, it was where he had grown up, and it commanded a beautiful view of the Starfall Mountains and the riverbanks flowing down from the western ridge. Miri had loved those mountains almost as much as Hal.

He let out a long, drawn-out sigh as he hobbled up to his apartment. Each step leading up to his second-floor entrance taunted him, but he dealt with each in turn with a grunt and a wince. After a great deal of pain and effort, he was finally home . . . and greeted with a bright red piece of paper nailed to his front door.

Eviction Warning: Failure to pay past-due rent will lead to forced eviction from this property if the balance is not paid in full with late fees by—

Hal ripped the piece of paper from his front door with a snarl. "Leave the world for a while and the world doesn't give a shit. Figures." He crumpled the notice up into a ball and tossed it down the stairs before unlocking his door and stepping inside.

The first thing that greeted Hal was the stench. The air was old and rotten, like something organic had been happily decaying inside for quite some time. "Ah, hell." Hal limped his way towards the small kitchen. Of course his apartment smelled like something had died; he hadn't taken the trash out in two months. Damn the continual march of time for not waiting for him to get back. A thin film of dust covered every flat surface in the apartment, testament to the unplanned period of neglect.

Hal spent the next hour impatiently taking care of simple house chores, though his leg made carrying anything other than a one-handed load quite laborious. Empty the trash, clean out the fridge, check the mail. All of it seemed so trivial and pointless. He tossed the overflowing stack of envelopes onto his bed and haphazardly sorted through them. Junk, bill, junk, bill, catalog, magazine, bill . . . He tossed them into different piles with barely a second glance. He started to toss another envelope when he realized it was from the university where he worked and studied. He paused.

With one sharp talon, Hal sliced open the envelope and pulled out the letter inside. *Mister Adhil,* the letter began, typeset beneath the Calypsa District University emblem. *Due to your continued absence, your position as a teaching assistant within the College of Arts and Sciences has been terminated and your enrollment in all doctoral studies has been canceled. Your pay period ends—*

Hal crumpled the offending paper into a little ball and tossed it across the apartment. "Damn it all!" he hissed in frustration. The world didn't care why he hadn't been around to pay the bills and go to work and deal with all the little inconveniences of life, but it punished him all the same. Hal grimaced as the paper ball made an entirely unsatisfying thud against the wall. He needed to figure out what to do next.

As Hal sat there alone with his thoughts, he became aware of just how deathly silent it was in the room. Silent, except for one sound. That clock. That old ten-lucre wall clock apparently had the best pendulum in the history of Anduruna, and it sat there on the far wall ticking away each second with a barely audible, but absolutely infuriating, *tick tick tick.*

He ignored the clock and sat on the edge of the bed with his head in his hands. He needed to figure things out. The Celestials were armed and willing to kill anyone who got in the way of their goals. He needed to be ready for that.

Tick tick.

Hal was physically compromised, but a springer worked plenty well as long as you could pull the trigger. Maybe if he could get his hands on a gun he would be able to handle things if everything went south again. Firearms were illegal for civilians to own in Anduruna; not like that stopped some criminals. Maybe he had no choice but to contact his old friends in the family, see what they could do for him. Marcus was AWOL, but Hal was fine keeping it that way. Maybe Jonny was still alive and kicking?

Tick tick.

Miri had always hated guns, and thought it was good they were illegal. Hal always disagreed with her fiercely on this point, but he'd grown up in a different world than she had. Miri . . . she had to still be alive. They'd captured her rather than killed her for some reason that he still didn't understand. If that was true, it meant she was being held hostage somewhere, and that she'd been a captive for quite some time now.

Tick tick.

The memory of that morning flooded through Hal, and he felt the burning sting of each bullet as he relived the last moments he remembered. *Hal!* Miri's screams echoed in his mind, her profound loss and despair giving weight even now to the memory of her voice. The cold shock of the river as he was kicked into it, fading darkness, and then . . . oblivion.

The clock chimed a happy little ding-dong pattern as the hour reached eight o'clock, snapping Hal out of his thoughts. Without any warning, a truly overwhelming anger crystallized in his heart and set his senses on edge. Before it reached the fourth "ding-dong" of eight, Hal was ripping it from the wall with a scream. "Enough!" Hal swung it onto the side of his desk with all his might, and it shattered spectacularly into a hail of glass and splinters. He continued to swing the broken remains against the wall until all that remained in his hand were the pendulum and chain. With one final cry of primal rage, he flung the pendulum down the short hallway into the kitchen, where it clattered on the floor and slid to a stop beneath the kitchen table.

When the dust settled, Hal stood alone amidst the wreckage, gasping for breath as tightness gripped his chest with icy tendrils. He scrambled to the bathroom sink and ran the cold water, splashing it on his face as he struggled to regain control of his senses and force oxygen into his lungs. He shuddered and looked into the mirror at his own reflection: his pupils were completely dilated; the lines around his eyes had set into the heavy burdened crags of a man who had seen too much and lived too long. His tail eagerly lapped at the stream of water, greedily drinking in the cold liquid.

After a few moments of staring at his own image, Hal gripped the sides of the sink and activated his power. The dim room was suddenly aglow in a pale blue light, a light that seemed to emanate from within his own chest. After the time spent recovering from his injuries, the meteor fragments in his body had spread further. Hal could see the corruption in his veins stretching throughout his entire torso, threatening to reach up into his neck and into his limbs. The cancer, if that even was the right word to use, appeared to be advancing at a steady pace.

As Hal used his Dreamkeeper power, he noticed that the tightness in his chest had disappeared. Likewise, the pain in his leg had all but vanished. Instead, each breath he inhaled was rich and fulfilling, infusing him with energy. On each exhale, a tangible cloud of condensation emerged, as if he were suddenly standing back up in the snowy mountains. He felt the whispers of the entire universe tug at the furthest borders of his perception, new colors teasing the very edge of his vision. This wasn't the same as before. It was *more.*

Hal blinked and forced himself to stop, snapping out of his power. With a sudden shock, the wider perception of the universe contracted around him and disappeared. He was left digging scratches into the sink with his talons, once again gasping for air as he stared at his own dull reflection. *What the hell?*

It was a few minutes before Hal even dared to move, so bewildered was he by what he had just experienced. The pain of his injuries returned, leaving him with a familiar throbbing in his knee that guided him back into reality. He took one final breath, fighting the tightness in his chest as he shut off the sink and returned to the main room.

The shattered remains of his outburst littered the floor, and with the clock destroyed, it was now truly silent in his apartment. All the anger from before was gone, replaced by a weary regret that he had acted so violently. That had been his only clock. "What in the world has gotten into you, Hal? You're losing it at the worst possible time." He spoke aloud to himself to break the silence, and his tail looked at him quizzically, offering no answers.

Hal gingerly kicked aside a few shards of glass with his toe-claws as he reached for a chair and sat down at his desk. He needed to get out of this apartment before he went truly mad. One hand unfurled his data scroll and powered it up. A couple of taps and he was making a data-call to his old associate, Jonny. Jonny's avatar flashed as the data scroll attempted to connect, leaving Hal wondering if the call would even be picked up. Just as he reached for the "hang up" button, Jonny's avatar stopped flashing, and a fuzzy-sounding voice answered.

"Hello?"

"Jonny? It's Hal."

"Hal? Hal! My old pal! What the hell have you been up to? Shit, it's been forever, man!"

Hal nodded instinctively, even though Jonny couldn't see the gesture. "Yes, it has been awhile. Look, I need a favor: a springer, to be precise."

"Wow, not wasting any time, are you? Sounds serious. Did you get in trouble?"

"No, I'm not in trouble." Hal paused. "Well, I kinda am, but it's nothing you need to worry about."

The line went silent before Jonny's voice responded with a good dose of humor behind the static. "Hal, that has got to be *the worst* explanation anyone has ever given me. Don't leave me hanging, man. Fill me in on the details!"

Hal sighed. "Look, it's a long story! I'll explain later. Are you free tonight? You working?"

"I'm always working, but that doesn't mean you can't drop in. Besides, I guess it's not smart to talk about business like this over a network connection. I'm at the usual office. You know the one. It's your favorite!"

"Yeah, I know the one. You'll be free soon? Maybe in the next hour?" Hal frowned at the remains of his wall clock.

"Anytime for you, man. It'll be great to see you! Hell, Marvin might even crack a smile if you walk in through the door tonight."

Hal shook his head and chuckled. "I highly doubt that. But all right, Jonny, I'll see you in a bit. Don't get arrested before I get there."

"Hey, that only happened once before!"

The scroll-call ended with a tap of one sharp talon on the semi-flexible display, returning the apartment to silence. In truth, Hal still wasn't sure if this was the right thing to do, getting back in touch with the elements of his old life that he deliberately had put behind him. Jonny was a good guy, though; if nothing else, Hal was confident he would help him out without too many strings attached. Besides, the underworld was the best place to get information if the police weren't going to be on his side. He needed to arm himself with weapons and knowledge before he could find Miri. If he was lucky, maybe he could handle the rest from there.

Given recent events, Hal wasn't sure if his luck was up to the task.

9

Before setting off into the night, Hal took a few minutes to change into some fresh clothes that had fewer bullet holes in them. Though he was feeling quite weary after a difficult day, just the simple act of wearing something clean and fresh gave him a second wind of energy. He opted for an older but comfortable leather jacket that blended well with the background of the nighttime city streets. His large raptor feet and claws made it impossible to wear traditional shoes or boots, but he wrapped his lower legs with heavy-duty cloth to protect his scales from the grime of the urban roads. His tail continued to look out the window attentively as he prepared himself.

He stood from the edge of his bed and retrieved his cane, steeling himself for the walk ahead of him with a few measured breaths. Jonny ran an illegal gambling den from the back rooms of a brothel in the center of Calypsa. Hal didn't care for that place very much, not because of the people who ran it, but because he wasn't the sort of person who gravitated towards such vices. Hal never indulged in the brothel's wide variety of services, but realistically speaking, it would be the most secure place to do illicit business, and he trusted the people who operated things there. Buying or possessing a weapon could put Hal in jail for a very long time, and he didn't want to waste what remained of his days behind bars.

With a creak he shut his apartment door and locked it behind him. The crack of thunder and flash of lightning split the sky for an instant, and Hal grimaced at the fact that in about two minutes he would be soaking wet. As apt as the weather might have been in representing his current state of mind, he sure wished it would pick a more convenient time to rain. Funny how life didn't seem to be all that convenient in recent weeks.

It was a twenty-minute trudge through the Calypsa streets to the bordello. Two minutes into the trip it started raining, as Hal had predicted, transitioning straight from a drizzle to a heavy downpour. He merely frowned and continued walking, taking comfort in the fact that the bad weather meant there were fewer people on the streets he had to be wary of. Throughout the hike he had to willingly fight the urge to activate his power to make it easier to walk. Using his power had felt so good before, and the temptation was strong to expand his senses; without them, the world felt so narrow. So muted. Too bad in public it could lead to his immediate arrest. Damned police state really knew how to make things difficult.

Soon enough, Hal reached the front entrance of the brothel. The building stood three stories tall, standing apart from the surroundings with flamboyant flair. The walls were painted in obnoxious pink and purple hues, and the name of the business was identified by a garish neon sign that read in flowery script: "Passion Lounge." His tail blinked at the buzzing sign that flashed and flickered in the rain, and Hal shook his head at the display. He doubted Miri would think very highly of him if she saw him walk into a place like this.

As Hal stepped out of the rain through the front door, his senses were overpowered by the weight of the air inside. It hung heavy and opaque like the velvet drapes along the windows, thick with the competing scents of smoke, sweat, and perfume. The muffled grunts and groans through the walls and ceiling left little to the imagination. The lighting was dim, and the sea of maroon, purple, and pink made it difficult for the eye to get a good sense of direction. An ornate chandelier in the center of the room only half-succeeded in splashing sufficient light into the foyer. Hal coughed as he inhaled the new air, dripping water into a rapidly growing puddle just inside the entrance.

"Welcome to the Passion Lounge!" a familiar voice with a hint of rural twang greeted him as the door was closed shut. "Well, bless my heart, that's not a sight I've seen in ages! That can't be little Hal. Hal Adhil? That is you, isn't it?" The out-of-place reptile was greeted with a warm smile from a dark-colored lagomorph. The woman's bright brown eyes twinkled with vitality beneath the sparkling light of the chandelier.

"Hello, Cassi," Hal said, blinking through the haze. Cassi was the madam of the Passion Lounge, and though pushing middle age, she carried herself well. While he didn't care for her line of work, Hal recognized that she was a good person and a savvy business owner who never treated him poorly. She wrapped her arms around Hal and gave him a friendly hug, awkwardly bumping into his cane.

"Oh, spirits, I'm sorry, Hal, did you hurt your leg? Look at you, coming in from the cold and I'm falling all over you causing trouble."

"I'm fine, just a little mishap a few weeks ago. Climbing accident." Hal adjusted his weight and tried not to grimace. "I'm actually here to see Jonny tonight. He should be expecting me."

"Oh, one of Jonny's boys did come out and mention you'd be dropping in. I just never expected to actually see you here after all this time." Cassi's expression blossomed into a knowing grin. "You can't *stand* being in here! Never could. I can tell right now you feel more out of place than a fish out of water."

"It's just the leg. I'm fine. Really. It's good to see you, Cassi." Hal cleared his throat and tried to be less glum, forcing a smile.

"You know, Hal, them boys always said you needed to learn to relax and loosen up. When you're done talkin' with Jonny, why don't you grab yourself a girl and enjoy the rest of the evening, on the house. Don't even worry 'bout that old leg. All you need to do is lie down and let my girls do the rest." Cassi smiled warmly, playfully poking at his tail.

Hal responded with silence, not sure how to react to what was both a joking and a serious offer all at once. Cassi raised an eyebrow and smirked. "Maybe you'd prefer the company of one of my boys instead?"

"Cassi. You have a true gift for comedy," Hal quipped dryly, wiping off the water that clung to his jacket. "I appreciate your generosity, but I need to speak to Jonny. Is he in back?"

"Yeah, right this way, hun. You change your mind, just let me know." She winked at him and led Hal beyond the main lobby through a back hall to a stairway known by only a select few. The steps led them downward from the brothel above, and the air seemed to get a hair cooler as they dropped below ground level. A sturdy wooden door sat at the bottom of the passageway, blocking any further advance. Cassi gave Hal a knowing smile and banged on the door with three authoritative knocks. The cover to the peephole slid open as the guard checked them over, and Hal heard him grunt in recognition before the door opened without further objection.

The two of them stepped down into a surprisingly large room that was buzzing with activity. A number of gambling tables dominated the center, as clusters of men and women leaned in, rolling dice, dealing cards, A number of gambling tables dominated the center, as clusters of men and women leaned in, rolling dice, dealing cards, and celebrating or cursing their luck in turn. Gambling was legal in theory, but this operation didn't pay a hefty cut of taxes to the state, which pushed it underground and away from the public eye. A few bouncers around the room maintained order, and this gambling den drew a good mix of the affluent and desperate willing to risk their wages for entertainment and the rare promise of striking it big. Cheaters were usually dealt with quickly and roughed up outside to learn their lesson. It was a profitable and mostly clean operation, from everything Hal remembered. From the looks of things, almost nothing had changed since he'd left all those years ago.

"Well, well, well, look what the lovely rabbit dragged in!" A tall and slim zebra stepped aside from the crowd and held out his arms wide with a smile. "Halcyon Adhil. You are a sight to behold, my friend!" Jonny's gold teeth flashed in the light as he offered a wide smile. The flamboyantly colored stripes on his mane made him look like a walking advertisement for rainbow-based money laundering services, but Hal's old friend nonetheless had genuine warmth and joy behind his grin.

"Jonny!" Hal smiled back and they exchanged a brief handshake that was quickly pulled in for a brotherly hug. "It's good to see you again. Thanks for taking the time to see me on short notice."

"Of course! Of course!" Jonny nodded to Cassi. "Thanks, doll. I'll take care of old Hal from here."

"All right, boys. Y'all know where to find me if you need me." Cassi gave Hal a sly wink before departing through the same door where she'd entered.

Jonny clapped Hal on the shoulders, giving him a once-over. "It's been years, Hal. Man, you look like shit!" Jonny laughed warmly, but Hal knew there was probably truth to his words. Recent events had not exactly been kind.

"You really know how to make me feel at home, Jonny." Hal smirked. "It honestly doesn't look like you've changed much. Business is doing well, I take it?"

"Yeah." Jonny nodded and guided Hal towards the back of the room. "Yeah, business keeps rolling along as usual. Step into my office and we can talk all about it." A handful of booths occupied the back of the room, separated from the rest of the crowd by heavy privacy curtains and the occasional strong man who discouraged the other patrons from getting too close. One curtain was pulled aside, and Hal gingerly took a seat, sliding into the semicircular booth as Jonny sat across from him. The curtain closed again, leaving just the two of them alone to talk face to face.

Jonny looked Hal over once more, his flashy and outward bravado reverting to more serious tones once they were away from the crowd. "All right, Hal," Jonny started. "I've got an awful lot of questions, so why don't you just fill me in from the top. Why are you here? It sounds like you're in a jam."

Hal sighed. His tail stared down at the table without looking up. "Well, Jonny, I have cancer. There's a lot I don't know about it, but to put it simply, things aren't looking too good." A moment of chilling silence passed between them as that information was absorbed. "I may not have a ton of days left to look forward to, and there are some things I need to take care of before I run out of time."

"Whoa, Hal, I had no idea. You shoulda told me sooner. That's heavy, man." Jonny shook his head, giving himself a moment to process the unwelcome news. "So you need a springer? This better not be some vengeful cleaning-house sort of thing. That ain't no way to live, trust me, Hal."

"No, that's not it. Let me explain." Hal went on to describe the whole predicament to Jonny, who listened with attention and concern. He explained the meteorite, the gunmen who confronted him, and his miraculous but costly survival thanks to the meteor shards now buried within his body. Though a somewhat outlandish tale, the truth was almost too fantastic to be made up, and Jonny seemed to take Hal's word at face value.

"So now I just need to find Miri and get her out of this mess I dragged her into. I never meant for any of this to happen." Hal leaned back in his seat, looking worn out.

"Damn, Hal, that's some heavy business you got yourself stuck in." Jonny's mood was more subdued than when Hal had first walked in. "So you need a piece to protect yourself through all this bullshit, huh? You know I can help you out more than that. I'll grab Geno and Marvin and we can be your backup. Just like old times."

"No. Absolutely not." Hal's voice was steely with conviction. "This is my mess, not yours, Jon. Helping me out more than you already are will just get you into trouble with the family. I know my old man meant a lot, but I'm not part of the family anymore and I don't want to be. I just want to get some of my life back while I can."

Jonny nodded. "Ok, Hal. Ok. We'll do this your way, but only because I trust you to not go do something stupid like get yourself killed for no good reason." He reached down and grabbed a suitcase that had been resting in the back of the booth and set it flat on the table between them. With practiced flicks of the latches, the case snapped open. Resting inside was a pristine double-barreled springer pistol, complete with shoulder holster and a box of twenty-five cartridges, pre-compressed and ready to be loaded.

Jonny removed the pistol from the case and held it gently for Hal to see as he explained the features. The pistol had a breech-loading over-under design, fixed sights, and was colored a dull silver with brass accents. The serial number had been filed away, leaving only a rough patch of metal where numbers and letters were once stamped. "This is a brand-new Smith and Damien officer's sidearm. Forty caliber. Two barrels, two shots, breech-loading break action." Jonny used his thumb to flip a lever and the barrels broke open at a hinge near the grip, exposing the back end for loading ammunition. "The spring strength in those cartridges has lethal velocity to about 200 feet, but you'll probably have a hard time aiming at anyone outside of twenty-five unless you're a crack shot. Might not get through trooper armor without a healthy dose of good luck, but it will get most jobs done."

Jonny turned the gun around for Hal to see the other side. "Button safety on the side by your forefinger. Black is safe, red is dead. You know the basics. Business end towards the guy whose day you're about to ruin, and pull the trigger to shoot." Jonny held the weapon by the barrel, extending the grip towards Hal. "If you ever get caught with this thing . . ."

"I know." Hal nodded. "I didn't get it from you." He picked up the gun and acclimated himself to the heft and balance of it. It was large enough to fit in his hands comfortably, but not too big as to be unwieldy. "Jonny, this means a lot to me. I know this is risky for you. Just let me know how much I owe you and I'll pay it."

"I'll give it to you on credit on account of you and Marcus sticking up for me back in the day when I needed it. You're like a brother to me, Hal. It hurts me to see you all laid up like this, especially after so much time. Just promise me you'll be smart about things and won't get me in trouble, and you don't owe me a single lucre."

Hal started to slip the shoulder holster on underneath his jacket where it was out of sight. "Thanks, Jonny, you're a good guy. I'm sorry I haven't kept in touch with you, but I've been trying to put this part of my life behind me ever since that night."

"I know, Hal. I can't exactly blame you for wanting out. Your parents never wanted this life for you or your brother. You were always too smart to stick around in this violent business. Smarter than me, at least." Jonny folded his hands together and frowned as he watched Hal load the pistol with two fresh rounds. "Have you even spoken to Marcus since that night? The two of you dropped off the face of the earth so fast after your family was killed, it's almost like you died, too."

"We spoke a little." Hal snapped the breech closed with a sharp flick of the wrist and double-checked that the safety was set before holstering the weapon inside his jacket. "But we both dealt with our grief in our own ways. I don't even know what he's up to anymore. I was actually hoping you would know."

"Nah, Hal." Jonny shook his head. "I haven't seen him in years. Last I heard he was working in some mine somewhere, but that was a few years back. Like you, Marcus wasn't exactly interested in being a part of this business anymore, and he didn't leave me a forwarding address." Jonny laughed. "And if we're being honest with each other, I don't think he ever really liked me as much as you did."

Hal grunted in disappointment. It sounded like no one had really followed Marcus's whereabouts after he left; either that, or Marcus was really good at escaping from the world. "Do you know anything about the Celestials? What they might be up to?"

"Sorry, Hal." Jonny shrugged. "I don't have my ear to the ground as to what goes on over in Theophanies, but if what you tell me is true, it sounds like they're doing all the right stuff to keep the local fuzz off their backs and stay under the radar. Only cause trouble outside of town where the cops don't care, pay them off to turn a blind eye to the stuff they do got going on inside. You need to be careful. It doesn't sound like an amateur operation." Jonny gave Hal a knowing nod. "You've seen yourself how corruptible everyone is in Anduruna, from the Viscount to the pawns, they're all just bureaucratic rats. Hardly honest businesspeople like us, even in the best of times."

"You're probably right about that." Hal's tail nodded as if in agreement as he tucked the extra ammo into one of his pockets, leaving Jonny with an empty suitcase. He regarded his friend with a wistful smile. "Jonny, you're a good friend. I really can't thank you enough for helping me out, especially after I come back out of the blue all of a sudden. It's good to know I'm not in this entirely on my own."

"You can thank me by getting through things in one piece, finding your girl, and letting me know you made it." Jonny was unusually frank with Hal. "Shit, we all know how short life can be. We all deserve to be happy while we can, right? Especially depressing little space cadets like you." Jonny stood and helped Hal from his seat, pulling him in for a tight, brotherly hug.

"Thanks, Jonny. You stay out of trouble yourself." Hal returned the hug with a strong clap on the back and gripped his cane to steady himself. "Assuming I get through this, I'll let you know how things go. Otherwise, well, see you on the other side, I guess."

"Amen to that, Hal."

Hal started to walk back towards the exit, but Jonny called to him before he made it all the way out. "Oh, and Hal! Remember the number one rule!"

"Yeah?"

"Don't fuck things up."

Hal chuckled. "Sage words, Jonny. Sage words indeed."

10

The wind howled at Hal, spraying a cloud of snow into his face and eyes. His feathers ruffled in the gale, each one hardened into a heavy black icicle that dragged in the wind and pulled him back. He squinted into the fury and forced his way through, fighting to put each foot in front of the other.

"Hal!"

He could hear Miri's voice echo through the wind from somewhere up ahead. Steeling his resolve, he put his head down and continued to march forward into the night. The darkness of the gully draped heavily on top of him like a fog, narrowing his perception and blurring his focus. The jacket he pulled tightly around himself did almost nothing to cut through the desolate chill that left him feeling brittle to the core.

Hal stopped and looked upwards. In front of him stood a sheer rock face that looked to be several hundred feet tall. The surface of the canyon wall was sharp and slick, looming down on top of him. Hal had never attempted to scale a cliff this difficult before without a full set of climbing gear, or with weather so absolutely treacherous.

"Hal!"

Miri's voice echoed once again from above, somewhere beyond the top of the rock wall. Gritting his teeth, Hal gripped his lone climbing pick tightly in one hand, his scaly fingers wrapping firmly about the contoured wooden handle. With a grunt he plunged the head of the pick into the stone and ice, getting purchase to pull himself up and begin the ascent.

The minutes felt like hours as he worked his way up the cliff, each movement risking death from a single mistake. A sense of urgency gripped his heart like a vise, pressing him ever harder for each foot he climbed. He was getting close to the top now, and each time he looked down, a lightning bolt of fear shot through his blood, tightening his grip even more. His legs and arms protested the exertion with searing hot flames of fatigue. Each foot seemed ten times more difficult than the last as he neared the top of the cliff.

Through the howling wind, Hal thought he heard Miri call out again just beyond the edge of the summit. The rocks above him angled slightly inward towards the empty air below him, making it difficult to find footing to anchor himself for the final push. Once he committed to the next leap up, it would be nearly impossible to go back. If he stayed where he was, he would surely freeze to death, alone and stranded on the cliffs of the Starfall Mountains.

With a heavy cry of effort and exhaustion, Hal swung his pick up and over into the ice, setting himself up for the final push. He pulled up on his pick and pushed with his feet, flinging his other hand up to grab at the ledge above. As his fingers tried to find a steady grip, he felt the climbing pick shift suddenly, and it came free of the rock face with a large chunk of ice buried in the tip of the blade. He let out a panicked shout as the pick fell from his hands, tumbling into the gully far below him. His feet kicked and scrambled to find something to rest on as he dangled from one arm over empty air.

Hal looked up to the sky and was greeted not with starry radiance but with an absolute and unfathomable darkness. His eyes went wide as he gazed up into an unfamiliar abyss that froze his heart and paralyzed his muscles. The emptiness pressed down on top of him with unrelenting silence. Even the howl of the wind disappeared from his senses as he hung frozen in that moment of time. His fingers started to slip, and despite the will to hold on, Hal was powerless to stop them. An all-consuming terror overcame him as his grip finally failed, and he fell back into the empty void below.

***

Hal woke with a jolt, flailing his arms at the air above him. His body was gripped with a cold sweat that sunk deep into his bedding and left him feeling clammy and chilled. He blinked and shuddered as he regained his composure; it had only been a terrible dream. A few rays of morning sunlight beamed through the window, illuminating dust that floated lazily in the still air of the room. Hal looked over to the wall to see what time it was, only to find the wall empty, remains of last night's fury still littering the floor.

He sighed.

Hal held his head in his hands as he shook off the last lingering memories of the nightmare, trying to ground himself back in reality. He swung his legs over the edge of the bed and gingerly brought himself to his feet. His joints popped and snapped as he did so, and his muscles felt tight and stiff after a long night of restless sleep. The familiar pain of his injuries helped dispel his grogginess as Hal sullenly went about preparing for the day ahead.

He dressed himself in comfortable layers for the late autumn weather, including a hooded sweatshirt and his well-traveled leather jacket. The springer was tucked in its holster concealed beneath his clothing, not easy to reach if he was all zipped up, but at least it was completely hidden from view. Today he would head back to the Theophanies district, and this time he wouldn't waste his effort trying to convince the police to do their jobs.

It was the middle of the day when Hal finally reached the Order of Celestia's cathedral, buried amid other grand structures in the heart of Theophanies. The cathedral stood maybe seven stories tall at the decorative peaks, and the front doorway was topped with what Hal assumed to be the symbol of their faith: an eight-pointed starburst with elongated vertical rays. The stained-glass windows depicted the same symbol within various scenes that in Hal's judgment appeared to be a world-creation myth. The cathedral was not as grand as the much more common Sacrare churches, but it was still suitably awe-inspiring in its unique sort of neo-Gothic architecture style. The cathedral's clean and unweathered appearance suggested it was constructed more recently. The placard on the door said there would be a general sermon at seven o'clock that evening.

Hal spent most of the day wandering around the immediate area, scouting it out and observing the people who came and left. Not very many people entered or left the church during the day, and those who did appeared to be plainclothes citizens, none of whom Hal recognized. As the day marched on, the shadow of the Sabbaton Tower crossed over the district, briefly transforming Theophanies into one wedge of a massive sundial.

The streets of this district were far too busy for Hal to have a good chance of sneaking into the cathedral through a non-standard entryway, so he decided to simply walk inside and blend in with the churchgoers later that evening. He didn't know if the "Archbishop" would be inside, or honestly *what* he would find, but there was only one way to find out.

Evening eventually settled over the city, causing shadows to dull and fade into the growing darkness. When the time came, Hal shuffled into the church along with the scattered faithful. He took a seat in one of the pews furthest from the altar so he could keep a good eye on everything around him.

The interior of the church was laid out fairly typically, with a long center aisle and rows of pews leading up to an altar at the front of the room. Judging from the depth of the exterior of the building, it looked like there was a good deal of real estate still hidden behind the doors at the back. Everything in here felt a little backwards compared to a Sacrare church. In those places, the audience sat "up" in sort of a grand lecture hall format, looking down at the priest. Here, the view of the audience was drawn upwards towards the elaborate paintings on the ceiling and carvings in the supports depicting shooting stars, destruction, and the blossoming of life. The lighting inside was dimmer than expected, giving the impression of being under a real night sky. Hal had never been a religious man, but he could understand the appeal of the stars, even if most people couldn't perceive the depth of their colors as he could.

Hal drew his hood up over his head and waited anxiously for the service to begin. After a few more minutes, a figure emerged from the back of the cathedral and stepped up to the podium. She appeared to be an onyx black panther with glowing cerulean eyes. She was wearing a white robe trimmed in brilliant blood red, and when she spoke, she had an ethereal inflection that made Hal's blood freeze.

It was *her*.

"Celestia be with you, now and forevermore."

"And also with you," the audience replied in unison, offering what Hal assumed to be the proper response to her greeting. His tail hissed and sneered towards the priestess before he forced his anger back beneath the surface, drawing a sidelong glance from one of the church-goers in front of him. At least he knew he was in the right place, but he would need to wait until after the service to make his move.

The woman in front continued her sermon while Hal internally simmered. "The scrolls tell us that when time first began, the old gods created the Dreamworld and everything within it. They created the oceans, the land, the mountains, and the heavens, and they filled this new world with life." The priestess's voice echoed sharply throughout the hall, lending an otherworldly quality to her voice. "But the goddess Celestia saw that the Dreamworld, for all its beauty, was incomplete. For all the life in this world was crude. It lacked creatures with souls, creatures who could share in the glory of creation, shape it into something more, and protect it from the evils that sought to tear it apart."

She pointed overhead to the image of a falling star. "And so she sent to the Dreamworld her gift: a falling star. A fragment of her divinity made real. When the creatures of the Dreamworld touched Celestia's gift, they ceased to become mere creatures of the earth, and instead became creatures of the divine. They were imbued with a soul, and with this soul came a unique inner power. It is this spark that made us all Dreamkeepers, so that we may serve the goddess and guard the Dreamworld we call home. Let us begin tonight's service with a reading from the scroll of prophet Sa'd Al-Malik."

Hal kept his head down, staring at the priestess from just beneath the crown of his hood. He only half-listened to the words she was saying. All he could think about was the hatred he felt towards her. The pressure of his rage welled up in his heart, straining against his ribs and lungs. He ran his tongue over the void in his mouth where his teeth used to be, and felt the sharp crags of the chipped fang. It sent a shot of pain through his jaw that sharpened his focus to a keen edge. She had robbed him of everything he had . . . but soon he would get it back.

Hal bided his time until it seemed the service was over. When the audience was starting to leave, he slid off to one side of the cathedral and lurked in the dark shadow of a pillar, blending in quietly with the ignored edges of the room. There he waited breathlessly for the last person to exit, leaving him and the priestess seemingly alone in the large chamber. She didn't seem to notice him as she began rolling up the scrolls.

With a long, cold exhale, Hal reached for his pistol and drew it from the holster with the faint sound of metal sliding across leather. He activated his power, and even from behind the pillar he could see her heat signature. A burning point of white-hot light emitted radiance from the necklace around her neck. It was a fragment of the fallen star. There was no longer any doubt in Hal's mind that these were the people responsible for his recent misfortune.

The pain in his leg swept away by the fortifying euphoria of using his power, Hal crept along the perimeter of the room, inching closer to her. He moved quickly and decisively every time she appeared to be looking away, carrying his cane with one hand and the pistol in the other. Soon he made it to the pillar closest to her, and the anticipation was palpable, almost unbearable. She was standing only ten feet away.

"Is someone there?" The woman looked over towards his pillar. Hal froze behind his cover and waited, trying not to breathe so heavily. Cold fog billowed from his nostrils with each suppressed breath. He could see her shape stand and move towards him. Three steps. Two steps. One step.

As she peeked around the column, Hal pivoted around the opposite side and raised his springer to point at the side of her head. "Move and you're dead." Hal's raspy voice carried the weight of conviction beneath it, and though she reflexively jumped in surprise, she did not run or call out for help.

The priestess's eyes went wide in astonishment as she recognized Hal, her mouth curling into a bitter frown. "You!" she hissed. "You're supposed to be dead."

"Life is just full of surprises, isn't it?" Hal bared his fangs with a feral grin. "Where's Miri?"

"She's nearby. And unharmed. Put that weapon away before you do something you'll regret."

"Not a chance." Hal gestured with the barrel of the weapon towards the door in back. "Take me to her. Now."

"You have no idea what you're getting yourself into." The priestess stared back at him with defiance in her eyes. "You've already caused me enough trouble with the Archbishop."

"Sorry for the inconvenience." Hal pulled the hammer back on the springer, and it snapped into position with a loud and final click that echoed in the open room. "I'm done talking with you. Take me to her now or I give you the same mercy you gave me."

"I don't know *exactly* where she is right now, but the Archbishop has been keeping a close eye on her. I will take you to him, if you prefer."

"It's a start." Hal nodded sharply. "Let's go. Any sudden movements and they will be your last."

The woman moved towards the rear of the chamber and led Hal through stone hallways and up a winding staircase. With his power, Hal could see the faint heat of other occupants of the church and another bright meteor-white light from up above. The woman seemed unsettlingly calm despite the weapon trained on her as they walked. "You can drop the bravado. The Archbishop doesn't want you dead."

Hal snarled. "Funny, you didn't act that way the last time we met. Why the change of heart?"

"I didn't know who you *were* at the time. If I had known that information back then, things would have ended differently." She led him to the top of the stairs and up to an ornately carved flo-wood doorway.

"Oh yeah? Who am I?"

The woman chuckled lightly, a playful maliciousness dripping from the sound. "Why don't you think about the answer to that question on your own?" She knocked on the door with one slender claw. "Your holiness, I have a visitor for you. He wishes to speak with you right away. It's *very* important."

"Hmmm? Very well, Vanir. Show him in," a muffled voice responded through the doorway.

Vanir, as the woman's name turned out to be, pushed the door inward and gestured for Hal to step inside. He did so, and found himself in an opulently appointed office, warmed by a small fireplace that snapped and crackled in the corner. At the window stood a robed man looking out onto the dark city streets below, his head turned away from Hal. In one hand he rested on an elegantly carved wooden cane, and on the top of the cane was an unmistakable remnant of the meteor. The heavy fragment of heaven provided the perfect shape for fingers to grasp. The hood turned towards Hal, revealing a white raptor snout that protruded beyond the shadow. The Archbishop noticed his visitor and quickly fought back a gasp of surprise. "Vanir. Leave us at once. I'm not to be disturbed."

"Yes, your holiness." The panther left quickly, shutting the door behind Hal.

The voice was uncomfortably familiar, and Hal felt his knees start to buckle, forcing him to lean heavily on his cane as he fought to remain upright. "No . . ."

The man reached up and pulled back his hood, revealing a smiling face that Hal had not seen in years.

"Hello, brother. It's been far too long."

"Marcus?"

Hal doubled over, leaning heavily on his crutch, feeling as if he had just been kicked in the solar plexus. Marcus was quite possibly the last person he expected to see in front of him.

Hal's brother turned from the window to face him, a wide smile stretching across his face. It was a smile Hal had not seen since before their family was murdered.

Marcus, like Hal, was a feathered raptor of the same height and build. Though they were technically twins, they were not fully identical in appearance or personality. Marcus's scales were a bright white with patches of red around his eyes and on his limbs, and a crown of crimson feathers atop his head. The color difference stood in stark contrast to Hal's black and green shading. Marcus's eyes were dark gray with brilliant yellow irises, somehow managing to look both muted and keenly sharp all at once.

The largest difference between the two brothers, however, was their tails. Whereas Hal had a single, semiautonomous snake-head tail, Marcus had a trio of tails, each ending not with a head but with a deadly looking spike made of sharp bone. Like Hal, Marcus lacked total conscious control of his secondary appendages, and they bobbed and hovered of their own accord, trailing out from beneath the back of his heavy robes. Of course, this meant being close to Marcus when he was angry was quite dangerous, and Hal had been cut more than a couple of times as they grew up together, fighting as brothers often do.

"Hal!" Marcus wrapped his arms around Hal to give him a warm embrace. "You're alive! After I learned about the end results of Vanir's excursion, I thought you were dead. What a terrible mistake that could have been. I'm so glad to see I was wrong!"

"No thanks to your goons." Hal was reluctant to return the embrace, and Marcus slowly stepped back after the less than warm reception. "What the hell is all this, Marcus?" Hal waved an arm in the air, gesturing towards the door he'd come through. His voice was angry and suspicious, and his tail snapped its focus furtively between each of Marcus's tail blades. "You're running an entire religion now? When did this happen? Why didn't you tell me?"

Marcus's expression of joy faded, and he took a step back towards the desk. "You made it clear last time we spoke that you had no interest in what I chose to do with myself. You seemed so content to run off on your own that I didn't think it was necessary to send you a card. Besides, you never did try to keep in touch."

"I was busy trying to live a new life, Marcus. A peaceful life. I moved on."

"You *ran*, Hal. You ran off trying to forget your pain, rather than doing something to make things right." Now Marcus's voice rose in anger, a snarl twisting his lips and baring his fangs.

"Make things right?" Hal was incredulous. "How the hell was I supposed to make the murder of our family right?"

"You could have started by not abandoning your family!"

"Our family is dead, Marcus! Nothing I say or do will ever change that!"

The two of them stared defiantly at one another for a tense moment before Marcus backed down and waved one arm dismissively. His expression suddenly looked weary. "Let's not have this fight again, Hal. I don't have the energy for it, and from the looks of it, neither do you."

Hal was gripping his cane with both hands, leaning heavily on it as he struggled to fight off the cold tightness wrapping around his lungs. Exhaustion settled over his body, and he had to put a lot of effort into simply staying upright.

"Let's just . . . start over." Marcus walked over to a cabinet set into the wall and pulled a pair of red fermentae bottles from inside. "Take a seat, brother. Make yourself comfortable." As Hal gingerly sat in one of the opulent chairs, Marcus offered him a drink. "You still like Fire Reed?"

"Yeah." Hal accepted the drink with a tired nod and leaned back in his chair, pulling the cork from the conical glass bottle. As he took a sip of the rich fermentae, Marcus followed suit, taking his own seat opposite Hal and indulging in a gulp of the delicious and intoxicating beverage. The two of them sat silently for a moment, each regarding the other with a look of pity and sadness for the lack of understanding they shared. The years hadn't been kind to their relationship.

"So, starting over." Hal squirmed in his chair, trying to rid himself of the adrenaline still teasing his bloodstream. "When did you start running your own religion?"

"Oh, that's a long story." Marcus sighed and looked up at the ceiling. "I've been Archbishop of the Order for a couple years now, though to be fair, the religion isn't my invention; I simply revived it. The Order of Celestia is actually an ancient religion dating back before the last War of Powers. It disappeared from the world after most of its followers were killed in the fighting. As the dust settled, it faded from public memory, and eventually became a historical footnote for academics to quibble over."

"You never seemed like the religious type, Marcus."

"What? Does it bother you that I've found faith?"

"I'm just surprised." Hal took another long sip from his drink and nodded to his brother. "Go on."

"I know it might seem unusual to you, Hal, but fate guides us in ways we don't expect. Five years ago, I never expected to be here." Marcus held his hands out to his sides. "But here I am, all the same."

Marcus took Hal's silence as a cue to continue. "After you left for university, I was lost, Hal. I'm not ashamed to admit that. I experimented with several different religions, trying to find some small little sliver of purpose for my continued existence in this dark and unjust world." He took a drink of his fermentae, looking at Hal with sadness in his eyes. "But unfortunately, none of them had any *real* answers. How can any one book, one scroll, one set of ideals or one doctrine possibly describe the truth when it stands in opposition to so many others?" Marcus sighed. "I decided they must all be wrong, and I found myself once again rudderless."

Hal frowned into his fermentae bottle as Marcus continued.

"I got a job working hard manual labor at the Koltech ore mine over in the north side of Ruskol. The pay was poor, the work was grueling, but it occupied my body and mind . . . and it put me exactly where I was supposed to be."

Marcus's eyes lit up, and he leaned over his desk towards Hal with hunger in his voice. "You've felt it, haven't you, brother? The chill. The silence. The undeniable feeling that there is something momentous and unknowable hiding outside the borders of your perception. A whisper in the back of your skull that makes you wonder, no, makes you *know*, there is something grand and eternal and true just barely beyond your reach. You can't explain it, but you know it's there, you're certain it's there, and it haunts you, tugging at your soul, calling out to you, yearning to be found!"

His voice rose in volume and passion, showing a fire that Hal had never before seen in his brother. Marcus smiled. "I was alone in a side shaft when I felt it, Hal. I felt there was something more. My pick chipped away the dirt and shadows and there it was: Celestia's gift. A gift that had been buried beneath the earth for centuries, just waiting to be discovered. Once I touched it, I knew I had found something glorious, and everything else was set in motion. The path in front of me was revealed."

Marcus grabbed his own cane and held it aloft, gesturing towards the heavy jewel-cut meteor fragment that rested on top. "All the other religions, all they have are books and myths. But this—this is real. This is tangible. This is *truth*. And whether you believe me or not, this is our future, brother."

A worried frown set itself across Hal's face. He scratched at his scars, his mind now racing, trying to figure out what the meteor actually was. It was certainly powerful, that much he couldn't deny. It had brought him back from certain death, but the exact implications weren't yet clear. His tail stared unwavering at the meteor chunk, transfixed.

How was it that of all the people in the world, only he and his brother had been the ones to find the fallen star and feel its otherworldly nature? He wasn't worried that Marcus might be insane; he was worried that Marcus may be right. That scared Hal, and he couldn't tell exactly why. He offered a cautious question, egging his brother on. "So what future is that, Marcus?"

Marcus grinned, his lips curling into a smile of proud certainty. "A better world, Hal. Where we don't need to deny what we are."

He walked over to the window and gazed out onto the darkened streets of Anduruna. "When I look outside, do you know what I see, Hal? I see an empty sky lurking over a corrupt and diseased city. It's filled with unenlightened hypocrites who cling to power only by outlawing and suppressing the one thing we all share as Dreamkeepers: our divine powers." Marcus rested both hands on his cane, turning his head slightly back towards Hal. "Imagine if we lived in a city where everyone was encouraged to find their power, rather than dragged into the night, never to be seen again. Imagine if Katya and Mother and Father all had their power and the knowledge to use it when the gunmen came. They could have saved themselves. They could have prevented the worst day of our lives from ever happening."

"You don't know that."

"Yes, I do! And you know it too, even if you don't have the courage to admit it!" Marcus shouted defiantly, his posture stiffening. "Change is coming, Hal. It's inevitable."

Hal grunted in response, shaking his head. "So all of a sudden you're a revolutionary fighting the good fight, huh? Rah rah, down with the establishment?"

"Of course I am. Why should we be complacent and settle for comfortable oppression when we have the power to do so much more?" Marcus shook his head at Hal's caution. "Trust me. We're not the only group in Anduruna that's interested in seeing change like this."

"Is that so?" Hal leaned back, absorbing the revelation. "So, what, you're building a coalition to overthrow the government?"

"Not exactly." Marcus sighed. "I thought about it, but let's just say that the others don't have the right amount of conviction. They lacked a certain faith that I found to be quite . . ."

"Disturbing?"

"Disappointing."

Hal barked a laugh at the whole ordeal. "You're talking about some pretty serious stuff, Marcus. What in the world makes you think you have even the coldest chance in hell of changing things?"

Marcus waved one arm as if physically brushing the question aside. "We can discuss the many answers to that question later on, but I think

I've indulged your curiosity enough for now. I have some questions of my own."

Hal grimaced, swirling the contents of his partially drained fermentae bottle. "This should be good. Got any really big ones I can answer for you? Like, what is beauty?"

Marcus frowned at his brother, giving him an unamused stare. "Oh, don't be an ass, Hal. I know that sarcasm is a defense mechanism for you, but I simply don't have the patience for it anymore." His sharp tone cut through the feigned levity in an instant. "Vanir told me that she shot you several times and kicked you into the river—"

"Thanks for that, by the way," Hal quipped, cutting his brother off.

Marcus stared daggers back at him. "Stop it. When I felt Celestia's new gift fall, I didn't expect anyone to reach it before my agents, let alone my own long-lost brother. Vanir was only following my instructions to not allow anyone else to discover the true power of the meteor. You don't have to take it so personally, Hal."

"Well, excuse me, Marcus, because being gunned down and left for dead sure as hell *felt* like a very personal and life-altering experience to me!" Hal didn't bother trying to contain his outrage. "It doesn't matter if it was me or Miri or some random other person out for a hike in the snow. You don't just murder people for being in the wrong place at the wrong time."

"When the stakes are this high, you do what you have to do," Marcus shot back. "This meteor isn't just powerful, Hal. It's power. *True* power. It can unlock the greatest ability from each and every Dreamkeeper! And if it got into the wrong hands before it got into mine, that would have been a catastrophe for the future of our world!"

Hal shook his head, muttering a sad little laugh. "If it's that important, why didn't you go grab the meteor yourself rather than sending your obviously evil little bitch after it?"

Marcus spun on Hal and grabbed him by the throat, pushing him back into the chair. His tail blades hovered dangerously close to Hal's eyes as his face leaned in, rage simmering behind the glare. "Because I'm a very busy man trying to change the world. That so-called 'evil little bitch' is my most devoted apprentice *and* my lover. I won't let you call her that again in my presence. Are we clear?"

Hal snarled back at Marcus and his tail bared its fangs, but he was in a defenseless position and didn't have the luxury of being able to argue the point. "Clear." As Marcus released him and stepped back, Hal rubbed his neck. "She's your lover yet she didn't recognize the family resemblance when she ran into me?"

Marcus sighed, taking a moment to swallow some of his own drink. "Believe me, Hal, when she returned with the girl and I realized that it was you who had been shot, I was furious beyond words. I asked the same question myself." Marcus sat back down and stared off at the wall, anger once again giving way to a look of sadness. "But everything seems obvious in hindsight, and I have myself to blame for her ignorance." He took another swig of fermentae, his gray and yellow eyes angling back towards Hal. "You see, after all this time, I had never told Vanir that I even had a brother. I told her the rest of my family had been killed years ago."

Hal finished off the last of his drink as he listened, finally setting the heavy glass bottle down on the desk with a light clank. "Why not tell her the truth, Marcus? Why hide my existence from her?"

"I should be asking you the same question, Hal." Marcus rested both elbows on the desk, leaning towards his brother. "I had a long conversation with Miri after she was brought to me. According to her, you never spoke about our family. She wasn't even aware that the murder of our family is what led you down the path you chose in the first place."

Hal looked at the floor, his lips twisting into a frown. "It's not easy to talk about. You know that."

"I know. It's not easy to even think about." Marcus's eyes seemed to water slightly. "Celestia help us, Hal. What has become of us? Are we so ashamed of each other that we can't even admit our existences to the ones we love?"

Hal looked back into his brother's eyes, Marcus's words hanging heavy between them. He had no witty remark nor honest words to offer that could deny the statement. It was tragic how large the gulf had grown between them since that one fateful night, and they both knew it. The look they shared said it all.

"Marcus," Hal finally said, his voice softer after absorbing that sobering question. "Can I speak to Miri now? I want to see her."

"Yes, of course. That's the whole reason you're here, isn't it? Neither of us expected a family reunion tonight." Marcus rubbed his eyelids. Weariness was taking its toll on both of the Adhil brothers. "I'll take you to her in a minute, but I still have one question that you need to answer first." He blinked at Hal, opening his hands. "How did you survive, Hal? Even if the bullets didn't kill you, you should have drowned and froze to death in that river."

"I was afraid you'd ask." Hal scratched at his chest. "I had a fragment of the meteor in my front pocket when I was shot. Shards of that fragment embedded themselves in my body. I guess your rock is the only reason I'm here talking to you now."

Marcus's expression barely changed; he had a good poker face, but Hal could hear the wheels begin to turn in his brother's mind. Hal continued, "I don't know if I actually died or was just in a coma for a few days, but the meteor is a part of me now, and I can feel it changing me. I can't describe it, Marcus, but it's like I'm being both sustained and torn apart all at once. My power is changing. Each day that goes by I feel it spread a little further, and it's . . ." Hal looked straight into his brother's eyes, his voice desperate and truthful. "It's terrifying."

"Indeed." Marcus's voice had an eager breathlessness to it. "Change is always terrifying, Hal, but this is all happening for a reason. It can't be an accident that we've been brought back together like this. Maybe . . ." Marcus allowed a small smile to cross his features. "Maybe if we learn to be brothers again, we can both make it to the other side of this coming storm."

Marcus stood and walked over to Hal, helping him up from his seat and handing him his cane. "We have so much more to talk about, so much more to do, but we can save the rest for a new day." Hal steadied himself as Marcus helped him up. "Come, brother. Follow me and I'll take you to your friend. I'm sure the two of you have a lot to talk about."

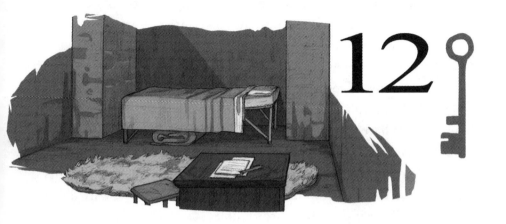

Marcus led Hal out of his stateroom and into the dimly lit halls of the church. They slowly weaved their way through corridors and down staircases, heading seemingly deeper into the labyrinth that served as Marcus's new home. Hal's energy was spent, and he leaned heavily on his cane with each step, his head sagging with fatigue. His eyes, however, remained alert as they walked and he did his best to mentally map the route.

Marcus walked calmly and patiently, leading Hal by a step. His footsteps carried little weight, and only the light taps of his own cane marked the time and distance spent. Those sharp yellow irises glanced sidelong at Hal. "It's fortunate that you're here, brother." Marcus's voice broke the cadence. "I've been in a difficult position ever since Vanir brought Miri back with her."

"What, is she too much for you to handle?" Hal smirked, remembering just how insistent Miri could be when she felt strongly about an issue.

Marcus sighed. "I can't trust her, Hal. She's an unwilling accomplice who already knows far too much about my operations." The eyes angled away again. "If she got out, she could interfere greatly with the plans I've been working for years to lay down."

"So she's a prisoner." It wasn't a question.

"In a manner of speaking, yes. For now." Marcus turned the corner and led Hal down another staircase. "In truth, I would have preferred for Vanir to have shot her and brought you to me instead. Everything would have been much simpler."

Hal grunted in displeasure. His tail bared the slightest flash of its fangs. "You don't seem to have a problem with violence. Why didn't you just kill her if she's too much trouble?"

Marcus stopped at the base of the stairs and turned towards Hal, blocking his path. "Because, Hal, I'm not some lunatic murderer. Killing is a very final and decisive choice, and as defiant as she is, she is still useful in certain ways." He stared directly into Hal's eyes for a few heartbeats before leading him onward. "I need you to convince her to join our side."

"*Our* side?" Hal snorted. "I'm not on anyone's side, Marcus. I just want to be free to go on my way and live my own life."

"That's precisely the problem, Hal." Marcus gestured with his free hand towards the air. "In this city of ours, we don't actually have the freedom to live as we choose. To embrace the powers that make us who we are. Until that changes, none of us will ever be free."

"I'm not a revolutionary, Marcus, or a politician." Hal shook his head. "I don't want to be involved."

Marcus's voice dropped a few notes. "We often don't have a choice when we discover who we must be."

The gravity of those words sustained a silence between them that continued until they reached their destination. They were now somewhere in the basement of the church, far removed from the opulent chamber where Hal had listened to sermons just hours before. Down here, the construction was much simpler, the air much cooler, and the rest of the world so much further away. In this simple corridor, another robed man stood guard in front of an unmarked door.

"Here we are." The guard seemed about to speak up at their approach, but Marcus silenced him with a sharp wave of one hand. "You can stay the night here; this is Miri's room. In the morning we can talk more about where to go from here."

Hal swallowed, a sudden dryness settling over his mouth. Anxiety tightened every tendon in his body. "Am I a prisoner now, too?"

"You're my brother, and our guest. I'll make sure my people know this." Marcus glanced over at the guard. "But I need you to stay here for now, until we can work things out. There are a lot of things we need to discuss, but I think the rest is better saved for once we're all rested and ready."

Marcus nodded towards the glimpse of Hal's holstered weapon, hiding beneath his jacket. "To prove to you that I'm willing to start over, I'll allow you to keep your springer. As long as you don't start shooting, my men will do the same. Causing trouble isn't in anyone's best interest right now."

"And if I disagree?"

Marcus sighed at Hal's habitual insistence on being contrary. "Then the story of our reunion will end rather abruptly and violently, I'm afraid. You're outnumbered and outgunned and you won't get far." He leaned in closer to Hal, voice low and serious. "But do me a favor, Hal, and just be patient. I know we've both made mistakes in the past, but that doesn't mean we can't learn to move past them together."

"Alright." Hal frowned, but nodded his understanding. The events of the past few hours had been so overwhelming, he didn't have the will to debate Marcus over his odds of survival. "I'll see you in the morning, then."

Marcus nodded and reached for the door handle. One taloned hand curled around the polished metal, and with a gentle sigh the door pulled open and Hal was ushered in.

"Damn it, can't you people ever kn—Oh!"

And there she was, dressed in the same style of garb as the other Celestials, her last word halting with a sharp cry of astonishment. "Hal?"

A flood of emotion welled up with a paralyzing rush, and Hal could barely manage a trembling smile. He tried to speak but all that emerged was a barking cough that quickly devolved into a sob. Miri nearly tackled him as she wrapped her arms around him, and they each stood there crying, heavily and freely, as they embraced.

The door shut behind them, dimming the room a shade as the two were left alone to cope with a reunion neither expected to be possible. For a few minutes there were no words, only the shared exchange of happiness, relief, and saline. Eventually, the flood subsided enough for Miri to speak, her voice muffled, buried in his shoulder. "Hal! I can't believe you're still alive. I can't believe it."

"Me either." Hal inhaled a deep shuddering breath, attempting to steady his composure. Just the subtle scent of her hair and the reminder of her voice triggered a flash of forgotten memories. Cold nights out among the wind and snow. A sky dripping with starlight. A gentle laugh and a wry smile.

She took a step back and wiped the tears from her eyes, looking Hal over as if she doubted what she was seeing. "It is you, isn't it?" Miri coughed up a relieved laugh, still blinking away tears. "I thought you were dead."

"Depending on what you believe, maybe I was, for a while." Hal nearly keeled over, his energy stores now completely expended by the outpouring of emotion. Miri helped catch him, and her face twisted into a worrisome frown as she absorbed some of his weight.

"Whoa, are you ok? You look terrible."

"I don't know. I could be better." Hal sat on the edge of the small bed, and Miri reached over to the end table and shook the glo-orb sitting there. The jar of bioluminescent liquid became energized by the sloshing, and spilled a little more warm light into the cool room. Only then did Hal even have the chance to take notice of his surroundings.

The room was small but well-furnished for a de facto prison cell. The floor, walls, and ceiling all seemed to be constructed of the same cold gray stone that did a poor job of reflecting light and made the confines seem less welcoming. The two of them sat on a comfortable but narrow bed nestled in one corner of the room. Along the opposite wall, a handsome wooden desk sat stacked with assorted scrolls, papers, and books. The path between the two was joined by a thick throw rug that offered a warm alternative to the heat-leeching earth. There were no windows, and the only way in or out was through the single heavy door.

Miri watched Hal as he caught his breath. She didn't say anything, but in her eyes he could sense the question that was waiting to be asked. She squeezed his hand that had been resting empty on one knee, a gentle encouragement to share his story. What happened? How did you survive? They were difficult questions to answer completely.

Hal took a deep breath, and once more did his best to answer them. "The river carried me all the way to the southern edge of the Eridu delta. A farmer's family found me and pulled me from the water." He shook his head slowly. "I was dead, Miri. I didn't have any heartbeat. I didn't dream. There was nothing."

Miri's face was pulled down into a concerned frown as he continued. "But before they could bury me, my heartbeat returned." Hal hesitated for only a breath. "One of the bullets shattered the meteor fragment I had in my pocket, and embedded the shards in my chest. Now, well, now it's a part of me. It's merging with my body, and it is the only explanation for why I was able to come back." He rubbed at the scars under his clothes. "I can feel it spread a little further as each day passes. It feels like it's lifting me up and yet killing me at the same time."

Miri's concerned stare became a look of devastation, as if she was realizing her greatest fear had come true. Tears once again started to well in the corners of her eyes. "No, this can't be happening!"

"I'm sorry."

Miri shook her head violently as if trying to deny reality. "No, Hal, you don't understand. The meteor is dangerous! It's powerful beyond anything we have seen before, and Marcus is *obsessed* with it! He's using it as a weapon and raising his own secret army. He's planning to start a war!" Miri sobbed. "And now you're telling me it's permanently embedded inside you? Does Marcus know?"

Hal looked away. "Yeah."

"Damn it, Hal!" She punched at his arm, sobbing in frustration. "Now he's going to try to use you in all of this madness, just like he's been trying to use me! As if keeping me here was bad enough, now he has you too!" He felt her tears dampen his side. "This is terrible."

Hal wrapped his arms around her as she buried her face in his shoulder. "It's ok, Miri. I found you. We're going to get out of here." He gave a gentle squeeze. "It's going to be ok."

She pushed him back with a shove, disbelieving anger in her glare. "No, Hal! It's not going to be ok!" She waved her arms in exasperation towards the remainder of the small room. "What did you think would happen when you came here? That we would be reunited, everyone would be happy, and then, what, we just walk out the front door?"

Hal was at a loss for words. What had briefly been a happy reunion was now spiraling into a heated argument. Miri continued, wiping away tears. "This isn't some fairy tale, Hal! You're not the knight in shining armor, this isn't the tall tower, and I'm not your damsel in distress! We can't just ride off into the sunset and live happily ever after. This is real life! And we are in some really deep shit right now!"

A dense sadness wrapped itself around Hal, resting heavily on top of the fatigue that already cloaked him. He didn't know what to do next. The day was completely overwhelming, and now the girl he swore to save was throwing reality back in his face.

"Oh, don't look at me like that, Hal, it's breaking my heart." Miri's anger faded, and all that remained was a shadowy silence that dimmed the air between them. They both looked at the ground, neither knowing what to say. After some time, Miri's hand reached out to find his, and her voice was much softer. "Why didn't you tell me about Marcus? About your family? You know I would have listened to you."

Hal grimaced. The memories flashed through his mind, and he blinked them away. "What do you want me to tell you, Miri? They're memories I've been trying to forget for a long time. It was the worst day of my entire life; I lost everything I thought I knew and loved." Hal's head drooped lower. "It's not really something I wanted to talk about."

"But no one should have to hold onto that pain on their own. You can't possibly keep it bottled up forever."

"Not easily."

Miri gave Hal a sad smile, resting one hand on his shoulder. "Hal, you're as stubborn as ever, but it's good to see you again." She leaned in, allowing the comforting gesture to morph into a warm hug.

"It's good to see you too, Miri."

Miri was quiet for a few heartbeats before speaking up. "I guess there's a lot we still don't know about each other, even after all this time." She glanced over at him, her expression softening. "Did I ever tell you that I lost my parents too?"

"What?" Hal pulled back in surprise. "No, I had no idea."

She nodded. "When I was an undergrad. Groundcar accident."

"Oh." Hal's tail coiled itself up, looking into the corner dejectedly. "I'm sorry, Miri."

She shrugged, as if trying to rid herself of the unpleasant memories. "Things like this, they happen sometimes. Life isn't perfect, Hal." Miri tried to fight a smile through the heavy atmosphere. "But, after that, I really focused on my studies, and it helped. Dr. Kincaid became like a second father to me. He's probably worried sick that we never came back from that last expedition."

"I know he is." Hal nodded. "At least we'll have a hell of a story to tell when we see him again."

Miri chuckled lightly. "You're right about that."

She pulled back, looking Hal over. He couldn't see himself, but Hal judged from her reaction that he was not the easiest sight to behold. "Spirits, Hal, you look tired."

He managed a smirk. "Is it that obvious?"

"You could say that." Miri patted the bed with one hand. "Here, lay down. You should rest."

Hal looked over the bed, judging its size. There was enough room for the two of them, but just barely, if they didn't mind sharing body heat. "I can sleep on the floor. It's not a prob—"

"Hal." Miri gave him that all-too-familiar "you're an idiot" stare. "You look like you're about to die from exhaustion. Lie down before I force you to lie down."

He snorted. For some reason he could never win the staring contests with Miri. "All right."

He kicked his feet up onto the bed and shuffled over to one side, easing his way down onto the pillow. The simple act of being horizontal flooded him with a sense of relief, and only then did he realize just how completely tiring the day had been. The cushions seemed to leech from him all the anxiety that had built up, and his eyelids closed without command.

Hal's mind was able to register the soft touch of a hand resting on his skull before the world melted away, and within seconds the world disappeared entirely as he settled into a deep, dream-filled sleep.

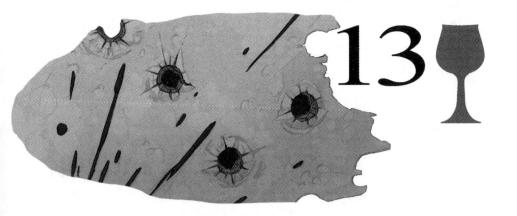

13

Hal rested one hand on the satchel that was slung under one arm. It hung loosely from the strap wrapped around his shoulder, and he patted the canvas with his talons as if reassuring himself that it was still there.

"Relax, Hal." Marcus chuckled at Hal's anxious tic. "We're almost there."

Hal let out a long breath and nodded to his brother. It was just another courier job. Nothing out of the ordinary. The two of them sat together on a ferry that glided through the canals of Calypsa; Marcus seemed to be enjoying the warm summer breeze that carried them forward. "I'm not worried about the delivery. I'm worried about being late for dinner."

Marcus laughed. "It was your idea in the first place to take the job on such short notice. Are you worried about Dad chewing you out again?"

"Aren't you?" Hal grunted. "Using 'it was Hal's idea' doesn't work for you anymore, remember?"

Marcus glanced at his watch, pulling back the sleeve of the nice shirt he was wearing. "Well, consider it an act of good faith that I decided to tag along and keep you company. It's six thirty. If you don't waste time chatting up the boys, we shouldn't be more than a couple minutes late."

Hal looked out at the banks of the canal, watching the scenery slip past. "What's for dinner tonight, anyways?"

"Risotto, I think. Plus the usual sides."

"Awesome."

The ferry was almost at their destination, but it was still a gamble for Hal to risk working on a Sunday evening. Family dinner night was an important event for the Adhil household, and Mom and Dad didn't like it when Hal and Marcus ate into family time by doing other things. A couple minutes late would be forgivable, but not by much. It would be close.

"Did you hear about Katya's test scores?" Pride gave weight to Marcus's voice. "She scored in the ninetieth percentile. She could get into the top schools of the city with results like that!"

"Wow, good for her." Hal was impressed, but he furrowed his brow towards his brother. "Wait, I didn't think the results had even been announced yet. How do you know?"

"They were released today."

"And she didn't tell me?"

"Come on, Hal." Marcus grinned. "I'm her favorite brother. We all know that."

Hal shook his head and chuckled. "Apparently so. I bet she's planning on making an announcement to the whole family at dinner."

Marcus's yellow eyes homed in on the satchel Hal was carrying. "School is great and all, but we're getting close to breaking into bigger and better operations within the family. We've proven ourselves over and over again." Marcus clenched one claw into a loose fist. "We're ready."

"I don't know." Hal shrugged as his tail looked off towards the sun that was gently angling towards the horizon. "Katya seems to be very happy with her scholastic pursuits. Maybe she's on to something."

"She's going to do well, I have no doubt." Marcus nodded as the ferry started to slow down. "But we're meant for even more, Hal. I can feel it. Together we can do anything."

The ferryman brought the shallow-draft ship into dock at the end of a tiny pier, deftly tossing a rope over the wooden pillar to anchor everything in place. The echo of splashing water bounced and bobbed in time with the rocking of the boat as Hal found his balance and stepped onto dry land.

"Heah we ah." The ferryman lifted the brim of his cap, revealing a bright green eye hiding behind a thin wall of wiry gray hair. The eye squinted as he looked up into the sunlight, watching the two brothers leave.

"Thanks, Lawrence." Marcus handed him a couple of crisp fresh bills. "Don't go paddling off on us. We shouldn't be too long."

"Whatevah floats yah boat." The old rat chuckled to himself, a dark smoky laughter that drifted in pursuit of the joke he had told thousands of times before.

The short dock led directly to the entrance of a handsome patio. The perimeter was circled by well-kept hedges and fencing wrapped with ivy. The vines wrapped upwards and over a loose lattice that served as a rooftop, providing a mottled and natural shade to the people underneath. It was a very nice backyard, especially for Calypsa, and it was only accessible through the home at the rear of the patio, or from the canal itself.

A stiff-looking rhino, nearly as broad as he was tall, and a bored-looking mantis, both well dressed, stood guard over the archway that led to the patio. "Marvin. Geno." Hal nodded to each of them in turn and patted the satchel. "I have a delivery for Mister Beneviedes."

Marvin held out one massive hand to halt Hal and Marcus, and spoke in a slow rumbling voice that seemed to send tremors through the ground. "Mister B is attending to important business at the moment." The horned head moved itself with heavy inertia in the shape of a negative nod. "He's not to be disturbed, presently."

"It's just the weekly take from ops on the north side," Marcus interjected. He tapped one talon on the face of his watch. "We're kind of on the clock right now. Can you cut us some slack?"

Marvin seemed ready to offer a rejection, but Geno spoke up with a sharp gesture of his claws. "It ain't no problem." His mandibles clicked as his voice buzzed underneath. "Jonny can help yaz and get yaz on your wayz."

"Thanks, Geno." Hal's tail smiled at the familiar faces. The twin raptors were quietly ushered in by Geno, who led them around the corner. On one side of the patio, a gaggle of well-dressed men sat around a large circular table speaking in hushed tones. The breeze carried from that corner the subtle scents of chilled fermentae and hot food. One of the entourage standing near the fringes of the discussion noticed the new arrivals and flashed a golden smile as he broke away from the main group.

"Evening, gents!" Jonny ran one hand back through his hair as he walked towards them, gesturing towards a free table on the opposite side of the patio. "Take a seat. Mister B is a little occupied, but I can take care of this business for you."

Hal and Marcus each selected a chair and sat down across from Jonny. The canvas satchel hit the center of the table with a soft thud, and Jonny immediately went about opening it up to get at the contents inside. The garish metal rings he wore clicked and clacked against one another as slender fingers deftly began pulling stacks of cash from the bag, arranging them in neat rows on the table.

"Here's the itemized breakdown." Hal pulled a folded sheet of paper from his front pocket and smoothed it flat for Jonny to double check.

"Uh-huh." Jonny licked at his thumb and finished flipping through the last cluster of bills before taking a look at the ledger. He muttered the names of the businesses to himself and began rearranging the sorted money into specific piles for each line item. "Thirteen fifty from Bruno . . . plus five hundred . . ." He glanced back and forth between the paper and the money before nodding in satisfaction. "Looks like it all adds up. We should be good."

Jonny pulled a few bills from one of the stacks and handed them over to Hal. "Much obliged, Hal. Here's your cut for 'services rendered.' Don't go blowing it all on, I dunno, stuff . . . and things." Jonny smirked and tilted his head sideways at Hal. "Shit, Hal, do you even have any hobbies to waste money on?"

Hal accepted the cash with a snort. "I've been saving up."

"For what?"

"I haven't decided yet." He shrugged and started to pocket the cash.

"Hey, what about my share?" Marcus spoke up, eyes narrowing in suspicion.

Jonny laughed. "I didn't see you carrying anything. What am I supposed to pay you for? Hanging out?"

"Come on, Jonny, you know how things work. It's a two-man job. I'm the muscle in case anyone tries to start something." Marcus gestured to Hal. "I mean, come on. Look at him. Hal can barely manage tying his own shoes. He'd be toast if someone started a fight."

"I don't even wear shoes."

"Exactly." Marcus shook his head. "You're terrible with knots. People can smell the weakness."

"Look, Marcus." Jonny held up both hands to quell the banter. "Even if you were worth paying, I can't hand you money, and for purely philosophical reasons."

"What?" Marcus looked confused. "Why not?"

"Well," Jonny leaned in across the table, as if he were about to share some deep secret. "I didn't want you to find out like this, but—" He held one hand up to the side of his face. "You're kind of an asshole."

"Hey!"

Everyone else had a good laugh at that, and Geno's buzzing chuckle seemed to cut through the evening breeze and stand out among the others. Marcus scowled, looking quite unhappy that he was the subject of the playful taunting.

Jonny checked his watch. "Hey, ain't it family night for you two? You should get going. I don't want to hear an earful from your mother about how I'm a bad influence and all that jazz."

"Yeah, you're right. I promised Marcus I'd make this quick." Hal gave Jonny a firm handshake. "Thanks for the help, Jonny. I'll see you around."

Jonny flashed a smile and winked. "Later, boys."

Hal clapped Marcus on the shoulder as he stepped back from the table. "Come on. Let's get going."

The two of them wandered back towards the dock, where Lawrence was still waiting with the ferry. Marcus was scowling, clearly still upset about the perceived snub. Hal let him fume for a couple seconds before reaching into his pocket. "Relax, Marco. Jonny paid both of us. He just likes giving you a hard time." Hal split the money and handed Marcus his fair share.

"Yeah, well, I don't appreciate it when it's in front of the rest of the family." Marcus stepped into the ferry and sat down with a huff, crossing his arms.

"Don't worry about it. Everyone knows it's just a joke." Hal stepped down off the dock and nodded to Lawrence. "Back where we came."

The ferryman grunted his understanding and set about undocking the ship and getting back underway. The narrow-hulled boat gently glided onward, bringing them back upstream towards the western side of Calypsa. Hal and Marcus each sat in silence; Hal once again watched the scenery pass by while Marcus frowned at his feet. Calypsa was many things: mysterious, dangerous, unforgiving . . . but it had its tranquil moments. In those waning minutes of daylight, the reflections off the river seemed to set the entire waterway ablaze with dancing light.

"Hey, Lawrence," Hal spoke up to pass the time, blinking the sunset from his eyes. "Do you ever get tired of pushing people up and down the canals?"

"Nah." The older man shook his head, adjusting the weathered cap that shaded his eyes. "It's a good job." His knobby knuckles gripped the oars firmly as he pushed against the current. "Good people-watching. People coming, people going, good stories. It doesn't mattah who you got. Everyone starts from heah, and tries to get to theah. No one is evah happy to be where they ah."

Hal raised one eyebrow. "But you're different?"

Lawrence gave a short laugh. "Heh, I just enjoy the journey." One of those green eyes briefly emerged from behind the brim, twinkling with life. "You'll undahstand someday."

By the time the ferry reached their destination, it was already a couple of minutes past seven. Hal paid Lawrence for the return trip, and he and Marcus set off along the last few blocks to make it back to their house. They were late, as Hal and Marcus had both feared, but there was no changing that now.

As the two brothers approached the front door, they were greeted with the sound of familiar dinner music. But they shouldn't be hearing it yet; they weren't even inside. The front door creaked and whined as it shifted in the evening breeze, left full open. Hal felt a heavy sense of dread fill his stomach. This didn't feel right. The entire street appeared to be empty of other people.

Marcus and Hal shared a concerned glance and hurried the pace, jogging up to the entrance of their home.

"Mom? Dad?" Hal stepped inside and was greeted with no response, save the music that continued to play.

"Katya?"

He turned the corner into the den, and saw that the couch had been flipped over. The upholstery was pockmarked with pinpoints of cushioning that exploded outward in the blossom of bullet impacts.

"No!"

Hal sprinted forward and vaulted over the couch. As he landed on the other side, he slipped and fell on a slick patch of still-warm blood. Next to him on the floor was his dad's own body, crumpled and motionless. A springer pistol, still unfired, lay inches from one outstretched hand. He scrambled to his knees, grabbing his father's lifeless form with both hands.

This couldn't be real.

This couldn't be happening to him.

"Dad! No!" He repeated those words over and over again, frozen in that moment, rocking his father's body back and forth. This had to be a dream.

"Auuugh!"

Marcus's cry of anguish snapped Hal out of his paralysis. The sound came from the kitchen. Hal released his father's body and ran into the next room.

The sight that greeted him was one he would never forget.

The table was fully set; food in the center, silverware all laid out. Each tall glass was filled with ice water, and a pair more still sat empty, waiting for wine that was never poured. The two candles in the center flickered as the calm jazz music continued to drift from speakers in the other room.

A few paces past the dinner table, near the back door, Hal's mother and sister, each dressed in their Sunday best, lay motionless on the tile floor in thick pools of crimson. One hand was outstretched in the direction of the door handle; a promise of escape that was never realized.

Marcus hugged the body of their little sister, sobbing uncontrollably. Each cry of pain was deep and hoarse, consumed with grief and the unbearable weight of truth. Hal could do nothing but stand there as the scene burned itself into his memory.

Marcus looked up at Hal, and the two locked tragic stares in that unbearable moment that was stretched out into an eternity. His lips twisted into the shape of a word. It was a question that Hal could never answer.

"Why?"

***

With a shuddering gasp, Hal opened his eyes. He was lying on his side of the bed, staring straight at the gray stone wall that rested just a few inches from his face. Reality offered no gentle greeting to his waking mind.

Hal lay there, breathing heavily as a throbbing pulse rapidly tested the veins in every limb. He blinked and shifted his weight as the nightmarish memory faded from his perception. It had been ages since his mind had relived that terrible day. Why now, of all times?

A gentle stirring brought awareness of a warm body behind him. One arm wrapped gently around his waist. The calm exhale of humid breath teased at the nerves in the back of his neck. Miri was curled up close behind him, making the most of the narrow space the two of them shared.

Hal closed his eyes, releasing a long, slow breath. This wasn't the past anymore. This was now. Now was good. Maybe he could just rest like this for a while. It was a moment worth appreciating.

Tendrils of relaxing sleep started to wrap themselves around Hal, but they were rudely interrupted by a sharp sliver of light that assaulted his eyes. The door to the room opened halfway, spilling more relentless light into the room with the groan of a hinge giving way. Both Hal and Miri winced and squirmed at the unwelcome interruption.

"Rise and shine, lovebirds." Vanir's smooth but haunting voice shattered the fleeting tranquility. "It's a new day." A malicious chuckle dispelled the last remnants of peace as the future beckoned once more. "We have so much work to do."

anir led Hal and Miri deeper through the underground level and into the largest room. There, Hal encountered a sight that was somehow both expected yet irreverent: the basement was wide and open, littered with punching bags, free weights, and training dummies. A rather long firing range stretched along one whole side. One corner nearby had an area with a modest kitchen, complete with some counter space, a fridge, a sink, and a few small round tables. Hal's tail blinked all four eyes as he struggled to process the disconnect between what he had expected and what he was seeing. It hardly felt like classical cathedral architecture.

At one table sat Marcus, relaxed and impeccably dressed, as he read the morning paper and sipped a hot mug of tea. A finished bowl of cereal sat just beyond easy reach, pushed aside to make room for the paper. "Good morning, brother." Marcus smiled and raised his mug in greeting, folding the newspaper into a neat rectangle. It was almost an absurd sight: there he was, Hal's long-lost brother and aspiring evil mastermind, eating breakfast in his secret underground training room as if nothing were amiss.

Hal struggled to speak as he looked around the room. "What the hell? What is this, Marcus? Your evil rec room?"

"I said the same exact thing," Miri whispered from behind him.

"Laugh all you want, Hal, but I'm actually quite pleased with it." Marcus wiped his mouth with a napkin and set his folded newspaper to the side. "Do you want some breakfast?"

Hal snorted. "I'm good."

"You'll be hungry in a while, Hal." Surprisingly it was Miri who countered him. "I tried that trick the first time, and I ended up hungry on top of everything else. Just eat some food."

Vanir laughed, causing the corners of Hal's mouth to twitch into a scowl. "You should listen to her. She's a smart one."

Hal didn't appreciate the unsolicited advice, but what troubled him more was the realization that he wasn't really that hungry at all. In fact, over the past few days, he had barely eaten more than a meal or two. Despite the lack of food, hunger was not a sensation he had felt very often, and he wasn't feeling hungry right now. Still, eating breakfast seemed to be the appropriate and inevitable choice.

Hal sighed, grabbing a bagel from a bowl that rested in the center of the table. He chomped half of it off in a single bite, and forced himself to go through the mechanical motions of chewing and swallowing. "All right. Breakfast initiated; you can all give it a rest now."

Hal turned away from the three of them to take in the rest of the room. They weren't alone. At the firing range, two men practiced their marksmanship, firing pistols at dummies clad in heavy trooper armor. The springer rounds pinged and ricocheted off of the sloped metal plating, but every odd shot or so would fly true, finding a gap in the protection or slamming into the target's pockmarked face.

At one of the heavy punching bags, a scarred and hulking Kodiak was quite literally beating the stuffing out of the defenseless target.

With every strike, his fists left deep impressions that were slow to rebound, as if he were a baker punching a soft ball of dough. The chains that held the bag aloft clanked and clattered in protest, barely up to the task of keeping the equipment suspended in place.

In the far corner, two lithe females wrestled and sparred with training knives. Every so often, one would succeed in executing a particularly lethal-looking takedown upon the other. All in all, Hal decided he didn't feel very comfortable around this new company.

"So, I guess this is the point where you're supposed to tell me all about your secret plans to overthrow the government, and through a combination of emotional appeal and/or veiled threats, convince me to help you?" Hal folded his arms; the snark seemed to be flowing freely this morning. "I don't exactly have all the time in the world, so why don't you just do your thing so we can get this show on the road?"

Marcus harrumphed at his twin brother's attitude and stood to his full height, smoothing out some imperceptible wrinkles from his fine clothes. "Don't you want to make some sort of wiseass comment about me starting my own fitness club first?"

"Good point. I'll start paying you for comedy lessons." Hal's tail made a sort of sneering expression as he looked away.

"Enough, both of you," Vanir interrupted before the feedback loop became insufferable. She took it upon herself to begin the inevitable conversation. One black-furred hand gestured to the training room before them. "Call this what you will, but here is where we can train for the conflicts to come, free from prying eyes or outside interference. The people here are all rejects of our good and just society. Ironically, we train these paroled outcasts into weapons to strike back at the tyrants who released them."

"Clever." Hal devoured the rest of his bagel, forcing himself to stop speaking before he said something else to goad them on. Miri rested one hand on his shoulder, the gentle gesture intended no doubt to keep him calm.

"Yes, it is," Marcus said, apparently ready to hit his stride. "I know you don't trust me, Hal. We've had our differences. But you'll see soon enough that we are destined to make something more of what we have."

Marcus walked towards the firing range, his elegant cane making distinct tapping sounds against the stone floor with each step. "Tell me, Hal. Do you enjoy using your special power? Is it important to you?"

"Of course. It's why I went into astronomy in the first place." Hal's eyes narrowed. "It's also something I remember you not handling very gracefully when I decided to start living my own life."

"Indeed." Marcus brushed aside the invitation for argument. "But the past is the past. I'm ready to look forward to the future." As Marcus reached the firing range, the two goons-in-training stopped firing and cleared some space for their leader. They apparently knew better than to interrupt Marcus during one of his dramatic monologues. "We each discovered our powers after that terrible night. Only after it was too late." A sour note flavored the words. "Do you remember what my power was?"

Hal shrugged. "It was some sort of limited telekinesis, right? You thought it was pretty worthless."

"Yes, I did, back then." Marcus set his cane aside and reached down to scoop a couple of spent brass springer cartridges from the floor. In one hand he held onto a single cartridge, and the remainder of the casings he hovered a few centimeters above his other open palm. "I can only manipulate materials I'm already physically touching, and my telekinetic strength is roughly equivalent to my normal muscle strength. It's neat, but really not useful for much more than parlor tricks." As if to demonstrate, he telekinetically hurled one of the brass cylinders downrange where it audibly plinked off of the trooper armor.

Hal didn't feel particularly impressed by the demo. "Your point being . . . ?"

"My point . . . *the* point . . . is that under normal conditions we have only scratched the surface of our true potential." Marcus retrieved his cane and rested one hand comfortably around the meteor chunk that formed the grip, keeping one shell trapped between two fingers. He smiled a self-satisfied smirk, and gestured towards the target with a flourish of his open hand. In an instant the remaining spent shells hurtled through space, slamming into the dummy with the force of a runaway groundcar. The armor exploded in a spectacular hail of metal and polymer, unable to withstand the energy input of projectiles traveling far faster than a normal bullet.

Marcus grinned. "Celestia unlocks our true abilities."

Hal frowned, his tail fidgeting uncomfortably. That second display certainly had got his attention. Had there been a person wearing that armor, all that would have been left was shredded flesh and blood. "Celestia. You mean the meteor."

"Celestia. Meteor. Mineral X. You can call it any name you want." Vanir smiled confidently, wrapping one arm around Marcus and sliding in close. "The results speak for themselves."

"Clearly." Hal furrowed his brow, thinking about the fragments of meteor buried inside his body. "So, what is it, exactly? A power source?"

Marcus nodded, looking past Hal towards Miri. "I think Miri can answer that question more to your satisfaction."

The purple and gray fox took a step forward, adjusting her borrowed robes. "In exchange for *graciously* letting me live, they've put me to work studying the meteor. Apparently none of their recruits are particularly well versed in the scientific method."

She gave Marcus and Vanir an unfriendly sidelong glance, but mostly kept her attention on Hal. "I haven't really had many resources to work with, but so far the best I can tell is that the meteor is more accurately described as a power amplifier, rather than a power source. As you just saw, physical contact with the meteor induces amplified power effectiveness, which varies based on the individual's specific Dreamkeeper power."

Miri spoke quickly and precisely, appearing relieved to finally be addressing another educated person. "The amplification effect is mass-dependent and nonlinear. It's difficult to quantify and measure, since powers vary so much from person to person. I don't have enough data yet to mathematically model it with confidence. Not everyone has a power that lends itself to easy physical observation, either."

Hal listened intently to Miri's explanation, but out of the corner of his eye he caught Vanir whispering something into his brother's ear with a sly smile. He couldn't hear what words were being said, but their smug confidence really pissed him off.

Miri continued. "Generally speaking, a meteor fragment the size of a half-lucre coin, an ounce or two, induces a three- to four-times multiplication of power intensity. Physical contact with the meteor seems to be necessary to obtain the benefits, as mere local proximity has no observable effects. I wish I had more instruments to run radioactive and spectrographic analyses, but *some people* don't feel comfortable giving me access to hi-tech equipment."

Hal scratched at his chest. "Any, um, biological side effects?"

"It's hard to judge since it's outside my area of expertise, and all the data I have is based on short-term exposure." Miri walked close and gently grabbed the hand that Hal was using to itch his scars, putting a stop to the activity. Her expression softened. "Maybe you should be the one to tell me, Hal." She looked up into his eyes, genuine worry hidden behind her square-framed lenses. "Does it hurt?"

"No. Well, not exactly." He blinked and looked away, feeling for some reason both embarrassed and ashamed. His tail looked the opposite direction, flicking its tongue down at the floor. "It's difficult to describe."

"Then show us instead," Marcus said, interrupting the brief moment Miri and Hal were sharing. "After all, you wouldn't be alive right now if it weren't for the piece of Celestia you carry around inside you. I think we all deserve to see how it is affecting you."

"Why? So you can learn how to make better terrorist soldiers? Or do you just have morbid curiosity about how it's destroying your own brother's life?" Hal felt anger quickly surge into his voice as he snapped back at Marcus. Miri took a defensive step away.

"Destroy you?" Marcus shook his head. "It's already saved you, Hal. Given you life when you should have perished. It's reunited us after years of distance and silence."

"It's brought you back to your beloved Miri," Vanir added with a malevolent chuckle.

"That's it! I've had about enough of your—"

"Hal." Miri was there again in front of him, her hands resting on his shoulders. "Don't worry about them. Relax."

Hal balled his claws into fists and relaxed them again, restraining his outrage. She spoke with that quiet but forceful tone that he had never been able to completely resist.

"Look. I need you to listen to me." She kept her volume low, meeting Hal's eyes. "The meteor that's inside you is powerful and dangerous. I need to understand what it's doing to you. If we learn how it works, we might be able to learn how to stop it." She relaxed her grip a little. "I need you to help me so I can figure out how to help you. Can you do that for me?"

Hal took a deep breath and slowly released it. She was right, of course. As much as he hated the situation, they needed to figure things out, and resisting would only put them both in more danger. Marcus wasn't going to just let him walk away. "All right."

Miri nodded and stepped back, offering a slight smile. She pulled a pencil and notepad from one of the pockets on the Celestial robe she was wearing. "When you're ready, activate your power, then tell me what you see and feel."

Marcus and Vanir watched with rapt attention. Even the scattered henchmen paused in their activities, and a breathless silence enveloped the room. Hal swallowed, nervousness gripping his heart. He felt the weight of so many unspoken expectations in that moment. In the end, there was nowhere for him to go but forward.

A prismatic and shimmering halo materialized over his head as Hal awakened his power. The entire world seemed to stretch as senses expanded and colors multiplied. He could see the body heat of all the people around him, the bright pinpoints of radiance from the meteor shards some carried, the faint ultraviolet from scattered glo-orbs. All of this was familiar to Hal, and yet, he felt more.

It was almost impossible to articulate with words; he didn't know where to begin. Sounds like the faintest of whispers echoed in his mind. Each living person around him seemed to have a magnetic pull that he could feel in his blood. When he closed his eyes, he could taste the cool dampness of the air, smell the barest hint of Vanir's perfume, hear Miri's subtle heartbeat.

Deep, voluminous arcs of fog billowed from his nostrils at the conclusion of every fortifying breath. The pain from his wounds was gone, replaced with a restless tingling of energy. It felt amazing. He was standing in the center of his world, surrounded by a kaleidoscope of life.

"Well?" Marcus's shape asked with expectation. "Don't leave us in suspense, Hal. What does it feel like?"

"It feels great." Hal began to walk around without his cane, boldly flexing his damaged leg. "The pain is gone. I can feel . . . everything. Light. Sound. Breath. Blood." His voice took on a manic edge. "I don't have words to describe the feeling. They're incomplete."

"Why is his breath so foggy?" asked Vanir's gravity. He tasted her eager curiosity. Miri's heartbeat moved closer to him.

"Is he extracting energy from the air around him?" Miri smelled like uncertainty. "That doesn't seem physically possible."

"This is more than I remember last time." Hal's tail looked up at the ceiling, tasting the air. He continued to pace around the punching bag that served as the center of his accelerating orbit. "I need new words."

"Hal, slow down." Miri paced alongside him, alarm sharpening her sound. Heat shaped like a hand grabbed his wrist, pressing firmly against a throbbing vein. "Spirits! Hal, you need to stop. Your heart rate is insane."

The words fell on the floor, unacknowledged. He kicked them aside to clear a path. The sound of static filled his brain, like sand pouring from a broken hourglass. The weight of the flow came from somewhere up above. He turned towards the white noise, the volume increasing as he homed in on the source. Somewhere, out beyond the invisible walls of stone and life, there it was.

The searing cold light of another fragment of heaven stared back at him, piercing his mind. The kaleidoscope stopped turning. All time and space became silence itself. The hourglass was empty.

"Hal!"

The universe snapped back in a shuddering instant.

Miri's open hand finished the follow-through of a full-powered slap to the face that shook Hal from his trance. Tears flowed freely from her eyes, running down to salt trembling lips that curled into an expression of desperate anger and fear. A warm tingling throb of pain spidered across one side of his face.

Hal blinked.

"Fascinating." Marcus approached Hal, his cane marking each footstep with a tap.

"Fascinating?" Miri was outraged. "Holy shit, Marcus! That was madness! He wasn't even aware of what was happening to him!" she sobbed, emotion filling the air. "That's not a normal reaction!"

"Then I suggest you take your data and figure things out." Marcus dismissed Miri with the wave of a hand.

"You son of a—" Miri looked ready to punch Marcus square in the face, but two of his minions grabbed her arms, holding her back.

Hal wanted to yell out in protest, but he could barely stand upright, wobbling unsteadily on his pained legs. Each breath was laborious and tight, as he had to fight for every molecule of oxygen forced into his lungs. The constricted world did not greet him gently, and he was slow to recover.

Marcus retrieved Hal's cane from the floor, stepping close to help steady his brother. He offered Hal the grip, yellow and gray eyes never wavering. A hunger hid beneath the words that followed. "Hal, tell me. What did you see?"

Hal curled his fingers around the handle of his cane, staring back into his brother's eyes. "The meteor." The terrifying answer flowed all too freely from his lips. "There's another meteor out there."

"**A**nother meteor?" The entire room fell silent. Marcus's tone took on a breathless quality. "Where?"

Hal shook his head, still struggling to regain his breath. "I don't know where exactly. It's somewhere in that direction. That's all I know." He waved one claw towards the wall where his tail continued to stare.

"This changes things." Hal's brother glanced over at Vanir. "We need to retrieve it at once. With just a little bit more, we will have enough shards to equip each and every one of us."

Vanir nodded, smiling confidently. "We'll finally be ready to move on to the next phase."

"Vanir, take Hal and determine its true location. Let's not waste any time. I'll spread the word for everyone to assemble."

"Wait. Hold on." Hal seemed to finally find balance on the legs underneath him. "I never said I was going to help with any of this."

Marcus narrowed his eyes, staring Hal down for a tense moment that seemed to stretch on while Miri fruitlessly struggled against the two goons that continued to hold her back. Finally, Marcus broke the silence. "I'll make you an offer, Hal. An offer that should give us both exactly what we want."

"I'm listening."

"Help me just this once. Help me find this last meteor fragment, and I'll let you and Miri go free. You won't ever have to talk to me again if you so choose. Just stay out of my way, and we'll be even."

"Even?" Hal snorted. "I don't owe you anything in the first place. You're holding Miri and I hostage, and you think I owe you something? If anything, it's the other way around. You're delusional."

"Am I? You may not think so now, but soon enough we will be living in a different world. One bigger and freer than you could possibly dream of." Marcus clenched his talons into a tight fist of passion. "Trust me, you'll be more thankful of the events that brought us together when you see how everything turns out."

"Sure." Hal turned away, bracing his weight with his cane.

Marcus sighed. "Look. That's the deal, Hal. Take it or leave it. If you leave it, I'll have to keep both of you under lock and key until all the dust settles, and it will take much longer without your eyes to help me."

Hal looked over at Miri. She looked uncertain. Maybe even a little afraid. Not afraid of Marcus or his gang, but scared, perhaps, that this might be their only clean chance to escape before it was too late. Time was not a luxury he could afford to waste. She gave him a silent nod, and that urged him forward.

He took a deep breath, letting the air out slowly before offering an answer. "All right, Marco. All right. Let's just get this over with."

"Let's." Satisfaction dripped from Marcus's single word of agreement.

Vanir approached Hal with a bone-chilling smile, slipping an arm around his. "Come with me, Hero. We have work to do."

***

A short while later, Hal and Vanir were standing outside in the blindingly bright sun of late morning. The streets were filled with the chaotic hustle and bustle of thousands of people going about their lives, blissfully unaware that there was some anarchist group getting ready to do who-knows-what to the city.

Vanir had changed from her more formal Celestial robes into comfortable street clothes. She wore a close-fitting pair of jeans and a light jacket that wrapped around her lithe frame surprisingly well. It was the first time Hal had really got a good look at Vanir since all this madness began. She was certainly fit, and many would say that she was strikingly beautiful. Her bright blue eyes contrasted severely with her deep black fur, and her ethereal accent only added to her air of mysterious and exotic beauty. She stood tall and confident among the crowds of the streets, as if the entire world was already her own to command.

It was difficult for Hal to guess her age, but she was probably a couple years older than he and Marcus. Whether that number was two, five, or eight years older, he had no way of knowing. It wasn't a surprise that his brother would be attracted to Vanir, but Hal wasn't sure how Marcus was able to overlook her less appealing qualities. Her eyes and her smile always seemed to have a subtle cruelty hiding underneath the surface. Likewise, her laughter, though light and pleasant to the ear, had an undercurrent of playful malice that Hal could always detect. She was a dangerous woman, and Hal knew she wouldn't hesitate to kill if it served her aims.

"So, where to, Mister Hero?" Vanir smiled at him with mischief in her eyes. She stood close to him, her body language friendly and familiar. To other observers in the Theophanies streets, they might look like lovers going on a pleasant stroll through the city.

Hal grunted, tightening his grip on his cane. "I don't know why you keep calling me that. My name is Hal." He frowned, looking down the main boulevard that ran through the center of the district. "The light came from that direction. It felt like it was a ways off. It could be in the Norvondire district." He looked around anxiously at the buzz of people that appeared to pay him no mind. "I can't take another look unless we're in private."

"I can take care of that." Vanir gave him a wink and stepped forward, beckoning him to follow her. "There's a luxury groundcar depot only two blocks away. Let's catch a ride."

The two walked together along the edge of the boulevard, moving at a modest pace that Hal could manage. It was an odd feeling, walking alongside the woman who just weeks earlier had shot him multiple times in the chest. He had reservations about even playing along with their plan to acquire more Celestial meteor fragments, but Hal didn't know any other plausible option for getting out of the hole he was trapped in. Fighting his way out would be incredibly risky, and in his mind, it ranked a very distant plan B. As much as Hal was loathe to admit it, Vanir had the right idea. A groundcar would be a good discreet way of traveling through Anduruna. The telepads that dotted the city made for faster travel, but privacy was not an option.

"So, this is what life is for you, huh?" Hal quipped, lowering his head so he didn't have to meet eyes with Vanir. "Wake up in the morning, eat some breakfast, go hunting for some miracle mineral that makes us all gods, shoot some people, go home, and then unwind with a nice cup of tea?"

"Some days." Vanir laughed, sending a chilly tremor down Hal's spine. "Don't tell me you have hard feelings about our first meeting."

"Me? No. Not at all." Hal didn't hide the unpleasantness in his voice. "As a matter of fact, I enjoy the limp. Life was just way too fast when I could walk around without constant pain."

"Cooperate, and we won't need to repeat the exercise." Vanir gave a quick glance over her shoulder. "Situations change. We don't have to be enemies, you know."

"Right." The dry sarcasm could almost be tasted. "I think we're already becoming fast friends."

Vanir merely laughed at Hal's less-than-friendly reply. Soon enough they reached the groundcar depot, where a small handful of comfortable enclosed carts were parked together, each one hitched to a well-groomed and well-trained manekale. Vanir paid the eager attendant on duty, and they were quickly ushered into the carriage of the lead car by a smiling, white-gloved driver.

"Take us to Norvondire. We'll give you more specific directions when we get there," she commanded the usher with a silky but forceful smile. Once they were off, she slid shut the privacy curtain between the front of the cab and the passenger compartment in back, leaving her and Hal in relative privacy and comfort.

"You don't need to talk to me if you don't want to. But you will need to use your power to guide us more directly." Her eyes were locked onto his own, a taut sense of expectation bridging the gap between the two of them.

Hal sighed. He felt nervous about activating his power again, but after a few measured breaths to steel his resolve, he sat back and half-closed his eyes, letting his awareness slip into another phase of reality. Barely a second had passed before Hal was almost doubled over in his seat, absolutely overwhelmed by the bombardment on his senses.

He could see all the indescribable colors of other ranges of light, but layered on top of that was a tingling pressure exerted by all the other Dreamkeepers nearby. He could somehow feel the intangible touch of life all around him: the sharp aggression of a gang of street thugs as they closed in on a target to rob. The bright, desperate flood of emotion from two young lovers curled together near the window of a nearby apartment. The dim boredom of a retail clerk as she counted down the long minutes until another workday was over. Somewhere, out beyond the wall of pressure that surrounded him, was that white-hot light of a meteor fragment.

"Keep going north to northeast. It's a ways off." Hal could barely hear himself as he spoke, and he inhaled deeply to keep himself from suffocating underneath the chaos that seemed to surround him from all sides.

Vanir watched Hal carefully as they continued. He could smell her curiosity intermingled with her delicate perfume. Calculations were being executed just out of his sight, deep inside her skull. The world was almost too bright for his dilated pupils, even in the confines of the carriage. No matter what direction he turned, he couldn't look away.

Soon tension welled up inside of his heart, growing tighter as the groundcar traveled forward. The pressure of life around him was permeated by overtones of fear, suspicion, and aggression. Quickly, the tension reached an unbearable level, and with a silent snap, Hal deactivated his power. Suddenly, he found himself sitting with Vanir back in the real world, gasping mightily for air. It took him a good while to regain his composure and his energy, and only after a minute of labored breathing did he realize the groundcar had come to a complete stop.

"Miss, it looks like we have a roadblock." The driver's voice drifted into the compartment from further up front.

Vanir sighed sharply, irritation apparent in her features. With a beckoning tilt of the head, she opened the door and stepped back out onto the streets. Hal followed behind her.

Just ahead of them was a barricade of troopers, heavy sloped armor reflecting bright in the sun. "SAFETY TROOPER" was painted in dark capital lettering along the full-length shoulder-shields they all wore. Those shields covered most of their body from a side profile, giving them near total protection when arranged in a firing position. Behind the barricade, other soldiers appeared to be finishing up an armed raid. Suspects were being dragged out onto the street and restrained facedown on the ground. Some of the detained shouted and struggled fruitlessly, while others were silent. One of them didn't move at all, a dark pool of blood seeping from underneath his prone form. Smoke billowed from a second-story window while shattered glass and spent springer cartridges dotted the sidewalk.

"This is a restricted area! For your protection, please stay back!" one of the perimeter troopers shouted at the scattered spectators, urging them away, while other soldiers stoically held the line. The trooper's face was concealed beneath the identity-guarding balaclavas they all wore, but his voice sounded young. Despite his apparent youth, the insignia on his helmet indicated he was a veteran noncommissioned officer. It was likely this raid was only one among many the soldier had experienced.

Vanir didn't appear fazed by the violent scene in front of them, and she approached the roadblock with the faintest hint of a superior smile on her lips. "Is there a problem here, Officer?" The last word emerged with a twinge of condescension.

"Hey! What part of 'stay back' don't you understand?" The trooper held one hand forward in the universal stop gesture. "This is an active crime scene. No one is allowed through until everything is over."

"Oh. I see." Hal watched Vanir's eyes narrow. "And what did these *criminals* do?"

"That's none of your business, citizen. Now back off!" His voice took on a sharper, more authoritative edge. The barrel of his springer rifle raised ever so slightly to point at the ground nearer to their feet. "Clear the area immediately, or I'll place you under arrest for obstruction! You won't get another warning."

Vanir seemed to be looking the officer over, mentally taking notes. Rather than goad him on, she relented, taking a step back after one last glance at the suspects on the other side. She turned and walked back to their groundcar, grabbing Hal by the arm and guiding him back with her.

"Go around," Vanir directed their driver with a firm tone as she shut the passenger door with a slam. Once the car was in motion, she regained her composure, forcing her obvious disdain back beneath the surface. Her attention returned to Hal. "Can you tell how close we are?"

Hal was reluctant to use his power again, but yet, at the same time, a part of him wanted to use it even more. To perceive the entire world even deeper than he had before. He dipped his toes once again, only briefly, and snapped back with another gasping breath.

"We're closer, but it's still somewhere beyond here. I think it's further north. It could be back in Calypsa even." Hal shook his head, gathering himself.

Vanir relayed the directions to the driver, who was more than happy to ferry them across two districts to collect a handsome fare. The groundcar soon settled into a steady pace, working its way through the streets of Norvondire, leaving the grisly trooper raid long behind them. She tilted her head to the side. "Now do you see why we need to change this city? Those people the troopers were arresting, shooting, shoving facedown into the dirt. They were just young men, teenagers even, assaulted for the so-called crime of being yourself."

"Yeah, you're right." Hal nodded in agreement. "Shooting people for touching a rock is a much more fair and just application of lethal force." The sarcastic smile on his lips devolved into an angry sneer. "Why don't you take a hint and just leave me alone?" Hal paused. "I'm not your friend, and I doubt I ever will be."

"My, my," Vanir said with a self-satisfied smile. "So certain of that, are you?" She chuckled a little. "You really are Marcus's brother."

"Marcus and I are not the same."

"No, you're not." Vanir nodded in agreement. "Marcus takes action when he sees something he doesn't like. He doesn't mope about and complain like an insolent little boy, hoping that everything will get better even though he does nothing."

Hal felt a surge of anger well up inside his chest, but he trapped it before it burst out. He wasn't going to take the bait in her verbal sparring match. He exhaled sharply and turned his attention back out the window.

They traveled in silence for quite some time; the only words exchanged were terse directions on how to navigate closer to the meteor-light. Eventually, though, a question broke through the forced quiet. "I know you don't like me, Hal. To be honest, I don't think I like you very much either." Vanir smiled, that hint of mischief showing through. "But we're going to be family someday. At least we can be civil with one another."

Hal felt his heart skip a beat, freezing his blood. "Family?" He asked the question he already felt he knew the answer to. "What do you mean by that?"

The smile widened. "I'm pregnant."

The sudden storm of emotions sent Hal's mind into a tailspin. He was going to be an uncle? An uncle to the child of his egomaniacal brother and his brother's murderous girlfriend? Hal didn't even know if his affliction would allow him to survive long enough to see the day when it became reality. That thought solidified the anger in his heart into an even sharper edge. "Congratulations. I'm sure you'll make a great, loving mother. Set a good example."

"Oh, I will." Vanir didn't acknowledge the obvious sarcasm. "We're going to burn down the old to build up the new, and I will give my child, your nephew, a world worth living in. He won't be constrained by the barriers of this society. He will grow up knowing only a city that allows him to be free."

Hal scowled. "I don't care about your little revolution, so stop trying to sell me on it. In reality, you're not so different from the troopers back there; you just wear nicer clothes and wrap your lust for power in the comfy veneer of religion and destiny."

"Hmm. Such an insightful young man." Vanir's eyes lit up. "So observant. But such talent is wasted without a cause." Her head tilted, the curl of a smile tugging at the edge of her lips. "I wonder if beneath that wit of yours you care about anything at all in this world."

Hal didn't answer her.

"Nothing?" Vanir's voice took on a curious tone. "I wonder what Miri would think."

The anger that was waiting beneath the surface finally burst through. "That's it!" Hal slammed his fist into the side of the door. "Why are you always teasing me about her? Why the hell do you care at all about our lives? My life was going fine before you showed up and took it all away from me." His vision blurred from the tears that started to pool in the corners of his eyes. "Stop toying with me and let me go back to living what short amount of life I have left!"

The driver's voice drifted from the front of the groundcar. "Is everything all right back there?"

"Yes, everything is fine," Vanir answered without turning from Hal. He fought back a sob and blinked the water from his eyes, turning away. His tail hissed at her, hatred apparent in its cluster of red eyes. When Vanir finally spoke again, her voice was lower, more guarded. "You don't actually know that you're dying. You think the meteor is a sickness? It's a gift that's giving you more power than you've ever had before. You think you're dying? You've *already* died. Your old life is gone, and now you're beginning a new one. Here. Today. This very moment, in fact." Her eyes narrowed sharply. "You may hate me for what's been done, but you need to learn that all life is change. You can either hide from it or embrace it. Celestia teaches us these things."

Hal shook his head, exhaustion replacing his anger like a slow-rolling wave. "I don't need your lectures." He crossed his arms and looked at the floor. "Just leave me alone."

"Our little trip can end as soon as you find the meteor."

And thus, that simple fact, that promise of release, guided Hal's focus back to the task at hand. It took him some time to get his bearings again. The groundcar had stopped at the intersection in front of Calypsa District University. Hal's alma mater. They were already out of Norvondire? They must have been traveling for a lot longer than Hal had realized.

The campus was a welcome and familiar sight to Hal, who had spent the last several years studying and working there. His days at school were a sharp inflection point in the course of his life, when he'd walked away from everything he knew before. The avenue up to the main building was lined on either side by those curious goblet-shaped trees that dotted the slopes of the Starfall Mountains. The old, hard, spiral-swept wood wrapped around a hollow core that was filled with a thick bed of amber leaves. Just beyond, the main building itself stood regal and proud, sturdy architecture wrapped behind a veil of ivy.

Hal summoned his power yet again. The white noise of the meteor was so much louder now, filling his skull with a deafening non-sound. The hot fragment of starlight was close. Very close. Hal blinked, making sure he was seeing it right. It looked like this final meteorite was actually somewhere inside the university itself. He snapped out of his trance, swallowing hard to erase the dryness that now flooded his mouth.

"I think . . ." Hal inhaled a ragged breath. "I think the meteor is inside the university. Fourth floor."

"Are you sure?"

Hal looked back with his normal eyes. Scattered pockets of students walked around in the distance, happily ignorant of the cursed stone that hid somewhere behind the walls. Even now, without using his power, he could feel the invisible tug against his heart. "It's there." He swallowed again. "I'm sure of it."

"I think I can sense it too, just barely, now that we're closer. All of us awakened develop a sense for it. Celestia's children recognize their own." Vanir struggled to hide her eagerness as she craned her head in an attempt to get a better look out the window. "All right. Let's head back, then. We can't have you go running in there, using your power during the middle of the day. We'll return at night to retrieve it." She pulled herself back, fixing Hal with that same evil smile. "Good work, Hero."

As the groundcar pulled away, Hal's stomach clenched into tangled knots. He tried to relax, leaning his weary body against the window and closing his eyes, but it was no use. No matter how hard he tried, he couldn't shake the feeling that he had just made another wrong decision.

By the time Hal and Vanir made it back to the cathedral, the day was transitioning from afternoon into evening. They walked down to the "evil rec room" saying little to one another. Hal honestly didn't have anything more to say to Vanir, and he was already beginning to feel the heavy onset of fatigue even though the day was yet to be finished. As they approached the room, they were met with the sounds of an argument. To Hal's ear, one voice was definitely Miri's.

"How the hell is this funny to you, Marcus?" They stepped inside to find Marcus lounging comfortably on one of the couches, watching the news on a large wall-mounted data scroll. Miri was standing in front of him, just barely to the side of his view of the screen. She gestured pointedly with one hand towards the broadcast.

"Just look at them. They have no clue at all. The blind informing the blinded." Marcus was unfazed by her outrage.

Hal turned his attention to the screen, where a grainy image seemed to show dark smoke billowing from a gaping hole in a government building as fire crews continued the long fight to extinguish the lingering smolders. From the architecture, it looked like it was a fire in Ruskol, the northernmost district of Anduruna. The scrolling info bar on the bottom of the screen confirmed his suspicions.

One of the usual talking heads continued his explanation next to the looping images that were being broadcast. "The fire crews have nearly finished putting out the blaze that started earlier this afternoon at a safety trooper training facility in the Ruskol district. Early reports have not confirmed casualties, but authorities at the scene say several trainees and facility staff are still missing. Initial reports lay blame on an accidental munitions release, leading to cascading detonations as it set fire to the rest of the weapon's warehouse."

Miri wasn't about to concede the argument. Despite her clear hostility, Marcus's small band of henchmen didn't move to restrain her, and merely kept a close eye on her actions.

"Do you know something about this?" She shook her head. "People probably died in that explosion! It's not something to laugh at!"

"Am I supposed to cry over a couple troopers dying? They're hardly my friends." Marcus smiled, a smug sense of satisfaction in his eyes.

"We take you now to an emergency press conference with Representative Nadir Bagaveyev of Ruskol."

The screen switched from looping footage to a live feed of a politician standing in front of a podium dotted with microphones. An aging but well-dressed crane rested his wings on either side of the dais, leaning close to the recorders. "My fellow citizens. Today marks a difficult tragedy in our district. I am sad to inform you that many of our brave troopers have been consumed by this terrible blaze. Troopers who risked their very lives to keep us all safe."

The flash of cameras and click of shutters punctuated the silence between remarks. "Risk is always part of the job for these courageous men and women, but that does not mean they should bear the burden of unnecessary danger when they are in the safe confines of their barracks." The politician straightened himself, his voice taking on a more aggressive edge. "Unfortunately, this makes the failings of the current administration far too clear. Our civil servants struggle to maintain peace with outdated and unreliable equipment. Dangerous even, if not properly handled." The representative grimaced, a practiced emotion that conveyed the perfect amount of gravity and displeasure.

"Three times now the Viscount has received bills on his desk to approve funding for new equipment and renovated facilities here in Ruskol. Three times he has vetoed the bill, claiming that Norvondire, of all places, was in more dire need of supplemental funding. I say to you that this willful neglect is no longer acceptable! I say—"

The data scroll winked off, fading to an unlit, transparent display. Hal and Vanir's arrival had finally been noticed.

"Hal!" Miri and Marcus called out to him in unison, her voice more relieved, his more eager. Miri was quick to rush to Hal's side, two steps ahead of Marcus as he did the same.

"Are you ok?" Miri looked more concerned than Hal expected. He nodded tiredly. As he opened his mouth to speak, Marcus interrupted with his own forceful question.

"More importantly, did you find it?"

"We did."

Vanir's silky voice offered an explanation faster than Hal could. "It's somewhere inside Calypsa District University. Hal says it's on the fourth floor." She paused only for a split second. "I think he's telling the truth; I could sense its pull when we were close."

"The fourth floor?" Miri adjusted her glasses. "That's where the earth science labs are."

"Excellent!" Marcus was obviously thrilled; anticipation and energy colored his voice in bright, expectant hues. "We're already getting our agents to trickle back in from around the city. We'll be ready to put the new meteor to use immediately once we retrieve it. We go tonight."

"Wait." It was Miri who interrupted. "What's the date today?"

Hal shrugged. Vanir tilted her head. "Friday the 30th."

"Hal, you can't go tonight! The earth-sci department has that faculty-student stargazing party the last Friday of every month. There'll be people there all night long!"

Marcus frowned, not too happy that anyone was offering a reason to not immediately venture out to seize the meteor.

"It wouldn't be very productive if we were detected breaking in, would it?" Vanir asked, the words more a statement than a question. "Plus, I'm pretty sure the Archbishop has a service to attend to tonight."

Hal could see the frustration mount inside his brother. He stared daggers at anyone who met his gaze, including Vanir. His trio of blade-tipped tails seemed to writhe and bob with more animation than just moments before. "Let's talk in private."

Marcus and Vanir walked off to the far side of the expansive room, well out of earshot. Though a couple henchmen still lingered nearby, Hal and Miri were left to their own devices. She moved closer to him, one hand reaching for his wrist as her deep violet eyes looked up with concern. Warm fingers gently pressed against a vein, feeling for his pulse. "Hal, are you sure you're ok?"

"What?" Hal turned his attention away from his brother's quiet but intense argument. "Yeah. I mean, I think so." He rested much of his weight on his cane. "Why are you so worried?"

"Don't take this the wrong way, but you look terrible. Like you've been awake for days. Come on, let's sit down."

She guided him over to the nearby couch. Hal couldn't help but sigh in relief as the supple upholstery molded itself around his weight. Miri sat next to him, reluctantly releasing her touch from his arm.

"I do feel pretty tired." Hal closed his eyes, allowing his muscles to relax. His tail curled into a coil on one of the couch cushions, taking advantage of the welcome rest. "It's funny, because I actually ended up sleeping for most of the groundcar ride back from Calypsa."

Miri didn't seem to find the news heartening at all. "How much did you use your power?"

Hal shrugged, the gesture less pronounced now that he was sitting down. He opened his eyes and stared out at the inactive wall-scroll. "In total, maybe fifteen minutes? It was a lot of off and on. Very . . ." Hal wasn't sure how to describe the sensation of snapping back and forth between his enhanced senses. "It was very difficult." He scratched at his chest. "There's too much pressure out there. Too much noise."

"Do you feel tired when you use your power?"

Miri sounded like she already knew the answer. Hal provided it anyway. "No, I feel great. My leg doesn't hurt. It's almost like I have more energy. Sort of like an endorphin rush combined with an electric buzz."

Miri frowned, silently collating the data. One hand rested on his shoulder. "It sounds, and it *looks*, like your power doesn't give you more energy at all. Well, no, that's wrong." She rephrased her hypothesis. "Rather, energy isn't created for free. You're just borrowing it. Like a short-term energy loan, you end up paying back more than you originally gained."

The analogy seemed to make a lot of sense. In fact, Miri may have been right on. Her face appeared close in front of his, her hands on both shoulders now. "Hal. You can't keep using your power like this. It looks—" She didn't seem to want to say the words that followed. "It looks like it's actually killing you."

Hal felt he had known this from the moment that Mordecai showed him that x-ray. He hated it, yet also felt like he had resigned himself to the inevitability of it. To see Miri discover the same truth, however, left him feeling emptier than he had ever felt before. "It's not that easy, Miriel."

"Please, Hal. You need to promise me." Her voice wavered a little. "I can't watch you be destroyed, slowly, in front of my eyes like this."

Hal wanted to find some comforting words, some easy line to dispel the fear that gripped them both. But he didn't know if any such words existed. If they did, they were eluding him. Hal wasn't sure how quickly the meteor was destroying him, or if the changes could ever be reversed, but there was one fact he did know for certain: There was not enough time in his world. It couldn't be spent carelessly.

"Miri, I . . ." Hal hesitated. A thousand different lines could complete that sentence:

I want to live.

I love you.

I'm sorry.

His heart wanted to blurt them all out at once, but his courage faltered. He blinked and swallowed. She had been waiting for his answer for far too long.

"Are we interrupting something?" Vanir's voice ambushed him from behind, startling them both.

Miri stood, her expression and tone colder than a whirling gust of Starfall snow. "Did you finish your discussion?"

"We did." Marcus appeared to be back to his usual self. Whatever words were said or promises made, they were no longer in conflict of opinion. "We're going to take the meteor back tomorrow night. We can't afford to reveal ourselves prematurely, and it will be less risky tomorrow."

Vanir smiled, sliding in close to Marcus as he did all the talking. "You should get plenty of rest. It looks like you could use it. Tomorrow will be a big day for us all."

Hal stood, steadying his weight with Miri's help. He was angry at their sudden reappearance, and turned that into fuel for his demand. "One thing first." His tail curled in close around Miri in a protective gesture. "If you want me to go back, Miri is coming with us."

"What?" Marcus didn't take kindly to the demand. "That wasn't the agreement."

"It is now." Hal forged ahead. "She knows the university better than any of us, and I won't let you keep her locked away like some bargaining chip. We both go, or neither of us goes."

Vanir quelled Marcus's rage with a squeeze of his shoulder. She gave Hal a serious, no-nonsense stare. "You wouldn't happen to be planning to do anything reckless, would you?"

"If you hold to your side of the agreement, so will I. Everyone still wins. You get your meteor, and we get to walk away." Hal smirked. "Or, you can just shoot us both now, and look through every single office, lab, closet, and desk drawer on the fourth floor of CDU. Assuming the meteor isn't moved somewhere else by then."

A tense silence marked time before Marcus responded. "Fine." He pointed one sharp talon at Hal's chest. "But don't make me regret this, Hal. You're far too bold for your own good."

"I wonder where we get it from."

Marcus stormed off quickly, leaving Vanir to linger. Her guard seemed to be elevated after that flexing of willpower. "Don't make me regret this either, Hero. One mistake can change everything in an instant. You would do well to remember that." She nodded to a pair of celestial henchmen who dutifully responded to her summons. "I think you two should call it an early night, rather than stay up and cause more trouble. These fine gentlemen will bring you back to your room."

***

When the door shut behind them in the same small room they had shared before, Miri finally spoke up. "Spirits, Hal! What was that all about?" It was as if she had been holding her breath until they were alone.

Hal wiped his face. "With you trapped in here, there's no way you can escape unless Marcus allows it. If you come with us, you might be able to slip away and break free."

"But what about you?"

"I'll cover for you as best I can. Marcus won't kill me. He might be an egotistical prick, but we're still brothers. Besides, once he has the meteor, I don't think he'll care anymore."

Miri sighed. "That sounds like a pretty weak plan."

Hal started to unzip his jacket. "Look. Worst case we just behave ourselves, get that damned rock, and finish the deal like before. I don't know if he'll abide by his word, but that's exactly why escaping is plan A."

He threw his jacket towards the desk, relieved to shed some weight off of his shoulders. Miri gasped in surprise.

"Hal!" She caught herself, lowering her voice as not to attract the attention of the guards outside their door. The question emerged as a harsh, alarmed whisper. "Since when did you get a pistol?"

His jacket removed, the shoulder holster he wore was now visible, along with the two-shot pistol Jonny had lent him. Hal was so accustomed to wearing it now, he didn't even think about it.

"Does Marcus know you have it?"

"Yes, though it's never come up again. I think either he forgot that I'm armed, or none of them consider me a big-enough threat to address." He pulled the weapon from the holster to show it to Miri. "It only holds two shots, and it's slower to reload than the fancier magazine-fed versions. There are a lot more people to fight than I have bullets for."

"Where did you get that?" Miri seemed almost afraid of the weapon. Unlike Hal, she hadn't lived a life around less-than-legal citizens in a place where black-market weaponry was a more common sight. Hal popped the breech open and unloaded the bullets, rendering the weapon inert.

"An old friend lent it to me." He held it out sideways. "Here. You should learn how to use it."

"What? No, I've never held a gun in my life! Besides, I could never shoot someone, Hal. That's terrible."

"Miri." Hal didn't have the energy to be impatient. Instead, he calmly talked her through his reasoning. "I know you don't want to shoot anyone. I truly hope you never have to." He stole a quick glance at the door to their cell. "But you've seen what these people are capable of. They'll kill without hesitation. If things go wrong, you might need to use a springer to protect yourself." Hal frowned. "A firefight is the last place you or I want to be, but you'll never get a second chance." He gazed deep into her eyes as he spoke the uncomfortable truth. "You either make it or you don't."

Miri reluctantly approached the outstretched weapon, hesitant fingers closing around the grip. As Hal pulled his hands away, the pistol dropped several inches. She was unprepared for the heft of it, but adjusted quickly after steadying her grip. "Ok then. Just give me the basics."

Hal did his best to find his weight beneath him as he helped her through the tutorial. Without his cane, his knee protested loudly, sending sharp rivulets of pain through his nerves. He tiredly but patiently explained the different features: how the bullets were loaded, how the safety worked, how she had to cock the hammer between each shot. She listened quietly, letting Hal demonstrate. She didn't appear to enjoy the learning process the same way an eager boy might, but she seemed to understand its importance and treated the lesson seriously with her usual concentrated focus.

"Ok." Hal stepped back and fell heavily onto the end of the bed, letting his leg rest. "Go ahead and practice shooting at the wall." She looked unwilling. "Don't worry. It's not loaded. Nothing is going to happen."

Miri turned slightly and took aim at an invisible point on the wall. She held the pistol with both hands like he had showed her, pulled the hammer back with her thumb, then flinched as she attempted to pull the trigger. "It's not working."

"The safety."

"Oh." She belatedly clicked the button over to the not-safe position and tried again. Her aim still flinched, but the hammer dutifully cycled forward, slamming into the firing mechanism with an audible snap.

"See? It's easy. The trigger is light once the hammer is cocked. Try not to flinch. Nice and smooth is all you need."

She handed the pistol back to Hal, eager to be rid of it. "All right, but I think you should hold onto it still. I don't want a gun."

"Fair enough." He took it back and carefully loaded it with bullets, setting the safety before returning it to the holster. Once it was done, he leaned back heavily, an obvious sigh of relief escaping his lungs as he tried to relax.

"You look tired, Hal."

"I know." His tail nodded. "I am."

"I know it's early, but I think you should sleep. You need your energy for tomorrow."

"I think you're right about that." Hal didn't argue. He worked his way down to a horizontal position, heavy head sinking deep into the pillow. It felt so good to lie down; Hal wasn't sure if he would ever have the will to stand up again. He could already feel his consciousness begin to slip away into merciful sleep.

"Hey, Hal?"

"Mmmm?" He couldn't muster the willpower to open his eyes.

"Thank you."

He felt the tender, gentle touch of Miri's lips on his cheek, as she offered a delicate kiss goodnight. Hal didn't have the time to ask why she was thanking him, or to even appreciate the kiss, before his mind slipped the last bond of consciousness and fell down into a deep, dark, and welcome rest.

"It's just not fair." Marcus scowled into the drink that he swirled around in his glass. The potent amber liquid whispered a promise of temporary and intoxicating release.

"I know." Hal leaned back in his chair, regarding his despondent brother with a sad smile. He tossed back the rest of his own glass, swallowing the last mouthful of brandy and allowing the slow burn to fill his body.

The two sat alone as the sole remaining patrons of the bar on a cold and lonely All Spirits' Eve. The shutters on the windows clattered and clanked as the gusting northwest winds swept sparkling powder down from the mountains and into Calypsa. Nearly everyone else in Anduruna would be enjoying a happy and comfortable holiday with friends and family.

Not them.

Hal raised his empty glass into the air and shook it, getting the attention of the bartender. "Another round, Hector."

"Comin' right up, amigo."

The old weathered jackal stopped wiping down the bar and brought them what remained of the bottle of vintage liquor. "You know, why don't I just leave this bottle here for you two to enjoy. It's the holidays, after all."

"Thanks, Hector."

"De nada."

Hal pulled the cork and took the liberty of topping off Marcus's glass before refilling his own. Marcus barely even looked up, taking an absent sip before returning to scowling and swirling. "It's damned thievery, Hal. They can't just seize everything we had because of 'an ongoing central investigation.'" Marcus mocked the condescendingly dry and official tones that the special investigator had used. "It's total bullshit."

"I know."

"I mean, I figured they'd pull some sort of stunt because of who Dad was, but didn't know how far they'd actually go." He looked up from the brandy, his yellow and gray eyes alight with hatred. "They took all the money. The house. All of our stuff. The things we grew up with. Absolutely everything."

Marcus let out a sharp sigh of frustration and took another drink. "I mean, how the hell is the furniture part of a criminal investigation? Our photo albums? The pictures on the walls?" He dug his talons into the wooden bar top, and the heavily lacquered wood creaked and cracked under the stress. "They're not just taking our inheritance. They're taking the only memories we have left!"

Hal frowned. Ever since the shooting weeks ago, everything had been a total mess. "That can't actually be legal. Did you talk with Sergio earlier today? What did he have to say about it all?"

Marcus laughed. "Sergio? Man, that lawyer isn't good for jack-shit. He just fed me a whole lot of legalese about how he can't do anything because City Central Authority is involved. Special laws and jurisdiction, blah, blah, et cetera, et cetera." The yellow eyes grew darker. "Bastard isn't worth the air he breathes."

"It's not all his fault," Hal disagreed. "Sergio's done a lot for us both over the years, but he's not a miracle worker, Marcus. Sometimes a jam is too big to slip out of."

"Yeah? Well, one way or another, it's not fucking good enough, Hal." Marcus looked down at the worn and tired floorboards. "It's just not fucking good enough anymore."

Hal didn't know how to console his brother; he was just as upset about the entire ordeal, but the circumstances didn't fill him with hate. Instead, Hal's only prize was that deep and vast ocean of regret. Regret that he couldn't stop his own family's destruction. Regret for not being a better son. Regret for not capitalizing on every single quiet moment when he could have let the people he held dear know exactly how much he loved them. Hal knew he would need to start the slow and difficult swim towards the surface or he would be trapped here in this prison forever.

"If there's at least one good thing that came of this," Hal began, "it's that we both discovered our powers. Somehow, the chaos of that moment unlocked the potential in both of us."

Marcus's angry stare locked onto Hal. "Our *powers*?" The well of outrage in Marcus seemed to go from a simmer to a boil. "You mean this joke of an ability?" He reached out to hold onto the salt shaker and a shimmering purple halo materialized over his head. Slowly, and a bit unsteadily, the pepper shaker began to levitate, suspended in air by Marcus's novice telekinetic ability.

"Please, allow me to season your food using only the power of my mind." Marcus laughed emptily as the pepper shaker sprinkled some of its contents onto the middle of the table. "Do you want salt too? Well, you can't have any because I need to already be touching the same sort of thing that I'm levitating." The halo disappeared, causing the pepper shaker to clatter gracelessly onto the table and roll towards one edge. "Practically useless."

Hal caught the shaker before it reached the floor, returning it to its proper place by the napkins. Normally it was a terrible idea for any Dreamkeeper to even think about using their power where people could see them and call upon the troopers, but Hector was an old friend of the family and didn't seem to pay any mind. He simply kept his head down, focusing on cleaning up the bar before they closed for the night, maintaining his legal plausibility that he saw nothing at all.

"At least you found your power. Not everyone does. Most people don't, in fact." Hal tried to stay focused on the benefits. "Besides, I'm sure it has its uses. You just need to get creative with it."

"Whatever." Marcus wasn't in the right attitude to listen to anything Hal had to say. "This power isn't worth the cost that came with it."

"Maybe not." Hal sighed, reaching again for the bottle and topping off their glasses. His head was buzzing with the comfortable hum of intoxication, but he wasn't so far gone that he couldn't share one more drink with his brother.

Inhibitions lowered, Hal leaned back and looked up, watching starlight spill in through the ceiling. It was a sight he kept coming back to again and again ever since he'd found it a few days before. A sip of spicy brandy complemented the view quite well.

"What do you even see when you do that?" Marcus asked, a twinge of envy hiding among the words.

"Spirits, Marcus. I don't even know how to begin to describe it." Hal tried to think of a good metaphor. "It's like trying to explain the concept of color to a blind man. There are no words for what I see." He started and stopped himself a few times, failing to find the right explanation. "I don't know how to share this sight with you, Marco, but it's beautiful. There really is no such thing as true darkness." He locked eyes with his disbelieving brother. "There is so much more out there than anyone even knows."

"Well, isn't that just great for you." Marcus's sullen voice echoed into his own glass, sounding a little slurred now as he inhaled a strong slug of the remaining brandy. "I guess little old uncomprehending me will just sit here and contemplate this drink instead."

The conversation stalled out after that, returning to silence. Marcus was clearly drunk and depressed, while Hal was drunk and disappointed that he couldn't do more to reverse their collective fortunes.

"Last call, boys." Hector spoke up from the other side of the room, interrupting the shared silence. "I'll be locking this place up at the end of the hour."

Marcus exhaled slowly and sleepily, steeling his gut for the final swig. "Well, I guess if nothing else we still got each other." A wobbly glass raised to meet Hal's. "Cheers, brother."

Hal reluctantly clinked his snifter with Marcus's. "Cheers." Hal was beginning to feel awkward now that he knew what he needed to say. He cleared his throat, trying to shed the discomfort. "Look, Marcus. There's something I've been meaning to talk to you about."

Marcus swallowed the last of his drink before letting his sharp yellow and gray eyes lock back onto Hal. "Anyone who starts a conversation with those words is about to say something really shitty." He frowned. "What is it?"

"So, I took the entrance exams for Calypsa District University a few months ago. Paid the fee with my own cash. Didn't tell anyone."

Marcus stared at him. After a pregnant pause, Hal took it as a sign to keep talking. "Well, the results came back a few weeks ago, and . . . I made the cut. Classes start in the new year. I made the first tuition payment yesterday."

Suspicious confusion morphed into surprise on Marcus's face. "What? You've been planning on doing this the whole time?"

Hal shrugged. "I wasn't actually sure if I was going to go through with it. It was just an entrance exam. But then," Hal sighed, gesturing to the empty room with his empty glass. "Then all this happened.

Everything changed. And now that I've thought about it for a while, I think it's time for me to move on to something new."

Hal's statement should have been positive news to share with anyone, but Marcus didn't seem too happy. In fact, his anger seemed to increase with each heartbeat. "So you're going to just give up the life?" He snapped his fingers. "Just like that?"

"Pretty much. Yeah."

Marcus's voice turned accusatory. "You think it's that easy, huh? How the hell do you expect to even pay for schooling? City Central Authority locked up our family's funds. And even if they do miraculously release them, the estate tax will eat most of it anyways!"

"I've been saving nearly every lucre I've ever earned running jobs for the Cordovas. It adds up after a while, and it's my own private account. It hasn't been touched by the authorities." Hal shook his head. "Look, Marcus, it's already a done deal."

Hal could see his brother's eyes take on a watery sheen. "So what the hell am I supposed to do, huh? I don't have the cash for that, and I don't want to go to fucking school again." Marcus clenched his talons into fists. "Our whole lives we've always done things together, Hal! We've toppled every obstacle side by side!"

"I know, Marcus, but this is something I need to do for myself." Hal gave his brother a serious stare, all levity—all illusions—gone. "If you're smart, you'll quit the life too. I've seen the writing on the wall, and it's been painted with the blood of our family. If we keep doing what we've been doing, someday it's going to be you or me, facedown on the floor, just like Dad. Just like them all. I won't accept that as my future."

"So what the hell am I supposed to do? I don't have anywhere to go, Hal! You're the only person I have left that I can trust, and now you're running off in a direction that I can't follow."

"I'm sorry." Hal pushed his seat back and stood, pushing his arms through the sleeves on his jacket. "I don't have all the answers, Marcus.

I can't find them for you, and you can't find them for me. All I know is I need to start forging my own path now. It's the right time."

"You coward!" Marcus kicked his chair off to the side, violently toppling it to the ground. "You're just scared, running away, hoping that everything will get better if you do. It's not right, Hal, and it's definitely not fair!"

"It's also not your call to make." Hal grounded his feet and his heart. Despite the alcohol coursing through his veins, or perhaps because of it, Hal knew he was doing the right thing. "Look, Marcus. You're drunk and angry, and honestly, just impossible to reason with when you get like this. Sleep it off, and we can talk about it tomorrow if you want."

"Fuck you, Hal!"

Hal grunted, nodding in agreement. "Yeah. Ok. Good talk." He pulled some crumpled cash from one of the coat pockets and tossed it onto the bar. "I'll pay for the drinks this time, since I'm such an ass-hole and all that."

He turned towards the door, prompting an aggressive string of expletives to be hurled in his direction. He barely even listened to them. The cold and sobering gust of wind that welcomed him as he opened the door helped keep the vitriol at bay. He hesitated for only a moment, standing in the middle of the threshold, letting the chill nighttime air leak into the building. He thought about glancing back over his shoulder and locking eyes with his brother one more time, but he didn't. Instead, Hal stepped forward into vast and winding streets, stared up at clear and endless skies, and shut the door behind him.

***

Hal awoke, returning once again to the real world as his eyes focused on the room in front of him. This time, he had slept on his other side, and instead of a dark stone wall, Hal was greeted by the sleeping face of Miri. She had done her best to curl up next to him and sleep close, avoiding falling off the edge of the narrow bed.

He had been having so many vivid dreams recently. This last one in particular seemed to linger in his waking mind longer than most. Some memories, it seemed, just wouldn't fade away, no matter how much he wanted to bury them.

Several strands of Miri's long violet hair rested delicately in front of her face, wavering ever so slightly as her breath kissed them with each exhale. In that small, still moment, Hal couldn't help but think of how truly beautiful she was.

Miri. He had met her not long after that dream, and through the years that followed, she remained his companion and friend. Despite all that had happened, and the differences between them, she was still here, resting peacefully at his side. If there was ever a person who deserved to live a happy life, surely it was her.

Hesitantly, he reached out and brushed the errant strands of hair aside, feeling the silky softness as his fingers slipped by. This caused Miri to stir, and soon she opened her eyes, giving Hal a sleepy smile. "Hey you."

"Hey."

She shifted her weight, rolling closer to him and closing her eyes again. If there was one thing that Hal knew, it was that he wanted to have more mornings like this. He would give anything just to hold onto this one.

The door to their room creaked open, letting a sharp wedge of bright light spill into the room. Hal sat up, preempting the words he expected to follow. "Rise and shine, lovebirds. So much work to do, big day ahead, creepy laugh, et cetera, et cetera. Got it. We'll be ready soon."

The door seemed to pause, frozen half-open for a moment before it closed again, without a single word being spoken. Miri propped herself up with a surprised laugh. "Hal! What has gotten into you this morning?"

His tail drifted over to her and flicked at her face with its forked tongue. He shrugged and smiled.

"I guess I just woke up on the right side of the bed."

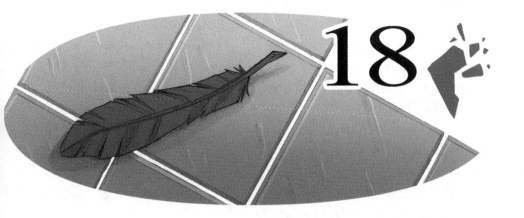

Hal zipped up his leather jacket, flexing his bad leg. His knee
made a loud popping sound that solicited a grimace.

"Are you going to be ok?" Miri asked the question Hal wondered himself.

"I hope so."

The two of them were now in the "evil rec room" again, but this
time the entire cathedral buzzed with activity. The network of agents
Marcus claimed to command seemed to be heeding his summons,
trickling in by the hour, usually alone or in small groups. All of them
looked fairly hardened, as one might expect from an army of ex-convicts. Many of them seemed eager to act, and were kept busy arming
themselves and preparing for the events to come. The air had a tension
to it that was impossible to overlook.

Rather than sally forth right away, Marcus preferred to sit tight
until later in the day, sending Vanir ahead of the rest of them. Though
the university was over in Calypsa, if they traveled by telepad, the

excursion would be shortened considerably. According to the clock on one wall, it was almost time to leave.

"Hal. Miri." Marcus approached them with a smile, genuinely beaming with delight. He seemed to be put in a chipper mood by the sense of imminent action. "Are you ready for a date with destiny?"

"Oh, I don't know." Hal pretended to be shy about it. "How does my hair look?"

"It looks like a sarcastic asshole," Marcus quipped with a smile, seemingly taking Hal's wit in stride. Undaunted, he turned his attention to Miri. "Now, don't say I haven't done anything nice for you. You have your old clothes back, and I even had them washed for you. No 'creepy ceremonial robes' for a day like today."

Miri ran one hand through her hair. "Thanks." She sounded at least partly grateful, though not particularly impressed. Hal caught her amused glance. Though it was more of a practical gesture than a generous one (robes weren't great for trekking through the city inconspicuously), it was still an important symbol. Miri certainly seemed a little brighter now that she was dressed in the comfortable and warm expedition gear the two of them wore just before the conspiracy began.

Marcus too was wearing new clothes. He eschewed his normal upscale clothing for a medium-weight trench coat that was subtly styled with epaulets and brass buttons. Paramilitary fashion was something of a recent trend that was making its way through various cuts of society. Marcus seemed to be no exception to that rule.

"I want to introduce the two of you to somebody." Marcus looked over his shoulder and called out to someone in the background. "Dubs! It's time."

Hal recognized the man that approached as the same hulking bear that had been beating the living daylights out of the punching bag the day before. He stood well over six feet tall, and his brown fur was interrupted in places with the stark line of a deep, healed scar. This man, whoever he was, had certainly not been a stranger to violence.

"Dubs, I want to formally introduce you to my brother, Hal. You already know Miri, of course."

The hulking beast offered one paw for a handshake that practically engulfed Hal's forearm. "So, you the brothah of the Arch. Respect." Dubs spoke with a deep booming voice that had the unmistakable accent of a man who lived his life in the inner city. Norvondire district, if Hal had to guess.

Hal gave Dubs a sharp nod as he finished the handshake. "Dubs, huh? Is that a nickname?"

"Yeah." Dubs answered the question as if he had done it thousands of times before. "My real name is William W. Wilson the Third. But that takes way too much work to say, and I ain't no 'Willie.'"

"Dubs it is, then." Hal cleared his throat. No doubt Dubs would be accompanying them as a little extra muscle to keep Hal and Miri from entertaining thoughts of heroism. In a close-in fight, Hal normally liked his chances pretty good, but between Dubs's sheer size and his bad leg, it wasn't an experiment he cared to run.

"Let's get going." Marcus stepped forward and waved for the others to follow. "We'll take the telepad to save some time."

The four of them walked out into the city streets to find that the sun was setting slowly into the final moments of daylight. The sky was already beginning to fade from sky blue into pastel hues of pink, lavender, and gold.

"Wow, look at the colors!" Miri smiled at the sunset, basking in the evening's fragile glory. After being cooped up inside for so long, it must have been a refreshing sight to take in. "They're beautiful!"

"Yes, they are," Hal grunted his agreement, contemplating the view. As the sun descended to the west, the moon was already up and shining in the east, half obscured behind the immensely tall spire that was Sabbaton Tower. As they walked past one of the main radial avenues that led inward towards the tower and the center of Anduruna, he glimpsed the anchor point for one of the several tension cables that held the massive structure steady. The spiral-wound metal cables were thicker than some tree trunks, and even under tension they visibly sagged under their own mass.

"Impressive, isn't it?" Marcus took note of the direction Hal was looking. "That a structure so grand could be built and held aloft securely." He chuckled as a gust of cool wind swept between buildings to chill them. "What a perfect symbol of all we can achieve, if only we sit down, lay back, and submit."

"You're a very cheerful man, Marcus," Hal scoffed. "Has anyone told you that?"

Marcus laughed out loud. "Oh, but I am." His smile had a cutting sharpness to it. "Now, I'm no engineer, but I wonder what would happen if those cables were to disappear all of a sudden and something unsettling were to happen to the foundation?"

"A lot of innocent people would die. That's what would happen." Hal narrowed his eyes. Was Marcus seriously bold enough to suggest toppling the Sabbaton Tower itself?

"Oh, it would be quite the destructive event. Tragic. I dare say it would be remembered for generations as a grand inflection point for the history of this city."

"You're insane," Miri muttered, her mood subdued by the grim topic.

"Am I really?" Marcus countered, relishing in the debate. "Think about this. When a forest becomes thick and overgrown, it begins to decay. New life cannot take hold because it is choked out, and the entire ecosystem falls into stagnation. Nothing changes, nothing grows, until one fateful day when a storm rolls through and strikes down with a flash of lightning to set everything ablaze." Marcus smiled. "The fire is destructive, yes. It lays waste to the old forest. But in that same stroke it fertilizes the land and sets the stage for new life to rise up, grow, and flourish." Hal's brother held his arms out to his sides. "Tell me, is the storm truly evil?"

"Good and evil are words we use to describe the actions of people, not nature." Miri was emphatic in her response. "The storm isn't good *or* evil. It just *is*. The lightning doesn't choose to strike the forest, and the trees aren't sentient creatures! It's just nature, and nature doesn't make decisions like we're capable of doing."

"But are we not all creatures of nature? Subject to the same natural laws?" Marcus sighed, shaking his head in disappointment. "I don't know why I waste my breath trying to illuminate you shortsighted people. We need to look past the familiar and accept its removal in order to discover a better world waiting beyond it."

"That makes for fine poetry, Marco, but that doesn't change the fact that you're suggesting the murder of thousands of innocent lives is in fact a noble endeavor."

"Someone has to have the courage to do what is necessary." Marcus pulled his jacket tighter as they approached the telepad station, his voice matching the temperature of the air. "If no one else will do it, let it be me."

Everyone fell quiet. Words weren't going to change the opinion of anyone present. Miri clung close to Hal, keeping him on the windward side to fend off the cold. His tail wrapped around her and rested on her opposite shoulder, not at all shy about the gesture.

It wasn't too long before the group approached their destination. The telepad itself was constructed of an elegantly engraved circle of stone set into the center of a large plaza. It was wide enough in diameter to fit several dozen people within its perimeter. The area was cordoned off such that you had to buy a ticket in order to get access to the inside, but for that nominal fee the average citizen now had near-instantaneous access to the center of any other district in the city. Telepad technology was relatively new, but in a short handful of years it had revolutionized intra-city travel, making the animal-pulled groundcars a utility item for distributing bulk goods rather than people. As far as Hal knew, telepad technology was controlled tightly by the government of Anduruna and not available for private use.

Marcus purchased tickets for the four of them and led the group into the circle where they waited with a handful of other people. A bored voice emerged from a loudspeaker as a telepad attendant announced their jump.

"Please keep all limbs and belongings inside the circle. This next jump is to Calypsa station. Calypsa station is the next jump."

After one more repeat of the same message, the attendant counted down to zero and initiated the jump.

There wasn't any sensation in the act of jumping itself. Hal merely blinked and found that he was standing in a new circle in Calypsa. The Sabbaton Tower that loomed over all of Anduruna was at a different angle to his orientation than it had been before, one of the few reminders that they had instantaneously changed locations. As convenient as teleportation was for travel, Hal never enjoyed the particular aftereffects he felt. While most people experienced no ill effects, or built up a tolerance, Hal always felt nauseated after using a telepad. As a result, he rarely chose to take advantage of the convenience.

"Ahh, home sweet home. So many memories from this place." Marcus waved them forward, stepping out into the now-dark city streets. "Let's keep going. Vanir should be waiting for us near the university."

Once they were free from the crowd of people at the telepad, Hal started up the conversation again. He was eager to learn more about the sorts of people that were loyal to his brother. "You've been awfully quiet, Dubs. How did you get involved in all of this?"

"Me?" The low bass of his laugh caused it to carry deep into the alleyways. "It start with beating the shit outta someone who done me wrong and gettin' thrown in the lockhouse for a couple. Then they come to me, say I can get out if I join this new 'second life' program. I took the deal."

"So you're behind all this 'down with the establishment, new world order' stuff?"

"Hell yeah." Dubs nodded with certainty. "Like the Arch said, if we wanna get ahead, we can't jus' play by the rules. You can't change the rules. That won't work. You gotta change the whole game."

Hal tried to keep his poker face intact. "But if they catch you, you'll be tried for treason. They'll execute you. All of you."

"That's why when you go, you go all in and get it done befo' they have that chance. And 'sides, I ain't afraid of dyin'. The Arch put a gun in my hand and say 'Dubs, you roll wit' me, ain't no one gonna step on you again.' I like that."

"If this is just a political movement, why the veil of religion?"

"Hey, if you got a problem wit' the goddess, you got a problem wit' me, aiight? Not everyone might care so much 'bout that sorta stuff, but I do." Hal was surprised by Dubs's impassioned response. "I don' know if she's like, real, and like, messin' with the world direc'ly and stuff, but she say she gave us our powers for a reason. She say we all got a purpose. An' we got her gift to give us power and to protect this world from evil."

Dubs certainly appeared to have a passion hiding beneath his bulk. "Ever since I sign on, Vanir been helpin' me learn to read by teachin' me the scrolls. They ain't so easy to read, but they mean somethin', you know? I like to believe that they ain't no lie. That we be actually more than we look like on the outside."

Hal furrowed his brows, falling into contemplative silence. After a moment had passed, Miri hesitantly spoke up, her voice no more than a confused whisper. "You didn't know how to read?"

Dubs was quick to lash out in anger at her disbelief. "Don't you judge me, pretty little fox girl! You ain't got no idea what it's like, growin' up on the streets! When you fightin' every night just to make it to the next day!" Dubs made a disgusted grunting sound. "You ain't never had to fight for nothin'. You ain't *never* gonna know what it be like livin' my life."

"Easy, Dubs. She didn't know." Marcus reined in his subordinate with a stern stare.

"Sorry, Arch."

Marcus nodded at Dubs's apology as he led them through a few more side streets until they reached the grand circle in front of Calypsa District University. Now that the sky was darkening, the tree-lined avenue leading up to the main building had taken on a more sinister appearance.

"Over here," a voice cried from the alleyway to their left, and Vanir stepped forward from the shadows out onto the sidewalk. "Have our guides been any trouble?"

"No, they're behaving." Marcus gave his lover a hug and a quick kiss while he had the opportunity. "What about on your end?"

Vanir's bright blue eyes almost seemed to glow in the dim light. "No trouble so far. Not much foot traffic on account of the wind and cold. Little activity entering or leaving the building. I have a groundcar waiting in the alley for our extraction."

"We're not taking the telepad back?" Miri sounded concerned.

"I don't know how big the meteor fragment is, but if it's the same size as the last one, it won't be easy to carry through public transport, especially if things go wrong and we need to get out quick." Vanir didn't seem to be in a very hospitable mood today, and her tone of voice was curt and condescending. "Don't you worry about the details. All you need to do is get us to the meteor without running into security."

Marcus nodded in agreement, turning to Hal and Miri. "Well, Hal, this is your territory. Why don't you lead the way."

Hal swallowed. "Ok." A nervousness settled over him, drying his mouth. "Our best bet is one of the side stairwells. No one really uses them."

"Then by all means, brother, lead on."

Hal and Miri started forward, walking up the side of the lawn to the edge of the building. Even without using his power, Hal could sense Miri's uneasiness.

"This is so weird, Hal. We shouldn't be breaking into our own school. I've got a really bad feeling about all this."

"I know, but let's just get it over with." Both of them were already whispering, a sense of tense caution present throughout the whole party. Hal tried the side door, but it moved only a bit before being held up by the locked handle with a rude, sudden stop.

"It's locked." Hal stated the obvious with a frown.

"Of course it is. Hang on." Miri searched the pockets of her jacket. "Where is—Oh! Here it is. I still have my ID. I wonder if they ever deactivated it." She slid the card through the little reader to the side of the door, and they could all hear a faint but distinct click as the lock temporarily disengaged. "I guess not."

Hal opened the door and stepped into the empty stairwell. The cold interior lighting matched the air now leaking inside as they all filed into the narrow ground-floor landing. Hal could already feel a weight pulling on his heart. They weren't far from the meteor. His tail looked straight up through the center of the spiraling staircase to the floors above, flicking its tongue rapidly.

Hal took a deep breath and looked at everyone around him. Dubs was following his tail's gaze, staring up through the center column of stairs. Marcus and Vanir were waiting with a look of impatient but fixated expectation. Miri bit her lip, looking as worried as Hal had ever seen her. He allowed himself one last exhale before activating his power and letting the unseen colors of the world wash over him.

The static was here. The gravity was here. He barely acknowledged the prismatic kaleidoscope of reflecting light that surrounded him and quickly ascended the stairs. Every inhale added to the tingling sense of energy that drew him ever upwards.

"Hal, please slow down," said Miri, her voice chasing after him.

"Be quiet, you fools!" A sharp whisper from Vanir gave further pursuit.

Every footstep echoed loudly in the confines of the tall but narrow chamber, barely registering in Hal's awareness as he passed each threshold. Second floor. Third floor. Fourth floor. The light was here. He stepped through the door into an empty hallway, and quickly paced onwards past doors to unlit labs.

"I don't think he can hear us." Marcus's voice had an urgency to it, but it lurked close behind Hal, waiting just over his shoulder.

The placard to the next room read "409 – Geology Lab." Hal didn't read the text so much as sense it, his eyes focused on the searing white orb of light that hid just on the other side. He pushed the door open, and the ceiling lights automatically turned on as a sensor detected motion inside the room.

Hal marched forward and came to rest in front of a long and deep work table. The light was coming from the center of a stone slab that lay in the middle of the workspace. Hal couldn't resist now that he was this close. He reached for the light, extending taloned fingers towards the source of his fixation . . . and touched only sandy, coarse stone. He blinked. This wasn't right.

"Hal." Marcus's hand firmly gripped one shoulder, and his forceful voice shook Hal out of his power. He blinked again, drawing a ragged breath as he adjusted back to normal light.

"Wha?" Hal looked bewildered, but it quickly became clear what he was actually looking at. The stone tablet in question was a fossil, roughly one arm's length wide and fairly thick. Visible on the surface was the well-preserved impression of two ryuu-nekos, partially entangled with one another in the shape of a rough circle. One appeared to have his jaws clamped around the neck of the other, as if they had died together, still locked in combat. The entire fossil was not yet exposed, and there was clear evidence that the caretakers of this ancient artifact had been slowly chipping and brushing away at it to reveal the remainder.

Miri saw the fossil and gasped in surprise. Vanir spoke up, an uncharacteristically unnerved quality woven among her words. "What is this?"

"It's here. It has to be here." Hal's tail flicked its tongue at the center of the circle between the two ancient creatures, kicking up a tiny cloud of dust as it tasted for his target. He looked around and found a miniature hammer and chisel sitting to one side of the table. He snatched up the tools and tapped away at the area where he remembered seeing the meteor-light. Normally fossil cleanup was a very slow and delicate process, but after only the seventh or eighth tap, a large flake of rock chipped away, revealing a dark and otherworldly core.

The second meteor.

"There it is!" Marcus eagerly watched as Hal continued to reveal it with the hammer and chisel, eventually freeing it from its prehistoric prison of rock and bone. "They must not have realized it was hiding within. I can't believe they came that close without feeling it."

"Maybe only certain people can sense the meteor remotely," Miri offered, her fear tangible now. "Were those ryuu-nekos fighting over it?" She was struggling to hold back tears. "They died battling over this?"

Everyone leaned in close to get a better look. Hal liberated the meteor from one last fragment of rock and pried it free, holding the cold familiar weight in one hand. It was the size of a grapefruit, and its hefty mass was already tiring the one arm that held it tight. The stone reflected almost no light, appearing in the sterile walls of the geology lab to be as black as black could be. It leeched heat from Hal's fingertips and palm with all too eager tenacity.

Marcus reached over and took the meteor from Hal's grasp, beaming with delight as he held it for himself. "Finally!" He wrapped one arm around his brother, giving him a tight hug. "I knew I could count on you, Hal. I always knew we were brought back together for a reason."

"What in the world is going on in here?"

A sharp, alarming voice startled them all from behind. Hal couldn't stop himself from instinctively jumping in surprise. Vanir and Dubs drew their weapons in a flash, pointing them towards the unwelcome intruder.

"Doctor Kincaid!" Miri called out, relief intermingling with surprise. It was none other than their old mentor, who had just unfortunately stumbled onto something he was never meant to see.

"Oh dear!" The aging cardinal gasped in surprise as weapons were pointed at him, and he held up his arms in surrender. His crimson feathers were fading from deep red to a pale pink and white, betraying his advanced age. He noticed his students not long after the weapons. "Miriel? Halcyon? You're alive!"

Miri rushed forward, heedless of the danger, and engulfed the old bird in an emotional, tear-filled hug.

"Oh, Miriel my dear, when you didn't return I feared the worst! We thought you had a terrible accident, falling from a cliff or getting swept up in an avalanche! We searched and searched, but never found you! I'm so glad to see you're alive!"

"Step away from him, Miri," Vanir interrupted the reunion with a sharp command. "Now."

"No!" Miri defiantly held her ground, holding her arms out in a shielding gesture. "I won't let you hurt him! I won't let you hurt any more people!"

"Dubs."

The bear grabbed Miri with one massive hand and yanked her away, tossing her back like a weightless ragdoll.

Miri screamed in desperation as she fell to the ground and slid across the waxed floor, coming to rest at Hal's feet.

"Get in the way again and I'll shoot you."

"Hey!" Hal and Kincaid protested in unison, both angry at the man-handling. The old professor huffed himself up in indignation, still looking impossibly small in comparison to Dubs. "Stop this at once! Who are you people? What in the world are you doing here? I demand to know what's going on!" He turned to Hal, anger and bewilderment clear as day. "Hal, who are these people?"

"Doctor—"

"Hal, shut up." Marcus pointed his own pistol in Hal's direction as a warning. "No one can know we were here."

"What?" Kincaid took a half step back, holding his hands even higher in the air. The atmosphere was beginning to feel far too chaotic to result in a sensible outcome.

"You can't just kill him, Marcus!"

"Don't say my name, you idiot!"

Vanir's voice grew taut to the edge of breaking. "Now we have no choice."

"No! Don't do this!" Miri cried out, her voice strained to the point of being hysterical.

Dubs aimed his springer at Kincaid's skull.

"Wait." Marcus cut through the mania with one authoritative word. Everyone held their breath as an odd silence fell upon the room. Marcus turned his yellow and gray eyes from Kincaid to Dubs, who stood like a statue, frozen in time, one moment away from pulling the trigger.

"No mess."

Dubs nodded and the hysteria was set back in motion. Setting aside his pistol, Dubs marched up to Kincaid, and with an engulfing grasp wrestled the old man to the floor, squeezing fingers around his small neck as he strangled the old professor in a display of complete and brutal violence.

Miri screamed at the terrible sight unfolding before them. Hal stopped her from running out by grabbing her and holding her close, pressing her head tight against his chest so she couldn't see. She wailed and sobbed, the only sound Hal could hear over the horrifying act.

A halo appeared over Dubs's head as the bear activated his own power, and arcs of blue electricity funneled down his arms and into his hands, where it delivered an intense electric shock into his victim. Kincaid convulsed beneath the onslaught, and even Hal had to turn away to stop himself from having the entire murder indelibly burned into his memory.

It wasn't long before the deed was done, and the air started to smell like burnt hair. Miri couldn't stop crying. Save for her, the room was now dead quiet. Hal continued to hold her close, his back turned to the aftermath.

"What now, Arch?" Dubs asked, his booming voice emerging without a hint of guilt or regret.

Marcus sounded disgusted and disappointed. "Hide the body in one of the closets. Then get ready to move out." Hal heard the sound of dead weight being dragged along the floor as his brother sighed in frustration. "We have what we came for. Let's go."

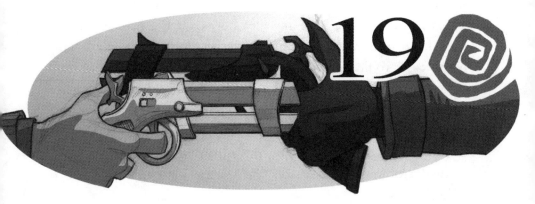

19

"**W**hat happened back there was murder, plain and simple! How the hell do you justify killing someone in cold blood like that?" After a sorrowful and silent ride back, Hal now found himself in a heated argument with his brother in the cozy top-floor office of the cathedral. Despite the comfortable setting, it felt like the argument could boil over at any moment. Vanir, Dubs, and Miri all played spectator to the unfolding fight.

Marcus sighed, uncorking a bottle of fermentae and taking a sip before responding to Hal. "Hal, you're angry. I get it. I really do. But what was I supposed to do? Capture him? Risk more people discovering us? Start a whole big collection of captives to keep you and Miri company? I can't afford that, Hal. One slipup when we're this close, and everything falls apart."

"Damn it, Marcus! He was my friend!" Hal couldn't restrain his outrage. "You could at least pretend to show remorse for all you've done."

Marcus threw his hands up in exasperation. "Words can't change anything, Hal. What's done is done. If an apology will make you feel better, fine, I'm sorry. I'm sorry it had to come to that. I really am. But I don't have the luxury of mercy under these circumstances." Marcus set his drink down and leaned forward, planting both hands on top of his desk. "Do you have any idea how hard I've had to work to keep the meteor's power hidden from the government? To establish my power base? To finally reach a point where we're ready to strike? Years of deliberate and methodical effort: collecting data, buying influence over important officers and politicians, building a network of agents in key positions." He shook his head. "I can't risk any rogue elements disrupting this delicate web, now more than ever!"

Hal stomped his cane on the floor. "That doesn't make it right, Marcus!"

"Maybe not, but that doesn't mean I'm wrong, either. Things just aren't that simple, and you know it."

Miri spoke up from Hal's side. "How many more people need to die before it is wrong, then? How many more people need to die before you're done killing in the name of this cause?"

"If we're smart about it, hopefully not more than is necessary." Marcus stepped around the desk, walking closer to the two of them. "If we want to save lives in the end, then we need to strike hard and end the revolution on the very same day it begins. Quick and clean." Marcus punched one fist into his other open palm. "Just think about it, Hal. The tower isn't just a symbol of our oppressors, it's the nerve center of all their operations! If we destroy it all in one momentous strike, they won't be able to resist us, and the people will finally learn to trust in the power of their own hearts rather than the power of the troopers and the Viscount!"

Hal grunted and shook his head, but that didn't seem to do anything but embolden Marcus.

"Just look at you. Look at us, Hal." Marcus placed a hand over his heart. "We are mighty. We have within us a beautiful and tremendous power. It wasn't given to us by the goddess so we could just sit back and merely exist as slaves. It was given so we could free ourselves. So we can remove our shackles and finally learn how to live again!" Marcus laughed a little. "Why do you think they make it illegal for anyone to use their power? It's because they *know* they cannot keep us contained once we've tasted the strength of our own souls!"

Passion dripped from each of Marcus's words, feeding the fire that crackled in the fireplace. Dubs nodded agreeably, but Vanir stood quietly in the corner, her attention uncomfortably focused on Hal and Miri's actions.

"Marcus," Hal shook his head, feeling his eyes water a little at the edges. "Do you really think you're a savior? Heroes don't murder innocent old men because they're inconvenient." Hal settled his weight on his cane. "Dr. Kincaid taught me how to study the stars. He introduced me to Miri. He gave me patience, helped me start my life over again . . . and now he's dead. Dead because of you and your bloody aspirations of revolution." Hal set his stance, the next words emerging with the weight of finality. "I don't think I can ever forgive you."

"I don't need your forgiveness, Hal." Marcus hefted the freshly-retrieved meteor fragment, staring at its center. "If you truly value his life, then we should work together to make his sacrifice worth the cost."

"No." Hal shook his head. "I'm done with this. All of it." Marcus appeared disappointed by Hal's stubborn refusal, but Hal didn't let that dissuade him. "We had a deal. You've got another meteor. Now let us leave. We don't belong in this nightmare anymore."

Marcus sighed, staring into the fireplace while he idly turned the meteor over in his hands. "All right." He hefted the black stone and tossed it between his hands. "Give me twenty-four hours, and then you're free to go. You won't ever have to talk to me again, if you so choose. We'll all be free to live the lives we want by this time tomorrow."

"Twenty-four hours?" Miri wasn't happy. "We deserve to be free right now!"

Marcus's lips twisted downward into a bitter scowl. "We all *deserve* it. But you can't leave until we've struck the first blow. No rogue elements."

"Come on, Marcus!"

"Don't even start, Hal! Don't you even start that 'Come on, Marcus' bullshit with me." Yellow eyes narrowed, cutting through the protest. "I just need enough time to organize my forces, distribute the meteor shards, and launch the operation. You can afford to wait just one day longer."

Marcus tossed the meteor to Dubs, who caught it in his massive paws with a cry of surprise. "Make sure it stays safe. We begin the ceremony of distribution as soon as possible. Everyone earns their shard tonight."

"Sure thing, Arch." Dubs eagerly marched out of the room, cradling the meteor like a fragile child as he disappeared down the hall.

Marcus nodded to Vanir, who drew her pistol and aimed it at Hal and Miri. "I'm sorry to have to do this to you, brother, but it will all pay off with just a little more patience. You need to trust me on this." Marcus placed his hand on Hal's shoulder, leaning in close. "You look like you could use some rest. Just relax. Spend some quality time with your girlfriend. Get some sleep. When you're ready to open your eyes again, you'll be able to look out onto a better world. I know we've been walking different paths, but we both want the same things. We always have."

Hal was far from happy. Marcus's words did nothing to comfort him. In fact, a bubbling pool of frustration and anger continued to simmer beneath his surface, one notch warmer than before. He was done letting people dictate terms to him. He wanted to return fire, maybe offer a witty one-liner about Marcus's definition of quality time if Vanir always had to use a gun, but instead he said nothing. Vanir had a pistol trained on him, and she looked to be in no joking mood.

"Get moving, you two. It's time to call it a night." Vanir urged them forward with a wave of her weapon.

"This will never end the way you want," Miri muttered under her breath as she grabbed Hal's free arm and helped lead him onward.

The three of them walked out of the office and down the hall in silence, leaving Marcus alone to plot the coming hours. Hal and Miri shuffled along in front of Vanir's steady aim, saying nothing to each other, nor to Vanir. They descended the spiral staircase and proceeded down another long corridor. The stained-glass windows watched them march on with twisted and shadowy shapes.

Hal and Miri shared a glance as they approached their room. Her brilliantly beautiful eyes shone with a determined fire he had never seen before. She gave him a subtle nod. They both knew what they had to do.

"Hold up."

Vanir's footsteps stopped, and they all paused in front of the door to their cell. Hal turned and found that she was aiming her springer straight at his head. "I think this is far enough."

"Far enough for what?" Miri asked, her voice mockingly indignant.

Vanir shook her head. "I'm not an idiot. And neither are you." Her expression was dead serious. "You're going to betray Marcus."

"I just want to get some sleep. I'm not in any shape to fight," Hal lied.

"Please." Vanir sighted the pistol in on Hal, shifted it to Miri, and focused it again on Hal. "You expect me to believe that you're going to play nice? After everything that's happened? Watching your mentor murdered like that?" She took a deep breath and brought the hammer to full-cock. "You're Marcus's twin brother, which means you're far too brave, far too stubborn, and wholly incapable of letting an injustice turn into water under the bridge. I'm afraid that your story ends here."

Hal held his hands up in a gesture of surrender. "So, what? You're just going to shoot me? Here, in this hallway? Kill the last family member he has left?" Hal narrowed his eyes. "Marcus and I may not agree on many things, but I promise you, he will never forgive you for this."

"Maybe not," Vanir agreed with a sober nod. "But at least he'll still be alive. At least we will still have a chance to build something new. I can't let you take the future from us."

Her aim settled over Hal's face. "I'm sorry."

"No!" Miri leapt into action, diving at Vanir in a desperate attempt to stop her. This took Vanir by surprise, and her aim shifted in that twitching half second as she pulled the trigger. The bullet whizzed by the edge of Hal's skull, missing by mere hairs.

Miri tried to get her hands on the gun, but Vanir batted Miri to the side with a sharp, skillful strike. Hal didn't hesitate and dropped his cane, letting his power come alight. He reached into his jacket and drew his own pistol, training it on Vanir just as she did the same to him. Time moved so slow in that moment. History could only be destined to repeat itself.

Hal fired first, his aim missing her chest, but instead clipping her springer with a metallic pang. It was knocked free from her grasp and spun across the floor, ending out of reach down the hall. They both took a sharp inhale of breath as time sped back up, snapping them into an accelerated reality. Hal cocked the hammer for his second shot. Vanir dove to the side. Guided by adrenaline, the bullet missed its mark, ricocheting off the wall.

"Shit!" Hal thumbed the breech release, and the barrel of his pistol angled down sharply as the back end hinged up to allow reloading of two new rounds. The spent casings and uncoiled springs shot out the back of the gun, nearly hitting Hal in the eye before falling onto the floor with a hollow metal echo. He reached into his pocket, desperately groping for fresh ammunition with trembling fingers. Every one of them was drunk on the intoxicating promise of survival.

Vanir rose to one knee and held her palms together. A shimmering blue halo lit over her head. As she separated her palms, a crackling, humming, throbbing sphere of black-purple energy grew into space, filling it with a tremendous singularity of doubtless destruction.

"Shit, shit, shit!" Hal muttered his way through the panic, struggling to load new bullets into the breech. His unsteady hand failed him, and a small handful of bullets fell from his grasp and clattered to the floor.

"Look out!" Miri propped herself up and kicked at Vanir just as the orb of energy was launched forward. Hal dove to the ground, hitting the deck as fast as he could. Gravity was barely strong enough to drag him out of the way of the projectile.

The orb sailed down the hall, crashing into a corner where the wall met the ceiling. It expanded in an instant, swelling into a massive black hole ten times the original size. It ripped at the universe itself, tearing fragments of matter in a final and irresistible implosion.

Wind rushed through the hall and sucked past them into the event horizon. Hal dug his talons into the floor, resisting the pull with every ounce of strength and will. The only sound he could hear was the high-frequency scream of molecules ripped asunder. All light seemed to bend, be absorbed, and rush past his shoulder into the roiling angry sphere.

Seconds later, after an eternity had passed, the sphere collapsed in on itself, leaving only a perfectly round imprint of nothingness where clean walls, floor, and ceiling once stood. The air dropped in temperature by a few degrees.

Miri wrestled with Vanir, disrupting her from summoning forth a new singularity, and buying Hal a precious few seconds to come to his feet. As much as it helped Hal, it was a losing proposition for Miri, and quickly Vanir emerged for the better, knocking the wind out of Miri with a sharp knee and hitting her head on the side of the wall.

Vanir was fast in neutralizing Miri, but not quite fast enough to be ready for Hal. His tail lurched forward and nipped at her with its fangs, creating the one opening that he needed to unleash a devastating combination of raw fury. The first strike caught her in the gut, liberating the air from her lungs and jackknifing her buckling body. The second strike snapped her head back in a dazing blow to the temple. His hands grabbed at her arm and twisted, rotated, and exposed her to the final third attack. Hal's palm slammed into her already extended joint, snapping it in the wrong direction and producing a wet, sickening scream.

She rolled there on the floor, writhing and howling in pain, effectively incapacitated. Miri was slow to gather herself. Hal smiled triumphantly, exhaling a deep cloud of vapor from his nostrils. His fingers, steadied now, easily loaded his pistol with two fresh rounds. He snapped the breech closed with a sharp flick of the wrist and the sweet metallic sound of imminent victory.

"How does it feel now, huh?" Colors shimmered in Hal's eyes as he stood over his oppressor. "It hurts, doesn't it? It hurts having your life changed in an instant, dragging you down from the place you thought you stood!"

He grabbed Vanir by the throat and lifted her up high until her feet were dangling over the floor. "I never wanted to be here!" He slammed her into the wall, pounding her skull against the stone as his fingers tightened their grip. "I never wanted to die!" His free hand pressed the barrel of his pistol against her chest, aimed straight into her heart. "I only wanted to be left alone. I only wanted to be happy!"

"Hal . . . ," Miri's voice weakly objected, but he could hardly hear her. The pressure of the moment was deafening. Overwhelming.

Inevitable.

Tears rolled down Vanir's face as she struggled to breathe. Her lips twisted and fought, struggling to form words. Hal's tail leaned in close, baring fangs that dripped venom. "Do you know what it feels like to lose everything you love?" His face hovered inches from hers and he pulled the hammer back with a satisfying *click*. "Do you know what it's like to be given no mercy?"

"N-n-no," Vanir gasped, her voice emerging as a weak whisper. She was in tremendous pain, and struggled to move her body. More than that, though, she was afraid. The desperate look in her eyes said it all. "P-please . . ."

Hal locked his eyes onto hers, drinking in her fear. "Let me teach you."

The gunshot wasn't loud. It heralded the end of her life with a faint, muffled crack of metal slipping through flesh. A small fan of blood emerged from the gap between the barrel and her heart, and the sanguine droplets fell like rain into the still and silent air.

Hal released his grip and took a step back, letting her body slide onto the floor. A trail of blood followed her down along the wall, ending where her back lay doubled over at an awkward and uncomfortable angle.

"Spirits, Hal!" Miri's voice was surprised, disbelieving, and sad. "You killed her."

The warm and comforting glow of revenge faded quickly, cooling and condensing into the bitter pit of panic. Hal's lungs sucked in air with an ever-growing greed, and soon he was hyperventilating, unable to escape the reality of an act that could never be undone. Vanir was dead. He killed her.

"Oh, spirits," Hal sobbed, unable to rein in the racing of his heart or the forward progression of time. Alarmed shouts echoed through the halls, pursued by the sounds of hurried footsteps. There was no way to go back. The only course that remained, once again, was to go forward.

"We need to go, Miri." Hal's panicked voice could not have echoed any truer in that hallway. "We need to go, now."

Hal sucked air deep into his lungs, fighting off the clamor erupting all around him. Through the walls, the floor, and the ceiling he could feel the pressure of the lives suddenly thrown into movement in reaction to his violence. No matter how hard he wished for it, the bees' nest couldn't be unkicked.

The giant void ripped into the world by Vanir's singularity prevented Hal from continuing down the hallway, which was probably a good thing. The evil rec room was down that way. He could already sense the IR heat shimmers of multiple people moving towards them from that direction. Miri ran to pick up Vanir's springer, but found the body of the gun to be badly damaged from the deflected bullet. It wasn't useful as a weapon anymore.

"No time for that, Miri, let's go!" Hal grabbed her by the wrist and pulled her along with him as he scrambled back towards the stairwell leading upwards to freedom. The sound of his own amplified and adrenaline-accelerated heartbeat made it difficult to hear her response.

"Easy, Hal! I'm right there with you." While his power washed away the pain from his old wounds, Hal still couldn't move as fast or as quick as Miri, who was healthy and nimble on her own. "You're the one with crazy super-vision. Lead the way!"

The heat from the bees was strongest down here. Hal needed to get up to the ground floor, and from there, out of the cathedral for good. A short sprint down the hallway led to the base of the spiral staircase. Its steps were hewn from alternating slabs of white marble and black granite, each deeply cold to the touch of his feet. It was no matter, though. He consumed them all in his haste, the sounds of frantic pursuit chasing them both towards the top. They had a head start, but that wouldn't last long if they hesitated.

Hal made it only a handful of steps past the top of the staircase before he stopped abruptly, causing Miri to crash into him awkwardly. "Ow! Hey!" she started to protest, but he silenced her without a word, dropping low to take careful aim with his springer. There was someone about to round the far corner up ahead. Even though Miri couldn't see it, he could.

The heat blur of a woman rounded the corner, but Hal was ready for her. He settled her shape in between the thin V-notch sights of his pistol and pulled the trigger. The bullet, launched by a coiled, high-energy spring, spiraled through the air, shedding vortices that shimmered brilliantly in its wake. It traversed the distance of the hallway in a flash, intersecting his target as she came into full view.

There was a short surprised scream of pain, and the woman lost her footing, half-tumbling, half-crashing against the opposite wall. Hal rose from his crouch and thumbed the breech release, exhaling a long-held breath of billowing vapor. The spent casings and springs ejected out of the back of his spent pistol. He reached back into his pocket for fresh bullets.

"Um, Hal?" Miri's worried voice caused him to look up. The woman was back on her feet, still alive. Blood dripped down her arm from where the bullet had wounded her. Her expression was one of pained fury, and with her good hand she drew a vicious-looking blade. A halo materialized over her head, and she started to charge at them. Her heat signature shifted, growing fainter as it morphed away from the spectrum Hal was perceiving.

"Hal!" Miri's voice jumped from worried to alarmed. "She's invisible!"

He reached one arm back, handing the gun and the loose bullets to Miri. He barked a single word: "Load."

"Wha—?" She accepted the weapon with surprise, nearly dropping the loose bullets onto the ground.

"Load the gun!" There was no more time to argue. Hal took a step forward, placing himself in the center of the hall between Miri and their attacker. His eyes flashed with all colors as he sequenced through every wavelength he could see, but at best all he could detect was a dim, indistinct cloud of color that rushed towards them at accelerated speed.

Hal could sense Miri's fearful but focused determination as she fumbled with the ammunition, forcing her untrained fingers to complete the delicate task. He could also sense the murderous intent of their assailant, and that intent grew into an ever increasing pressure as the sound of static began to fill his mind. "Come on," Hal muttered, balancing his weight between both legs, opening his stance. "Come on!"

The faint shape was almost in reach. It jumped sideways, launching off the wall and then up into the air. Its trajectory, in a few more tenths of a second, would fall directly onto Hal's chest. From behind, the sound of a breech clicking shut prompted delayed movement into action.

Hal leapt forward with all his might up towards the falling field of color. As his feet left the ground, he punched his sharp talons towards the center of the pressure that shoved against his heart. He felt the momentary flicker of surprise, like a candle flame wavering in the wind before it was snuffed out. Talons slid effortlessly into flesh, only stopped as fingers reached bone, wrapping around her spine. His momentum pivoted forward, and the jump ended by slamming her head down into the marble floor.

As the spark of life faded away, her form returned to normal, becoming visible. Hal's fingers were speared deep through the cultist's throat, and one clench of his grip would allow him to grab onto her upper vertebrae. Miri gasped in surprise as she saw the results, and Hal could do nothing to stop the blood from spraying onto his face and wetting his hand with its warm and violent flow.

"Oh, spirits!" Miri sobbed, holding the pistol loosely in one hand as her knees buckled. There was no hiding the raw results of the battle for survival in which there could be only one victor.

Hal let loose a primal cry of triumph and pulled his talons free, releasing her neck to close around the handle of the curved machete-like weapon.

More alarmed shouts echoed from the stairwell behind them. The night would not wait patiently for them to proceed. "Come on, Miri! We need to keep moving."

Despite her shock, she was able to get her legs to obey, and the two of them stepped past the body of the would-be Celestial assassin and rushed onwards towards the front door.

It was a short sprint down the corridor and around the corner to one of the doors that led into the main chamber of the cathedral. Hal paused at the door, taking a few precious seconds to scan the room beyond with his sharpened perception. In the chaos, the Celestials hadn't had much time to secure the area, but two humanoid shapes roamed amidst the pews, each carrying a military-grade springer rifle. The business end of those weapons scanned across the space where they were set to emerge.

"Ok, Miri." Hal breathed deep, sucking in every molecule of oxygen his lungs could hold. "We have maybe sixty seconds before we're caught. Two men in the other room. Both have rifles. I'm going left, you go right. Split their fire, make it easier to get close. Use the columns for cover and only shoot if you have a good shot. You have two bullets."

Miri's eyes were wide, and her fingers gripped the handle of the springer as tight as she could. It was clear the moment was threatening to completely overwhelm her. "Hal, I've never . . ." Hesitation and fear caused her words to falter.

"Miri." Hal looked into her eyes, placing both hands on her shoulders. "Do you trust me?"

Her confusion wavered, and she ever so slightly nodded her head. "Yes."

"Do you want to live?"

She nodded again. Her voice found its foundation, this time more clear. "Yes."

"We can make it through this, but only if we work together. I'm not going to let you die, and you're not going to let me die. Right?"

"Right."

Hal allowed himself the luxury of two seconds to give Miri a strong hug and a kiss on the cheek. There were so many things he wished he could say, but now was not the time. Despite his hopes, somehow it seemed as if time was never on their side at all. The precious seconds continued to pass.

"Ok." Hal swallowed, trying to wet a throat that was suddenly far too dry. His fingers wrapped around the handle of the door, gripping the metal with finality. "I go left. You go right."

Miri raised her pistol to rest at the ready, pointing it upwards alongside her head. "Right."

"Three, two, one, go!"

Hal pushed the door open and surged through, ducking low and diving to the left. He rolled towards the partial cover of the wooden pews as springer bullets whizzed through the air where his center of mass should have been. Miri didn't hesitate either, darting into the main chamber and angling to the right to take cover behind a sturdy pillar of white marble.

The two Celestials shouted out in alarm, and their large-bore rifles splintered wood and chipped stone with relentless ferocity as each one of them cycled round after round downrange. Miri screamed as she cowered behind cover. Hal screamed as he scrambled low behind the pews. The gunmen screamed as they traced differing targets, struggling to hold their weapons on track behind the massive recoil. The intensity of the moment overtook them all, like a storm overtakes a coastal village. Everyone knows what's coming, but not one can do a thing to stop it.

Fragments of wood splintered against Hal's face as he traversed sideways, narrowly avoiding a direct hit. Soon he reached the opposite row of marble columns, and was able to turn, heading deeper into the room, closer to his attackers. The Celestial targeting Hal did not relent, holding Hal in his sights as best he could. Every round springing forth from the barrel of his rifle hit hard, pulverizing stone into a fine white cloud as Hal weaved between the columns. The tricky landscape offered only fleeting windows of a clear shot. Miri let loose a primal bark of emotion as she pressed her body tight against the first column, pinned down behind the flurry of oncoming fire.

Hal stopped at the column closest to his gunman, hiding behind cover as the bullets meant for him found obstacles instead. He could sense the fear in his attacker, and that fear quickly turned to panic as the magazine of his rifle ran empty. One finger reached up to depress the magazine release, and that faint click triggered Hal's all-or-nothing charge. The gunman realized his dire situation as Hal turned the corner, just as the empty clip hit the ground with an echoing clank of metal on stone.

The second enemy seemed to realize the new trouble, however, and turned towards Hal. The barrel of his weapon angled towards Hal midcharge, and started to stitch a trail of bullets across his axis. The first bullet hit the back of a pew, sending forth a spray of wooden splinters. The second bullet whizzed inches from Hal's body with a sharp, high-pitched whine. The third bullet never came.

Miri took that moment to peel out from cover and fire a shot at bad guy #2. The bullet narrowly missed behind her novice aim, clipping the very top edge of a wooden bench to shower the man with stinging fragments of debris. It wasn't much, but it was just enough to buy Hal the time he needed.

Bad guy #1 was slapping home a fresh magazine into the side of the rifle when Hal reached him. With a ferocious scream, Hal swung his machete diagonally in a chopping motion. The blade carved into the gunman with disturbing ease, and it passed straight through his collarbone to rend the center of his torso in a single terrible strike. The blade found more bone and finally caught, stopping the cleave and awkwardly pinning Hal's weapon into the dying enemy, who lost his balance and fell forward.

The second gunman wasn't dissuaded for long. Rather than return fire at Miri, he continued to fire at Hal, who was much closer. The next few bullets slammed into his dying comrade, whose body shielded Hal's from the attack, if only for that one moment. The metal slide of the springer rifle kicked forward a bit too fast between shots, and it jammed onto a spring that had yet to clear the firing mechanism.

Hal struggled to free his machete from the dead body of his attacker, but with each millisecond that passed, the blade seemed to become more trapped between splintered ribs. Instinct took over, and Hal abandoned his weapon to charge at the sole remaining survivor, rushing the gunman before he could clear the jam.

Unfortunately for Hal, this one was well trained, and he cleared the stovepipe jam with a swift and forceful chop of one hand, allowing the bolt to finish cycling forward and load a new round. The barrel of the weapon trained back towards Hal, but the sheer bulk of the trooper-rifle made the action less swift.

That momentary disruption was enough, as it afforded Hal the precious additional second to get into melee range. With one hand he batted away the rifle barrel that attempted to home in on his chest. In that same step, Hal kicked out with his good leg, plunging his wickedly curved foretalon into the abdomen of his target before ripping sharply downward. The man screamed in pain, but was quick to fall. Within seconds, he had been reduced to a writhing bleeding mass on the floor of the cathedral.

Hal gasped, dragging in a ragged breath. The carnage of the brief but bloody battle was impossible to ignore, and already he felt his stomach clench and revolt against him. He closed his eyes and tried to swallow down the bile that simmered underneath the surface. Miri hesitated before realizing that they were clear, and quickly jogged forward to join Hal. She tried her best to avoid looking down at the blood that slicked the floor and stained Hal's clothes. "Are you ok?"

Hal nodded absently, using his forearm to wipe blood away from his eyes. Whether it was his own, he wasn't sure, but the strong metallic taste of iron lingered in his mouth. "I'm alive. You?" His heartbeat was almost deafening inside his skull.

"I'm ok." Miri was clearly shaken by the violent ordeal, but she nodded with certainty.

"Ok. Let's get out of here." Hal started to run towards the exit to the streets beyond, but he was halted by an electric shock that gripped his whole body and sent him tumbling to the ground. Miri screamed and dove off to the side, out of his sight.

"Aww, yeah! Get some, bitch! Get some!" The booming voice of Dubs erupted from behind them, and a fresh arc of brutal electricity leapt forward to wrack Hal with spasms of pain. He lost all control over his body and convulsed helplessly on the cold stone floor of the cathedral. Every muscle in his being clenched involuntarily as he flailed in the aisle, powerless beneath the supernatural assault. Hal could barely hear anything save the sounds of his own screams.

"That's what you get!" Dubs continued. "That's what you fucking ge—"

Dubs ended mid-syllable, and the room fell oddly silent. The onslaught of electricity disappeared. Hal waited a few seconds to gather himself and make sure he was still alive before he managed to angle his head. As his eyes focused, he saw Miri, standing with both arms outstretched, still holding her pistol in firing position. Delicate arcs of friction smoke wafted from the barrel as tears streamed freely down her cheeks. Dubs was shot dead with a bullet placed clean through his skull.

Miri wiped away her tears and ran to Hal's side, reaching down to help him stand. "Get up! Come on, get up!" Though they both struggled, Hal eventually found his feet and was able to limp towards the door. Miri kicked the entrance open with a decisive strike, and the two of them fled into the dark and empty city streets.

At this time of night, almost no one was in sight. The grand and open streets of Theophanies were awe-inspiring during the day, but now, under the scattered halos of intermittent streetlights, darkness seemed ready to engulf the whole city with shadowy tendrils. There was nowhere for them to run except deeper into the abyss.

The two of them fled the scene at a dead sprint, Miri leading the way ahead of Hal, who labored hard to keep up. They darted down alleyways and crossed boulevards, seemingly at random, and soon Hal lost track of where they were. Despite that, the sounds of pursuit never seemed to lag very far behind them. While neither of them could see their pursuers, Hal could feel their pressure urging him onward even as his body cried out for rest.

Miri dragged Hal around another turn and they were greeted with a view of the Eridan River, the primary waterway that flowed through the western core of the city. Ahead, a transport barge was steaming hard on its way upstream, pulling away from the riverside dock where it had just picked up cargo. The open deck was littered with crates, ropes, and tarps.

"Hal!" Miri pointed to the barge without breaking stride. "The boat!"

Hal felt his spirits both buoyed and sunk by the form of their salvation. "Miri, I need to tell you something!" It looked like at least fifteen feet of water between the shore and the ship. "It's really important!"

"Make it quick!" she called back breathlessly, not slowing at all.

"I don't know how to swim!"

Hal heard a winded laugh from up ahead. "Then you better be good at jumping!" Miri put words into action, and scrambled up the stairs to the wooden dock with surprising grace. Three more light strides and she reached the end of the platform. Without hesitation she hurled herself out into empty air, uncoiling her body to get every last erg of energy into her forward movement. She landed onto the deck of the barge with a controlled shoulder roll and finished on her feet, no worse for wear.

"Just do that, Hal. No problem," Hal muttered to himself under labored breaths. He clambered his clumsier and heavier body up to the dock and ran as hard as he could towards the edge. Miri held her arms out at the narrow wall of the deck, ready to help catch him. His tail looked back behind him, towards the pursuers that had yet to round the final bend.

"Don't look back, Hal! Just jump!"

"Grrrraaaah!" He felt his left foot curl around the final plank of wood, and he shoved forward with all of his might, letting out a feral cry. Hal's body floated out over the dark water, his arms stretched out in front of him, his feet trailing far behind. Hal was strong, but he wasn't nearly as light as Miri. Only now that he had committed to the leap did Hal realize that he didn't have enough altitude to clear the wall of the deck of the barge.

There was no time to brace himself before his body crashed into the side of the boat. He barely managed to get his arms above the ledge before the rest of his body hit, and he rocked his head against the metal hull, which sent stunning shots of electricity into his skull. Dazed, he slipped downwards, barely managing to close one claw around the lip of the wall. His fingers gave way, but the fast and firm hands of Miri quickly reached down to grab at his jacket.

"I got you. Come on!" She pulled with all her strength, and it was just enough boost to help Hal get his other arm up. It was a mighty struggle to pull himself over onto the cold and damp deck, but with Miri's help, he survived. The two escapees gathered themselves and retreated into the maze of crates and equipment. Hal was quick to collapse onto the deck, his injuries and his spent adrenaline finally catching up with him. It didn't take long before the dock was well behind them, as were the sounds of their pursuers. The two wayward astronomers were safe, for now.

Hal deactivated his power and the world contracted around him. The shock was so severe, he couldn't do anything except gasp for air for the next several minutes. Miri watched him with worry, resting one hand gently on his shoulder. "Are you going to make it?"

Hal nodded, swallowing loudly between breaths. "Heh, I'm alive. I can't promise anything more than that."

"Well, we lost them. But I don't think it's over yet." Miri looked deeply concerned, her face twisting into a frown. "Marcus is still going to try to destroy the Sabbaton Tower tomorrow. We need to let the police know."

Hal shook his head and coughed, wiping at his mouth. "That won't work. Marcus has the local authorities in his pocket. At best, the warning will be dismissed or delayed until it's too late. At worst, they'll arrest us." His tail looked back towards the roiling wake that passed through the water behind them. "We can't just go to the police."

"We have to do something, Hal! Thousands of innocent lives are at stake!"

"I know, Miri." He closed his eyes for a few heartbeats, taking a precious moment to think about the situation. The sound of the lapping water helped calm his nerves. "This barge is heading north, which means it's probably going to stop in Calypsa soon. We're moving at a good clip. I have an old friend there. He knows people. A lot of people. Hopefully we can use that to bypass the cronies and get the troopers alerted."

Miri's voice softened, and she leaned closer to Hal, smoothing the frayed and blood-spattered feathers on top of his head. "What about us, then?"

Hal opened one eye, looking her over, and then closed it again, leaning back with an exhausted sigh. "I don't have much fight left in me tonight, Miri. I'm sure Jonny will let us crash at his place until everything blows over. It might not be your cup of tea, but at least we'll be safe there."

Her voice grew suspicious. "What do you mean by that, exactly?"

Hal let out a weak chuckle. "You'll understand when we get there."

"Ah." Miri bit her lip as they approached the entrance to the Passion Lounge. The pale pink light from the buzzing sign flickered in the night like a beacon. "I think I understand what you meant." Her ears twitched, arching one eyebrow high as she gave him a look. "Spend time here often?"

"Hardly." Hal's tail shook its head as he wrapped his fingers around the handle to the door. "But I know the people who run this place. We go way back."

"How far back are we talking here?"

"Far enough."

Hal pulled open the door to their unlikely sanctuary. The hinge emitted the faintest of creaks as it swung outward to let them into the foyer. The brothel's velvety but heavy aroma was quick to overtake their senses. Miri coughed on her first breath as they stepped into the building and left the cold of night behind.

"Welcome to the Passion—Oh, spirits!" Cassi and Jonny were standing behind the front counter, but neither was prepared for the sight that had just walked through the door. "Sugar, what in the world happened to you?"

"Don't just stand there like an idiot, Hal. Get your ass out of sight!" Jonny grabbed Hal and hustled him away from the entrance, dragging him across the foyer into the back office. Here, they were no longer at risk of being seen by other customers.

Once the door was closed behind the four of them, Jonny gave Hal a good once-over. He whistled in awe, brushing some imaginary dust off of Hal's shoulders. "Wow. Ok. I never thought I'd have to say this, but first thing's first, I guess." Jonny looked Hal in the eyes. His trademark golden smile wasn't anywhere to be seen. "Hal. Why the hell does it look like you just killed a couple guys with your bare hands?"

"Um." Hal cleared his throat. In the bright light of the office, he noticed for the first time just how shocking his appearance was. Blood stained deep into his clothing, and dried remnants still clung to his legs, arms, and face. In the darkness of the streets it was easy to miss, but here there was no hiding the evidence of the violence he had so recently survived.

"That's not important right now," Miri butted in rather boldly, cutting short the question-and-answer session. "Hal says you can help us. Marcus is going to destroy the Sabbaton Tower, and we need to get word to the troopers outside of normal channels."

"Wait, come again? What's Marcus up to? And who the hell are you?" Jonny looked to Hal with surprise. "Is this that girl you were telling me about?"

Hal nodded tiredly, scraping at the dried blood around his eye.

"Here, hun." Cassi handed him a fresh towel. He muttered his thanks and did his best to clean himself up.

"It's true, Jonny. It turns out Marcus was the leader of that crazy zealot group all along, and he's planning on starting a revolution. Like, the whole 'He's dead and I'm in charge now' kind of revolution. In the next twelve hours. We barely got away with our lives."

Jonny shook his head in disbelief. Clearly it was a lot to take in all at once. "A revolution? That sounds like it could be messy for business. Doesn't Marcus know not to rock the boat around here?"

"Apparently not."

"Kid's damned crazy," Jonny scoffed, shaking his head. "Why in the world would Marcus try to kill you, Hal? You're brothers. You're the only family he has left. You used to be so tight."

"I know, Jonny. I know." Hal's voice was strained, stretched close to the breaking point. "Look, everything's totally screwed up right now. I can't even begin to talk about the shit we just went through. And now, I don't have anywhere else to turn. You two are the last living souls in this city that I can trust."

Jonny and Cassi shared a look. "All right, Hal," Jonny said. "Let's just say for the sake of argument that I believe you. Your brother might be crazy in the head, but what's his plan of attack, and how do we stop him? That tower isn't going to fall over on its own, and as much as Marcus loves huffin' and puffin', he ain't gonna just blow it all down."

"It's the meteor." Miri adjusted her glasses, willingly launching into the explanation. "It greatly amplifies an individual's Dreamkeeper power. He has a whole army of power-awakened ex-convicts equipped with shards of it, and between the lot of them, they probably have what it takes." She gave Jonny a sharp nod. "Look, let's be realistic. We're way out of our league here. This isn't some action movie where we win by launching some stupidly brave and heroic assault against the forces of evil. We need to let the troopers handle this. It's what they're supposed to be trained for, after all."

"Man, screw those guys. I hate the troopers."

"*Everyone* hates the troopers," Miri agreed. "But *they* have the tools to handle it. We don't." Hal wiped the towel over his eyes, nodding in silent agreement. Miri continued, undaunted. "You're Jonny, right?

You look like a guy who knows people. The kind of guy who gets deals done in back rooms with a handshake and a smile. Maybe there are people you can call to get the warning to City Central Authority in a way Marcus's agents won't detect. They need to send a full company to the Church of Celestia and stop this uprising before it starts."

"Damn, Hal." Jonny whistled. "You sure know how to pick 'em." Cassi gave Jonny a jab to his ribcage. "Ow! Hey, watch it, girl!"

Cassi smiled warmly at Hal and Miri. "What Mister Riggazoni meant to say is that he is delighted to make your acquaintance, hun, and it would be his absolute pleasure to make some calls for you and sort everything out."

Jonny ran his fingers through his rainbow-dyed mane. "Yeah. Um. Exactly. I think I know a guy who might know a guy who's friends with a dude that can help. It might take a little while, but I can make a few calls. See what's up."

Hal felt a wave of relief wash over him. "Thanks, Jonny."

"Hey!" Jonny pointed a finger at Hal with a sly grin. "You already had your free lunch. You seriously owe me now."

"Yeah. Yeah." Hal nodded. "I know. I'll buy you dinner or something."

"Dinner? Are you kidding me?" Cassi pushed Jonny towards the door, and he shouted over her shoulder as he was forced out of the room. "You better have, like, a full-on Zen revelation about the nature of existence *and* invent a better glo-orb or some shit, because I am getting too old to be bailing your ass out of every little two-bit 'blow up the tower' conspiracy you find yourself swept up—"

Cassi shut the door on Jonny before he could finish his rant, leaving the three of them alone in welcome silence. She placed her arms around Hal and Miri, giving them a warm, matronly smile. "Now that *that* unfortunate business has been taken care of, are you two all right? Poor little Hal here looks like he's about to keel over dead. And I'm sorry to say it, sugar, you put on a good game face, but it looks like you could use a breather as well."

Miri didn't argue the point. "I guess we could use a place to lay low for a while. It's been, well, it's been kind of crazy tonight."

"I bet." Cassi walked over to her desk and consulted a large floor plan of the building. Each room had colored tokens placed on top, representing their occupancy for the evening. "I think you two are in luck." She pointed to the top room with a smile. "It looks like our penthouse suite was just cleaned up, and no one's booked. Why don't you head on upstairs and make yourselves at home. I'm sure it'll take ol' Jonny awhile to get everything sorted out. Just don't hang around in the lobby for long. It makes my customers nervous seeing people stumblin' about all covered in blood. You just make sure little ol' Hal here gets some rest."

"Thank you. I will." Miri offered her sincere thanks. "I know it's all of a sudden, but I really appreciate your help, miss . . . "

"Cassandra DuPuis." Cassi offered one arm for a handshake. "But you can just call me Cassi, hun. Ain't nobody got time for formalities in a place like this. Y'all go do your thing. If you need anything at all, just holler. I'll be here all night."

With their business concluded, Miri helped Hal struggle up the stairs. With his energy stores nearly exhausted, Hal couldn't do much else than let himself be led by Miri's steady grasp. Soon enough they reached the top landing and the suite that would serve as their refuge for the evening.

The room was broad but lavishly furnished, making it feel far more cozy than the dimensions would suggest. A wide, king-size bed sat at the far end of the room, covered by crimson sheets of shimmery, skin-hugging satin. A control panel sat at the edge of the bed, the many buttons controlling features Hal could only begin to imagine. The windows to the room were obscured by thick velvet drapes that completely hid any view of the outside world, and the ceiling seemed to have a reflective finish, no doubt for the benefit of certain patrons.

One door off to the side led to an attached bathroom, which was decorated in a similar manner.

Their current lodgings would normally be rather uncomfortable for Hal, but he frankly didn't have the energy to care. He crashed down on the bed with a heavy sigh, finally surrendering to the weight of the day.

Miri shook him gently to prevent his immediate fall into slumber. "I know you want to sleep, Hal, but maybe you should get cleaned up first."

Hal gave Miri a muffled grunt of acknowledgment, and eventually summoned enough energy to get back on his feet and shuffle over to the bathroom. The cold, mosaic tile that decorated the floor shocked Hal into action, and he soon had the shower running with the hottest water he could bear. Steam quickly filled the air, giving it a rejuvenating weight that he could drink in with each deep breath.

He shed his clothes and stepped into the stream of hot water, pushing through the initial sting as he adjusted to the high temperature. He leaned one arm against the wall and dipped his head, letting the world finally grow quiet, with only the sound of simmering water to keep him company.

Here, at one with his thoughts, the events of the past few hours flashed through his mind: Dr. Kincaid's spasming end. The slippery sensation of talons tearing into flesh. The cold touch of a trigger against his finger as he smiled with vengeance.

Blood washed off his body and swirled lazily into the drain between his feet. Despite the water that ran into his eyes, Hal found himself mesmerized by the whirlpool. Over the minutes that passed, the crimson swirl gradually lightened, and eventually became clear when there were no more memories to be washed away.

Hal blinked the blur from his eyes and urged his body into motion again. He grabbed a bottle of body wash without bothering to read the label, and proceeded to take his time scrubbing away any last remnants of the fights he had survived. Soon the steamy air had the tingling sweet smell of tropical fruit.

Eventually, the faucet was turned off with a sharp metallic squeak. A luxuriously thick white towel waited for him on the rack just outside the frosted shower door. Hal stepped out and used it to wipe himself dry. The languid air grew quieter still, and a blanket of calm silence wrapped around him as snugly as the towel he wrapped around his waist.

He stepped over to the sink and ran the cold water, splashing some onto his face, shocking his nerves back to alertness. Looking up, he was greeted with the misty shadow of his own reflection. Hal reached out with one hand and wiped at the condensation, clearing a diagonal path to more clearly see the image of his own face.

The man that looked back was one Hal scarcely recognized. His eyes were sunk deep into his face, rung by heavy darkened eyelids. His lips curled involuntarily into a dark, unhappy scowl. His tail, normally quite animated, merely hovered, staring unblinking into the image presented to them. It looked almost like Hal had been through a week-long alcohol and amphetamine bender, with maybe one wild night of chemotherapy mixed in.

Was this the face everyone saw when they looked at him? Is this who Miri saw?

Hal was hesitant to touch his power again, but he had to dip his toes one more time, just to see. After the world grew out around him, Hal finally saw his true state. Neon blue tendrils of color glowed brilliantly from nearly every vein in his body. They spidered out, transitioning from a complex web in his chest into long, winding avenues down each limb and up his neck. Even the tree-branch network of capillaries in his fingers, toes, and face glowed brightly for him to see. The meteor's corruption was nearly complete.

The world shrunk back around him and the glow faded to dark. Hal couldn't bear to see it any longer. He was left with his own sad reflection staring back in silence. He swallowed desperately between deep breaths; the face in the mirror looked as scared as Hal had ever seen. It was exactly the same face as Vanir had given him one heartbeat before he had gleefully shot a bullet through her chest.

Like the one delicate snowball that eventually grows into an avalanche, Hal felt the weight and finality of that gunshot wash over him and rip his heart to pieces. She had been just as scared as he was. She had wanted to hold on to what she had just as badly as he did. And now Vanir was dead, along with her unborn child. Hal could never face his brother again. He had no family anymore.

He took one more breath, but the shuddering exhale became a snow-ball, and the snowball became the only thing it was destined to be. The avalanche hit hard, and Hal had no power to hold it at bay. His legs buckled, and soon he was leaning heavily over the sink and sobbing deep into the drain. The heavy, gut-wrenching bursts of emotion flooded the basin and spilled over into the other room.

A knock at the door failed to interrupt him. "Hal, are you ok?" When Miri's question received no response, she opened the door to find Hal crying into the sink. After a few unanswered sobs, she gently pulled him away from the mirror. "Come on, I got you." With soothing words and a light touch, she guided Hal back into the bedroom, sitting him down on the edge of the mattress. Miri didn't interrupt his grieving, but instead she patiently waited it out with one arm resting tenderly on his shoulder.

It took a minute for the flood of emotion to subside. When the over-flow was reduced to scattered sobs, Miri reached out and wiped the tears from his face. Hal looked up, staring deep into her eyes as the blur slowly cleared. "Miri," Hal's voice wavered unsteadily. "Am I an evil man?"

"What?" Miri shook her head. "No, Hal, of course not. Why would you even think such a thing?"

"Because Vanir . . ." Hal blinked away fresh tears that threatened to blind him. "I murdered her."

"She was trying to kill us, Hal."

"No, Miri!" Hal cut her off with a loud bark. "You don't understand. I didn't just kill Vanir. I murdered her."

Miri offered Hal a sad frown, but he continued. "Her body was broken. She wasn't a threat anymore. We could have just left her behind. But I . . ." Hal shook his head violently, as if trying to deny the truth he was speaking. "I wanted her to die, Miri. I wanted her to feel pain. My pain. The pain she first gave to me when we fought at the river's edge. The pain I felt when she took everything away."

Hal laughed bitterly. "You know, I wanted to savor her end. I wanted to see the scales balanced. I thought it would liberate me." The laugh devolved into a cry. "But it didn't, Miri. It didn't. All I feel now is the emptiest I've ever felt in my whole life. I wish with all my heart that I could go back in time and change it all. Do everything over again."

"Oh, Hal." Miri reached forward and pulled him in for a hug. She whispered in his ear as she held him close. "That is exactly why you are not an evil man. Evil men don't regret their mistakes. They let it harden them and turn their heart into stone. That's not who you are."

"Then who am I, Miri?" Hal pulled back slightly so he could see her face. "I don't even recognize my own reflection. I thought I knew where my life was going. I thought I'd escaped all this violence. But now," Hal blinked, shaking his head. "The only thing I know is that I don't know anything at all about my life. I don't know if I ever knew anything to begin with."

Miri reached out and smoothed the feathers on the top of his head. When she spoke, her voice was calm, gentle, and soothing. "Oh Hal, can't you see how special that makes you?" She smiled at him. "Your life is a miracle because you've built no walls around your heart. You have no affectations, no self-made illusions of who you are. You live every day entirely open, entirely vulnerable, and because of that, the world can hurt you sometimes. I think it might hurt you more than anyone else."

She leaned closer, brushing the last remnants of tears from his face. "But that also means that you can experience life in ways that no one else can. You can see things, feel things, that no one else even knows." Miri's own eyes began to water. "Let me tell you a story about a person I met. A few years ago I met a man. At first, I didn't think I liked him that much. He was kind of funny looking, a little shy, and he struggled at first with the simple things that the rest of us students took for granted: taking notes, doing homework, learning how to use a telescope for the first time. But he learned quick, and he didn't let anyone stop him from doing the things he loved."

Miri continued. "Soon enough we were working together, and through countless nights, some of them darker and colder than any can be, he taught me who he was. When I felt down, he would make me laugh, always ready to offer some witty remark. When I was lonely, he would keep me company, talking with me deep into the dead of night." She laughed as she relived the memories. "When I was hungry, he made me breakfast. When I was cold, he built me a fire. And when I was tired, he gave me an extra blanket and his only pillow so that I could sleep soundly."

Miri smiled at Hal, caressing his face. "And when that man thought I was asleep, when he thought he was truly alone, do you know what he would do? He would walk outside onto the balcony. He would stand out there, alone, against all the cold and all the wind and all the darkness of the world, and he would look up at the stars."

Tears started to roll down Miri's cheeks. "And do you know what happened when he did that? He smiled, Hal. He smiled with such raw and rapturous joy, like a little child discovering the tremendous beauty of his universe for the very first time."

She laughed and cried, looking into his eyes. "That man is the person I fell in love with. That man is you, Hal."

"Oh, Miri." Neither of them could hold back the flood that carried them both. Hal pulled Miri close. "Miri," Hal sobbed, finally unable to hold back the words he'd always meant to say. "I love you. I've always loved you."

"I know." Miri returned his embrace, crying over his shoulder.

They held each other for a long time, letting the years of pent-up emotion finally spring forth. It seemed like such a simple thing to acknowledge: love. And yet it took them an eternity to finally reach that admission. Eventually, Hal pulled himself together. "Why did it take us this long, Miri? Why is it that only now, near the end, are we able to say the things we mean?"

Miri pulled back, wiping at her face, clearing the water from her eyes. "I guess no one's perfect."

Hal laughed, shaking his head. "I don't know how much time I have left, Miri. The meteor inside of me . . . it's spread so far. I can feel it and I can see it. If I have to use my power for one more night," Hal said, not looking away from her eyes, "I may never wake up from it. I'm already so tired."

Miri nodded in sad recognition of the truth. "I don't know what's going to happen tomorrow, Hal. Truth be told, I'm scared to find out." Her hand fell to rest on his shoulder, giving him a comforting squeeze. "But no matter what happens, whether it's good or bad, whether we make it or not, we still have right now."

"Yeah. I guess we still have that." Hal nodded in agreement. "When did you figure me out so well, Miri?"

Hal's remark was met with an honest smile. "I guess you could say I've been an interested observer for a long time."

"I must have been pretty dense."

Miri chuckled. "Don't worry, Hal, you still are."

The two of them laughed at the joke, the emotion lightened by a giddy nervousness that overtook them both. But after a few more heartbeats, the laughter faded, and an expectant silence settled over the room. The air seemed to hang still, trapped in a moment of suspended animation. When Miri spoke again, her voice was much softer, almost a whisper.

"Hey Hal?"

"Yes, Miri?"

"Do you want to see my power?"

Hal's heart froze in surprise. In all the years he had known her, not once had Miri even hinted that she had found her Dreamkeeper power. "You found your power?" Hal was unable to hide his astonishment.

Miri nodded softly. "I found it after . . ." She hesitated. "After you were shot. After they killed Tesla. When I held him in my arms before they dragged me away." Her composure seemed to tremble. "I haven't used it since then, but I think I'm ready to show you, if you want to see."

Hal nodded, still speechless.

"Ok." Miri took a long, deep breath, letting it out slowly. She placed both hands on Hal's shoulders, finishing the exhale. "Close your eyes."

Hal wasn't sure how he was supposed to see with his eyes closed, but he did as she asked. They sat there in silence for a few more heartbeats. Then, all of a sudden, Hal's world changed. His one heartbeat became two heartbeats. His one breath became two breaths. He saw an image of himself through Miri's eyes. He could feel not only his own senses but everything she felt as well. Hal opened his eyes, and instantly he had a dizzying overlay of double vision as he saw the room through twin perspectives, all at once. Vertigo quickly overtook him, sending his sense of equilibrium reeling as his brain struggled to process competing inputs. Miri broke the link before things got too far out of hand.

"What the hell was that?" Hal asked, gasping for breath as he placed both hands down on the bed to regain his balance.

"I told you to close your eyes," Miri whispered, blinking away the disorientation. "It's a sensory link. Full two-way transmission. If I touch somebody else, I can feel everything they feel, see everything they see, and vice versa." She looked down at the ground. "The first time I used my power, I felt Tesla die in my arms."

"I'm sorry, Miri."

She shook her head. "That day has come and gone. I don't have to focus on the bad memories. I don't think that's what my power was meant for. I can build good ones as well." Her eyes found his again. "Do you want to try it one more time?"

Hal swallowed, bracing himself for the second wave. "Ok."

"This time, actually keep your eyes closed."

He closed his eyes and felt her hands back on his shoulders. In the next breath, he felt his senses duplicate, and the two of them were breathing with shared lungs, holding with shared arms. Her eyes were closed as well, letting them each wade into the pond slowly. He felt them both lean forward with care, adjusting to the waters. When the ripples began to subside, they each tilted forward just one more inch, and felt their lips touch.

It was so faint at first, like the gentlest breeze or the softest whisper. A mere memory of a kiss. They parted for just a moment, each grabbing on to a thread of that memory before coming back together. The second kiss was deeper, more yearning, and soon all hesitation had drifted off into the night. They drank deeply of each other, breathed deeply, and let themselves fall back onto the bed, entwined in mutual embrace.

There were no words Hal could use to describe the experience. They lost themselves entirely, and instead they found each other. Here, alone together in the deepest dark of night, they remembered that they were alive.

***

Sometime later, after their hearts and their bodies had been spent, after the fire of passion faded into the glowing embers of comfort, they rested. Miri slept soundly next to Hal, her head on his chest. Her warmth flowed into his core with a tender softness. One arm, wrapped around her back, held her close.

Hal felt his body, so tired now, sink deep and heavy into the mattress. Even if he wanted to move his toe with all the will in the universe, he wouldn't be able. There were no more words he could say, no more energy he could spend, no more minutes in his day. At the end of it all, there was nothing left that Hal could give.

He looked up at the ceiling and the dim reflection of the two of them, feeling his eyelids close as he welcomed the end of the night.

Before he drifted off into a long and welcome rest, Hal couldn't help but understand that in this one fleeting moment, perhaps for the first time in his life, his soul had found some measure of peace.

22

A dull tremor gently shook the floor, stirring Hal out of his slumber. He lay in that murky miasma of half-sleep: barely even aware that he was no longer unconscious. It was almost impossible to wake any further on his own, and he lacked the energy to open his eyes.

"Hal." Miri's hand on his shoulder jostled him awake. "Did you hear that?"

"Mmmm?" He rolled over, slowly forcing his eyelids to open. The room was dark and blurry, but Miri soon reached over to shake a glo-orb, and the needle of new light poked sharp pain into his skull. Hal winced, hoping his eyes would adjust quickly.

The room was well soundproofed by design, so Hal couldn't hear much of what was going on outside. He thought he heard the muffled sounds of commotion, like a violent argument was happening on the floor down below.

CLACK. CLACK. CLACK.

The distinct sound of springer fire pierced through the heavy walls, sending a jolt of adrenaline into Hal's heart. They were under attack.

"Oh shit!" Hal rolled over and instinctively reached for the nightstand, grabbing for his pistol. His talons found nothing but empty air and polished wood. The gun was nowhere in easy reach. It still lay among the pile of his bloody clothes that sat in a heap on the floor of the bathroom.

"Miri! The gun!" Hal was slow to move, half-tangled in the sheets of the bed, but Miri was faster. She rolled onto her feet and ran for the bathroom door. She only made it two steps before the door to their suite exploded inward, blasting free of its hinges and slamming into the far wall. Miri screamed and fell to the ground, covering her face from the shower of timbers that blew past her head.

There, standing in the doorway, was the last person Hal wanted to see. Marcus's eyes were alight with raw fury, and a swarm of his cronies filled in behind him as he strode into the room, violence giving speed to every step. The business end of mixed springer rifles and pistols trained onto Hal's chest, pinning him in place at the edge of the bed.

"Hal!" Marcus's face was twisted into the darkest hate-filled scowl Hal had ever seen. In one hand he clenched the shaft of his cane with a white-knuckled grip. In the other, he held a compact, easily concealable pistol. "I knew you would go crawling back to Jonny and the rest of these assholes! Did you really think you could get away after what you've done?" In a burst of telekinetic rage, the fragments of the door scattered outwards to slam against every wall.

Despite the armed intruders, Miri scrambled to her feet and tried to run for the bathroom. One of the cronies grabbed her, yanking her back and holding her rudely in place. "Let go of me, you bastard!" She didn't stop struggling despite being outnumbered and overpowered. For a moment, she actually squirmed free, elbowing her captor firmly in the face and spinning away. She started to reach for a weapon, but a swift strike of a rifle butt to the base of her skull knocked her out cold just as quickly as her struggle had begun. Two of Marcus's henchmen held her limp body up, preventing her from collapsing on the ground.

Marcus growled, pointing his gun at Hal as he walked closer. "Do you have any idea what you've done to me?" Tears rolled down Marcus's cheeks as he thrust the barrel of his gun at Hal's face. "Do you have any fucking idea what you've done?"

Hal's tail lashed out, biting Marcus in the forearm. "Gah!" His own tails flailed in response, slashing at Hal, slicing into his skin with their sharp, bloodletting edges. The hilt of the pistol was quick to follow behind, striking Hal in the temple and shooting a sharp flash of pain through his skull.

Hal tried to move out of bed and stand on his feet, but Marcus's fury was too relentless to withstand. The pistol slammed down against his face again and again and again, smashing teeth, cutting scales, and pulverizing cells into a pulpy ruptured mass. Marcus only relented when Hal collapsed helplessly onto the floor, coughing out crimson saliva with labored breaths. Hal felt the barrel of the gun press against one swollen and blinded eye.

"It wasn't supposed to end like this, Hal. We could have been brothers again. We could have changed the world together. But now . . ." Marcus sobbed between furious breaths. "Now that's all over, you goddamned bastard of a brother!"

With a surprisingly strong grip, Marcus grabbed Hal by the throat and dragged him back upright, pinning him against the wall. "I should kill you for what you've done. But a man like you doesn't deserve that mercy."

"Marcus . . ." Hal coughed, barely managing to utter the word. A sharp punch to the gut halted his protests, causing him to wretch violently.

"I don't care what you have to say, Hal. You don't matter to me anymore. You don't matter at all." Marcus's face was inches away, breathing toxic clouds of hatred into the air between them. "I'm going to make you understand the new pain you've given me." With his good eye, Hal looked past Marcus and saw Miri hanging naked and limp in the arms of her new captors. "You like learning new things, right? Let me teach you what it feels like to forever lose the person you love."

Marcus released Hal and took two steps back, letting Hal collapse weakly onto the floor. He looked over at Miri, then back at Hal. "Mmm, she is beautiful, isn't she?" A twisted smile crossed Marcus's lips. "My boys are about to go into battle against our oppressors. What better way to reward them than to give them the uninterrupted company of a beautiful young woman. I'm sure they'll enjoy her just as much as you did."

Hal fought mightily to push himself upright. "Marcus, don't . . ." His protests were far too feeble to reach across the room.

"Look on the bright side, Hal." Marcus smiled a pained and tragic smile. "I'm not going to kill you. I'm going to let you live on. You'll have the rest of your life to live in our new world, as a miserable little cripple, alone, abandoned by the people who once loved you." The smile disappeared. "It's the only fate you deserve."

Marcus trained his gun on Hal. "But, just because I won't kill you doesn't mean I won't shoot you. After all, I can't have any last-minute heroics spoiling our moment of glory."

Hal didn't have time to move or to protest before Marcus pulled the trigger. The bullet whizzed through the air in a millisecond, striking Hal in the thigh with a bloody, meaty *thwack*.

Hal screamed, rolling over onto his side and clutching his wound. It bled freely, bubbling thin rivulets between his fingers. Marcus and his companions ran out of the room without another word, leaving Hal to bleed deep into the carpet.

"Fuck!" Hal cursed out loud, blinking away the tears of pain that blurred the vision of his remaining good eye. He pulled himself up and pushed forward towards the door. He made it one step before his doubly-injured leg gave way beneath him, dumping him back down onto the ground in a graceless heap. Hal barked another curse and crossed the remaining distance in an awkward crawl, pulling himself forward onto the top of the lobby staircase.

Through the posts of the railing, he saw Marcus and company had already reached the base of the stairs, and they were about to reach the double doors of the front entrance. Miri was slung loosely over one crony's shoulder, completely unconscious. One of the accomplices fired a few rounds blindly into the central chandelier, causing the scattered patrons brave enough to watch to duck their heads back down. The dark nighttime wind blew cold air in through the shattered front door.

"Attack!" Jonny's voice echoed in pursuit of the intruders, and he erupted from the back hallway with Marvin and Geno, each one of them holding a military-grade springer rifle. They surged forward and fanned out, opening fire on Marcus's entourage. A quick flurry of bullets and shouts were traded between the two sides, but one of the cultists quickly activated his power, erecting a shimmering, translucent shield of energy to stop the bullets launched their way. The shield bearer stood firm while the rest of his compatriots conducted an orderly retreat back through the entrance.

"Screw you, Jonny!" Marcus said, offering a parting shot of words. "I always knew you'd never move up in the world!"

"And I always knew you were a special kind of asshole, Marcus! Thanks for messing up my shit for no good reason!" Jonny fired a few more impotent shots into the energy shield, which flashed brilliantly with each impact.

Marcus merely grunted in response, walking back out the door and out of sight. The last remaining Celestial reached into his pocket and produced a glass orb filled with blue liquid. He lobbed it into the center of the room and quickly escaped from the building.

"Sparker!" Jonny shouted, ducking behind cover just in time to escape the blast. The grenade exploded in a brilliant blue-white flash of light and sound, sending a concussive, dazing blast through the entire lobby. Even at the top of the stairs, Hal was not fully protected, and he felt the pressure wave pass through his body. It scrambled all of his atoms in a split second, stirring and rearranging them into a loose facsimile of their original state.

Perhaps it was because of the sparker, but the entire building became completely silent. Hal blinked, barely able to move, as he watched muted, delayed fragments of chandelier fall down onto the floor below.

One by one, like reluctant lemmings, Jonny, Marvin, and Geno poked their heads back out of cover. They were followed by other patrons and employees, and even Cassi emerged from the back office, where she had been hunkering down. Everyone seemed lost, as if they were unsure of what they were supposed to do next. It was a good dozen heartbeats before Jonny looked up and spotted Hal lying helplessly on the ledge above. "Hal!" The word echoed faintly through overloaded eardrums, barely acknowledged.

Hal tried to pull himself up along the railing to get back onto his feet. Jonny and Marvin rushed up to meet him, and were quick to grab and steady his balance before he tipped too far over the railing.

"He's shot, boss," Marvin rumbled in his usual stoic tones, prompting another cry of alarm from Jonny.

"Spirits, Hal! You're bleeding all over the place. Come on. We gotta staunch that before you pass out."

Marvin's engulfing grasp was strong enough to lift Hal clean off his feet. He cried out in pain at the sudden movement, but soon enough he was being whisked down the stairs in the arms of his acquaintance. He was gently deposited onto the narrow counter of the lobby, where Cassi normally welcomed new visitors and arranged their accommodations. Hal could barely fight to stay conscious through it all. The electric fire of pain stretched up through his leg and down from his face, converging in the center of his being. Adrenaline and endorphins were all that kept his heart beating.

"Hang tough, Hal. You ain't dyin' on me now, of all times." Jonny offered encouragement, retrieving a medical kit from underneath the counter. "You're lucky your brother uses a pea shooter. If that had been a trooper round, it would have broken your whole damn leg."

Hal cried in pain as Cassi applied pressure to his leg with a fresh pad of gauze. Blood quickly seeped through the fabric and colored it a deep, soggy red. She didn't seem all that encouraged by the results.

Hal screamed at the ceiling. Why was this happening to him? How could one forsaken night go from the worst one of his life, to the best one of his life, back to the worst again so quickly?

"Damn it, Hal, stop squirming!" Jonny held him still with a firm grip, giving Cassi a bit more space to work. The loop of a tourniquet constricted around his thigh, its pressure seeming to build like that of the night. Hal wasn't sure if it was tears or blood flowing freely from his eyes and drying in a small pool next to his skull. Whether it was his body or his heart, something inside Hal felt like it was about to give out.

Cassi worked quickly, fighting against the tide with practiced fingers and a strong touch. It seemed like this wasn't the first gunshot wound she'd dressed.

Hal had no more words left in him. To utter one would break the fragile wall of the dam that kept him on the high side of consciousness. With his one working eye, Hal glanced around the room, blinking through his tears. Everyone was watching him. Not just Cassi and Jonny. Marvin. Geno. Faces he didn't recognize.

Here in the quiet eye of the storm, employees and customers also watched on in silence. They were too scared to leave, but not brave enough to return to hiding, and instead remained trapped here in the lobby, looking on as the owners of this sanctuary treated a naked, broken, and bleeding man. The cold air of the night continued to blow in through the broken front door, wrapping around Hal's body like a thin blanket. It wouldn't be hard to just close his eyes and surrender. Let the night finish on its own without him. He had already given it so much. How could he possibly give it any more?

Cassi finished wrapping his thigh, pulling the bandages tight with a strained grunt. Their eyes made contact for only a second, but Hal saw her expression soften a bit. He couldn't bear to hold it, and looked away, blinking salt from his eye.

Her hand reached out to rest on his head. When she spoke, her voice was motherly and calm, despite the violence scattered about them. "Hey, sugar. You're going to be just fine."

Hal didn't acknowledge her. Lying exposed on the counter, surrounded by friends and strangers alike, one emotion seemed to swell the most within his heart. It wasn't fear, and it wasn't anger.

It was shame.

Such an overwhelming feeling drowned out even the pain that consumed his body. Hal couldn't remember the last time he'd felt like this. Never before had failures hollowed him so deeply. He wasn't able to save his family. He wasn't able to save his brother. He wasn't able to save the woman he truly loved. They were all gone, whisked away like a gentle sound carried by a strong wind.

"Awww, hun." Cassi seemed to understand his emotions through her touch. "You don't need to be ashamed." He angled his eye back towards her face, and Cassi gave him an honest laugh and a smile. "Do you really think you're the first man I've found naked in this lobby? Trust me. You won't be the last one, either."

Jonny looked around the room. "Why the hell ain't the cops here yet?" He started barking at Marvin and Geno, who were waiting attentively for orders to be given. "Don't just stand there, guys! Hide those weapons and get downstairs cleaned out! Do you wanna end up in jail for a night or ten years?"

Hal heard them scurry into action, moving further out of sight without complaint. Jonny looked back down at Hal, offering a forced smile. "You doin' ok, champ? It looks like Cassi was able to get the bleeding under control. We have plenty of time to get you to the hospital now."

Hal levered himself upright with Jonny's help. With a grimace, he angled his feet over the floor, taking a breath to brace himself for the second flood of pain that was sure to come.

"You able to walk?"

"No."

"It's all right. I gotcha."

Hal shook his head, fending off Jonny's attempts to help him stand. "No."

Jonny's face transformed into an expression of incomprehension as to why he was being shrugged aside. Hal looked out through the front door to the empty streets beyond. The night seemed to beckon for him with the atonal siren song of hinges swaying in the wind. The evening was not yet over, and even now it was not going to give way to morning easily.

Neither was Hal.

"I'm not going to the hospital."

Jonny looked at Hal like he was insane. "For fuck's sake, Hal. Do you even know what you look like right now?" His voice was quiet, low, and grim in its tone. "You need a blood transfusion and about a hundred stitches." The dark pool of blood waiting mere inches below Hal's feet offered silent agreement to the zebra's words. "You're in no condition to host a goddamn tea party, let alone fight."

Hal acted as if he didn't hear Jonny's protests. "I need help getting my clothes back on."

"Hal. Just think about what you're doing for a second. You're not gonna—" The words were halted by Hal's silent, serious stare.

"Jonny." Hal grabbed his shoulder with one free hand. "If you're truly my friend, you won't stop me. I can't let things end like this. Please, just let me go."

Something in Jonny's face changed. Behind the mask of bravado, Hal could see something softer in his eyes. Was it empathy? Sadness? Or just the sobering realization of truth laid bare?

Jonny blinked, gently clapping Hal on the back. "All right, Hal. All right." He nodded, as if convincing himself that it was the right call. "But after tonight, you're a big boy. So I won't be helping you with your underwear anymore."

Hal grunted a pained laugh. "Duly noted."

It was such a simple task: clothing oneself. Hal had done it countless times across countless days of countless years. And yet now it was the hardest possible action he had ever asked of himself. Moving his leg took every ounce of willpower in every fiber of his being. Hal had to fight hard to stop from howling out in pain at each touch, each twitch, each brush of cloth against skin.

Jonny and Cassi helped him dress, neither one willing to offer more words. Hal armored himself with the clothing of the streets, like a broken old knight readying for one last joust. Cracked leather, stained fabric, and dried blood. These were his protectors now. If only the morning could come when Hal wouldn't need them anymore. What a great morning it would be.

Hal slipped his arm through the last sleeve on his jacket and felt the leather groan a little as it settled along his back. The familiar sensation felt so alien in its starkness. Would it be able to keep him protected now that everyone had seen his soul exposed? Maybe it didn't matter. Maybe it wasn't supposed to be hidden. Maybe . . .

Hal chuckled to himself, shaking his head. Maybe this really was his destiny. Maybe Miri had been right about him all along.

Jonny dusted off Hal's shoulders, holding him at arm's length to give him a look over. "All right, Hal. All dressed in Sunday best. Just like old times." He inspected Hal's pistol, making sure it was still in working order. "Since apparently I can't stop you, do you mind telling me the game plan?" The pistol was offered to Hal, grip first, and Jonny leaned in closer. "You do have a plan, right?"

Hal closed his fingers around the handle, letting the weight settle into his palm. "I can't say I've thought that far ahead."

"Huh. And people say *I'm* the reckless one."

"I learned from the best." Hal took a deep breath and slid himself off of the ledge onto his feet. That lungful of air was quick to get exhaled again in a sharp, pained hiss. Jonny allowed Hal to wrap one arm around him as he settled in to help support the weight. "Marcus is going back to his church. He'll probably have some stupid ceremony and dramatic speech while he's at it. He's always craved attention. He needs to be seen and he needs to be heard. Now that his moment has finally arrived, he won't pass up the opportunity to feed his ego. I guess all I need to do is get over there somehow."

"The telepads are closed, but that ain't ever stopped me before. Think you can walk a couple blocks?"

"That depends." Hal winced, adjusting his weight. "Have you been working out?"

Cassi and Jonny both laughed at that one. "If you still have the energy to be a smartass, I'm sure you'll be fine."

Jonny and Hal started to limp for the door, but Cassi halted them for just one more moment.

"Hey, sugar." Cassi pulled Hal's tail close for a soft hug. "You take care of yourself, ok? I mean it."

"I've never been very good at that, Cassi."

"I know." She gave his tail a kiss on the head. "But it's never too late to learn. Just do be careful."

"I will." Hal offered a weak smile. "Thanks, Cassi."

241

She took a step back, clearing the way once again. "Get along now. Go do your thrillin' heroics before I change my mind and stop the two of you."

And just like that, the goodbyes were over. Jonny dragged Hal out into the streets, marching him forward with each shuffling, lurching step. The telepad wasn't very far from the brothel, but it might as well have been miles away for how difficult it was for Hal to move. Still, they never stopped walking, and Jonny kept him supported every step of the way.

"Hey, Jonny."

"Yeah?"

"I've been thinking, and I believe I have a confession to make."

"Oh yeah? What's that?" Jonny glanced over with a curious smile.

"You know the number one rule?"

Jonny nodded.

"Well, I think I'm pretty bad at it."

Jonny laughed, the sound echoing off of the walls of nearby buildings. "Hal. Sometimes you just don't know how smart you are." The zebra smiled wistfully, tightening his grip on Hal as they marched along. "If it makes you feel any better, Hal, just remember." The smile widened into a golden grin. "Rules are meant to be broken."

They both laughed at that one, and it helped to take the edge off. Truth be told, Hal's heart was beating a mile a minute, and by this point, "running on fumes" was an overstatement. Exactly what he was running into, Hal had no idea, but here he was, running all the same.

Soon they reached the telepad plaza, finding it entirely abandoned. The lights were on but not a soul was to be seen. Normally there would at least be a security guard or two loitering around to keep the riff-raff at bay. A section of low fencing around the pad was toppled over, and the door to the control vestibule was left open to sway and clatter in the wind.

"Well, this certainly isn't foreboding," Jonny quipped, frowning at the scene. "You sure you don't wanna just take a breather? Let the troopers sort everything out?"

Hal shook his head, even though Jonny already knew what the answer was going to be. "I can't just make a mess for others to clean up. One way or another, I'm going to see this through. I've spent an awful lot of time running, and I think I'm ready to finally stop and stand on my own two feet."

"Oh, well, in that case." Jonny released Hal and stepped to the side, leaving the raptor to support his weight entirely on his own.

Hal cried out in alarm, struggling to keep his balance. "You're very funny."

"Bad metaphors hurt, don't they?" Jonny laughed and made his way to the control room. "Stop being all profound and just get on the damn pad already. It's nearly four in the morning. See earlier comment marked 'this shit,' 'getting too old for.'"

"Jerk." Hal limped his way past the gap in the fence to take his place at the center of the telepad. The circle felt so large and empty without a crowd of people crammed in alongside him. The cold wind stung his eyes, causing him to blink.

From the booth ahead, Jonny made a sour face. "Hal, I think Marcus and his merry men came through here recently."

"Why do you say that?"

"Well, for one, there's a dead guy in here who looks like he was killed by some supernatural face-melting laser beam. That, and there ain't any cops swarming the area. Some crazy shit is definitely going down. City Central is going to have a field day when they get the coffee pot goin' in the morning."

Hal frowned. "Do you know how to work that thing?"

"Hal." Jonny looked over through the window, shouting to make sure he was heard. "Haven't you learned by now that I know how to do everything?"

243

Hal smiled, fighting off the arcs of pain that danced through his body. He couldn't hold back any longer. Even though he didn't have a winning hand, it was time to go all in. With a relieved sigh, Hal activated his power, and let the clamor of the world wash over him. The pain in his body bled away, replaced only with a tingling energy and the subtle bass of his own heartbeat.

Hal inhaled deeply and looked up at the clear night sky. Showering down on him was a silent display of brilliant light and nameless hues. The stars were still there, like they always had been, just waiting for him to look up. It was a sight he had almost forgotten in the past few weeks, but the heavens waited patiently for him. In the end, those beautiful colors had never left his sky.

An almost imperceptible glow from beneath the horizon heralded the morning that would be coming soon. Here, in the opening seconds of astronomical dawn, Hal was the only man to know it.

"Are you ready, stargazer?" Jonny called out to him, his hands resting on controls unseen. The voice tried to sound brave, but Hal could sense his hesitation.

"Yeah."

Jonny looked down and nodded, delaying the inevitable as he fiddled with the telepad controls. A few hesitant breaths marked the passing of time.

"Hey, Jonny," Hal called out, causing Jonny to look up from his procrastination. "I'll see you on the other side."

Jonny smirked, and the two of them shared a wistful smile for one more heartbeat. "I'll see you there, Hal."

And with that last breath, Jonny flipped the switch, and the telepad winked to life.

Hal materialized on the Theophanies pad with a sudden sound-less jerk. Vertigo washed over his body, but he managed to keep his balance in spite of himself. This pad was just as abandoned as the last one, but evidence of violent conflict wasn't hard to find. Small spatters of blood waited by the pad's exit, leaving a macabre trail that led off into the streets. Hal didn't need to find the body to know what methods his brother had used.

Hal took a step forward and tested his weight on his unsupported legs. His power washed away any semblance of pain, but he still had to be careful. Pain or not, throwing his weight around wouldn't end well if he asked too much of bruised bones and torn muscle. Somewhere along the way, he had lost his cane tonight.

Step by step, Hal worked his way into more empty streets. During the day, these avenues would be filled with the hustle and bustle of commerce. Vendors selling wares. Preachers selling faith. Everyone clamoring for attention all at once. But now, at this seemingly forsaken hour, even the wind held itself still in a self-imposed curfew. He sensed the urgency of life from up ahead, only a few blocks away. There was only one place it could be. Marcus was not far.

Hal moved with a slow and steady pace, measuring his balance with every shuffling step. His pistol felt like a lead weight: a burden he couldn't yet discard. Between the gaps of the large spires overhead, stray beams of moonlight spilled down onto the streets. Somewhere beyond those rays, the Sabbaton Tower still remained. It's hulking and erect form, often the subject of so many lowbrow jokes, failed to inspire any sort of feeling in Hal's heart. It didn't render him mute in awe. It didn't weigh on his soul. It was nothing to him, and yet, in spite of his apathy, tonight it had become the nucleus of all of his misfortune. The night drew Hal ever onward.

Hal slowed his march and leaned against the wall of his alley, stopping to listen to the world. Around the bend, just across the street, waited Marcus's cathedral. Inside, so many souls were caught up in rapt attention. Filled with anxiety. Hope. Fear. Confidence. The cold but inevitable wind of a storm ready to be unleashed upon the unsuspecting world.

One dim soul waited glumly outside the front door. Hal could feel him. A young man filled with doubt, wondering how he had been rejected among all the others, forced to guard the entrance alone. It was a thankless job, delegated down to the very lowest man on the totem pole. He was missing the dramatic speech, and no one in the world cared at all.

Hal pulled the hammer on his pistol back to full-cock, but something inside his heart caused him to hesitate before rounding the corner. Was this right? He didn't sense any violent intent from the teenager left alone in the dark. Only doubt. The desolate but resonant sensation of not belonging where he was. It was a familiar feeling that Hal knew all too well. Half-forgotten memories danced through his mind, brought back to life for one tiny instant.

The gun felt heavy and cold in Hal's hands. It too didn't really belong. Hal let his thumb ease the hammer back up, de-cocking the weapon. Hadn't enough people been shot tonight? The survival instinct in Hal clamored out, demanding that he kill his potential attacker, but somehow his muscles didn't hear it. With tremendous difficulty, the pistol was tucked into his jacket pocket by one begrudgingly cooperative hand.

Hal swallowed, waiting one more heartbeat before stepping out onto the street and into view. He walked towards the church, forcing himself to keep the weapon stowed and unfired. The young recruit was quick to notice the wounded raptor, and Hal could feel the alarm wash over him with a shuddering inhale.

"H-hey!" The kid drew his pistol and waved it in Hal's general direction. The barrel danced about with furtive uncertainty. "Don't come any closer!"

Hal didn't heed the warning and continued his slow, unsteady march. This caused the level of fear in the air to swell higher, threatening to flood the street. "I mean it!" The wavering barrel kicked back, unleashing an errant bullet to bite at Hal. It clipped a frayed shoulder of the leather jacket before skipping off further into the dark.

Fingers desperately clenched on the hilt of both pistols, but Hal kept his in check. He looked over at his graze wound and then back at the kid, finally pausing in his steps. After a short moment of silence, Hal offered words instead of his own bullet in response. "Are you going to kill me?"

The question took the young man by surprise. This wasn't how people were supposed to respond to being shot at. "I'm supposed to stop you."

"And I'm supposed to be asleep, lying comfortably in a hospital bed with all sorts of tubes sticking out of me." Hal shrugged. "But I've never been very good at doing what I was supposed to do."

The youth didn't know how to react to Hal's apparent indifference; that much was clear. He wasn't supposed to have a polite conversation and argue the finer points of appropriate behavior at 4 AM. The gun, rendered mute by the mild debate, pointed aimlessly in Hal's general vicinity. "Why aren't you scared? I could kill you right now."

"You could." Hal nodded, looking his opponent in the eyes. "Since that's the case, why are you scared?"

The young man's confidence seemed to falter, and he placed another hand on the grip of his pistol, steadying himself. "Because." His eyes narrowed as he found his resolve. "I don't want to die."

"Huh." Hal felt the corner of his mouth curl up into the edge of a smile. "That's funny."

"What's so funny about that?" The kid aimed his pistol with more precision, hovering the sights over Hal's chest with an uncomfortable focus.

"I don't want to die either. I think . . ." Hesitation halted Hal's words before they inevitably fell from his lips, one by one. "I think the idea of dying scares me."

And there it was: a simple truth, floating between the two wandering souls that stood lost together in the cold predawn air. They each watched it in silence before a gust of wind sent it drifting off, out of sight. The would-be gunman lowered his pistol a hair, unsure of whether he should chase after it.

"Look." Hal returned his attention to the conundrum at hand. "I need to walk through this door, and I'd prefer that you didn't shoot me before I even got that far. I don't know what's going to happen when I walk in there, but I don't think it's something you really need to stick around for. It might be in your best interest to go your own way."

"Like you know." The kid aimed his pistol at Hal's head. A defiant sneer was quick to replace the confusion on his face. "I don't have anywhere else to go. You think it's just that easy to walk away?"

"No." Hal shook his head. His tail stared up at the sky. "No, I'm afraid nothing like that is ever easy at all." The pistol didn't waver, which prompted the final question that had been awaiting resolution. "So, what's it going to be?"

The recruit glared, his finger teasing the trigger of the pistol at the apex of each heartbeat. The bullet wasn't going to miss its mark at this close range. Hal wasn't sure if he was even breathing anymore, so still his body had become. Every muscle, every last adrenaline-kissed nerve, screamed out for him to grab his own weapon, but the call went unanswered. The paralysis of trust was too foolish and stubborn to be overcome by instinct. Hal could feel the flood of conflicting emotions wash through his unwilling companion.

"Screw this shit." The pistol fell, as if acknowledging the pull of gravity. One arm guided it back down into its former hiding place. The kid gave Hal one more passing glance before pulling up his hood to hide his face and marching off into the alleyway. Where he would eventually end up, no one could guess.

Hal finally released his breath with a heaving, shuddering gasp. His lungs screamed for air, quickly accelerating to a greedy series of labored inhales. Hal leaned forward against the wall of the church and closed his eyes, coughing hoarsely at the ground. His stomach twisted itself into a knot of belated panic. He experienced all at once the primal punch of delayed emotions now that his potential executioner had walked away. Hal's remaining eye watered quickly as a broken sob of relief spilled down onto the street.

It took a minute for the wave to subside. He was alive. He was alive. Hal repeated those words in his mind like a mantra to give him the strength to stand again. Despite his power, his body was weak, and even his willing soul was having trouble with the effort expected of it. With tremendous difficulty, Hal pushed his forearm against the wall and levered himself back upright, drawing in a long, ragged breath of air. "Come on, Hal, keep it together." Muttering to himself seemed the only way to keep a new wave from washing ashore. Hal could have been killed so easily, but somehow, it didn't happen. It was strange how such a twisted and confused life could still be punctuated by small miracles. In spite of all that had happened, he was still alive.

The muted echo of his brother's booming voice focused Hal's attention on the present. That dramatic speech of his must be getting to the good part. It wasn't too late for Hal to confront him. Miri was somewhere inside there, too. He could still save them both. In the story of this night, there were still a few more pages that were waiting to be revealed.

Hal found the weight of his pistol pressing into his palm again. The grain of the grip reassured his hesitant fingers that indeed, he could write those final pages himself if he had the courage to try. His other hand gripped the elegant brass handle to the doorway. The threshold was here, ready, waiting to be crossed.

Hal didn't know if he was ready. In truth, he wasn't. Hell. It seemed he was never ready for anything, and yet some unknown force from within always pulled him relentlessly towards the future. A surge of emotion welled up in his throat and forced him ever onward.

Ready or not, it was time.

"Marcus!" Hal pushed through the door and stormed into the room, screaming out his brother's name like a challenge against fate itself. Inside, a hundred heads turned to face him all at once.

Marcus stood at the altar at the front of the room, one fist still raised in a dramatic gesture. The meteors rested on decorative pedestals, many chips and fragments already hewn from their bulk. An army of converts, some dressed in ceremonial robes, but most wearing street clothes, turned from their positions among the pews and targeted Hal with a hundred different weapons. The metallic clicks of hammers being cocked and safeties being released echoed in the wide chamber.

"Wait! Hold your fire!" Marcus leaned forward over the altar, welcoming Hal's surprise visit with eager expectation. He smiled wide, grinning at the sight of his brother before him. "You really are tougher than you look, Hal! I should say I'm surprised to see you, but that would be a lie. You missed most of the ceremony, I'm afraid."

"Enough, Marcus!" Hal marched down the central aisle, past the columns of underground soldiers and the stains of blood he so recently left behind. "I'm done playing games with you!" He fired a shot from his pistol into the stained-glass window that arched across the ceiling high above. It shattered into several heavy fragments that crashed down onto the marble floor between the two brothers. A rogue beam of moonlight finally had an opening to spill down from above, illuminating the scene that was unfolding. Hal aimed his weapon back down and stretched his arm towards Marcus. "Where's Miri?"

"Why, she's right here, of course. She didn't want to miss the big event either." Marcus gestured off to the side. A few cronies shuffled around behind a marble column and emerged with Miri in tow, her body hanging limply between their arms as her legs dragged weakly along the ground.

She was still as naked as when they stole her from the Passion Lounge, only now she sported several more bruises and looked far worse for wear. At first, Hal thought she was unconscious, but Miri soon stirred and lifted her head to see what was happening. "Hal?" At first her voice was weak, but realization dawned on her quickly, giving her strength. "Hal!"

"I'm here, Miri."

She took in a deep breath, and for a moment it looked like she was going to break down into tears. Instead, the words that followed surprised everyone. "Hal, you idiot!"

The raw anger in her voice hit Hal in the face like a scornful slap.

"Why did you come here? Why?" She didn't want to believe that she was actually seeing Hal standing before her. "Can't you see? Now we're all as good as dead! You could have saved yourself!" She hung her head, letting it droop down as she screamed at the floor. "Now none of us are going to make it out of here alive!"

"Aww," Marcus said, feigning sympathy. "She doesn't seem all that happy to see you."

"Damn it, Marcus, what have you done to her?" Miri's anger was quick to feed Hal's own.

"Me?" Marcus shook his head. "I haven't laid a finger on her. She would be in much better shape if she hadn't tried to claw the eyes out of every one around her."

Hal grit his teeth, fighting against the anger ripping at his chest. "Let her go, Marcus!"

"Or what?" Marcus turned towards Hal, and his smile darkened into something far more bitter. "You'll *shoot* me?" He stepped out from behind the altar, exposing the whole of his body. He held no weapon, but one hand gripped the top of his cane with an intense pressure. "Will that make everything better, Hal? To put the final nail in my coffin? Is that how you want our story to end?"

Marcus's silhouette wavered behind the sights of Hal's pistol. "All I want is to be able to live my own life. Why can't you accept that? Why couldn't you ever accept me for wanting that?" There was no stopping the flood of repressed emotions now, and neither Hal nor Marcus were able or willing to hold anything back.

"Because you left me alone in the dark, Hal! Because at the core of it all, you're only a selfish, useless coward!" Marcus didn't bother to hide the contempt that dripped from the final word. "What have you done with your life other than run away? Who have you ever stood by other than yourself? What have you ever accomplished other than ripping my heart to pieces time and time again?" The rage in Marcus's face illuminated the room as bright as day. "Do you even believe in anything at all?"

"I believe that there's more to life than this!" Hal's scream echoed through the walls of the chamber, reflecting off of every marble pillar, every stunned person, every shard of glass. He surprised even himself with the weight behind those words. Miri lifted her head, watching in amazement as the echo of Hal's voice refused to fade away.

"What does existence look like through your eyes, Marcus? Do you see the world as a battlefield to be conquered? Do you view your life as a war to be won? It is so much *more* than any of that, can't you see?" Hal shook his head and felt tears free themselves from his cheeks. "Please, look down the road that you're on and understand where it's leading. If you destroy the tower, you might kill the Viscount. You might even succeed in overthrowing the entire government. But what will that make you?"

Hal took another step forward into the field of broken glass and brilliant moonlight. "If you impose your will on everyone, you'll just be another tyrant. You might fly a different flag and wear different clothes, but that won't change what you are."

Marcus growled at the accusation, but Hal continued. "The only things you will create are sons without fathers. Daughters without mothers. An entire generation of tortured souls that scream out at the universe, their hearts filled with hate to replace the things they've lost." Hal's voice cracked. "All you'll create . . . is a city filled with more broken children like us."

"That's not who we are!"

Hal shook his head, undaunted. "It's not too late to stop this madness, Marcus. You don't have to be a prisoner to your pain forever. We can learn to live our lives again if we're just strong enough to try!"

Marcus laughed. It was a dark, empty, and humorless sound. "Oh, that is rich, coming from you, Hal. If I'm a prisoner, it's only because you were the one standing next to me, laying every brick of those walls with your own two hands!" The words stung Hal with the keen edge of truth. "After all that you've taken from me, this fight is the only thing I have left!"

Marcus's voice took on a sharper, more manic edge. "With the meteor, I have the power to change the world. We all have the power to change the world!" He gestured towards his assembled men, who despite all reason had obeyed his wishes and not shot Hal full of holes. "It's not a curse, Hal. It's a blessing! Just look how *strong* it's made you! It's an opportunity for real change that this city has never experienced, and I'll be damned if I let it slip away!"

"But the way you're going about this is all wrong!" Miri interjected, struggling weakly against the men that held her back.

Marcus sneered. "Do you have a better fucking idea? What am I supposed to do instead, vote for the mythical politician that will allow us to be our true selves? To live freely without fear?" Marcus shook his head decisively, chopping through the air with his empty hand. "You don't need to be afraid of this power. It isn't evil. It's just a rock! It has absolutely no notion of the concept. If there is any darkness to be found here, it is the darkness that you find within your own hearts."

Marcus stood up to his full height, as if daring Hal to prove him wrong. He was a commander in full control of his domain, and he wasn't about to let anyone dictate any terms to him. "If you think that stopping me is the right choice, you'll have to do it yourself, Hal."

Miri and Hal shared a glance. Neither one was ready to accept that course of action. It would mean certain death for the both of them. Hal clearly didn't want to die, and neither did Miri. It was an impossible situation, but they needed to find a way out of it somehow.

The gun felt uncooperatively heavy and imprecise in Hal's outstretched hand. "I'm not here to kill you, Marcus. I'm here for Miri. I don't care what happens to me, but you need to let her go."

"Oh?" Marcus stepped forward towards the edge of the ceremonial stage. "And why should I let her go?" His voice did not hide the angry hunger that lurked underneath.

"Because she deserves to live!" Hal felt his throat constrict a little as he said those words. "I've made a lot of mistakes, Marcus. I'm sorry for hurting you. I'm sorry for not being a better brother. But she has done nothing to you. Please. She deserves to live. Just let her go."

"We all deserve to live, Hal. That's not why you're here. If it were up to you, you would ignore everything you didn't like about the world, including me." Marcus looked unconvinced, as if Hal was lying to his face. "Why are you really here?"

Hal's lips trembled, and he watched the world blur as his eye teared up. There was no point holding back the truth. "I'm here because I *love* her."

"Love?" That didn't seem to be the right answer for Marcus, and it set him off like a spark to a powder keg. "Love?" Marcus snarled at Hal, every syllable dripping pure venom. "Do you want to know what I've learned about love?" Using his powers of telekinesis, Marcus shattered the wooden altar into a million splinters and sent them scattering about the room.

"I loved our family, and then they were taken away from me. I loved Vanir, and then she was taken away from me. I loved *you*, Hal." Marcus's words could not have emerged with more sadness. "I loved you, my only brother, until you showed yourself for who you really are. You were never my brother at all." Tears flowed down his cheeks without restraint, and the words that followed echoed long in their finality. "You're my destroyer." Marcus nodded. "That's all you ever were. That's what you are. That is why you're here."

Hal didn't know how to respond. A strange pause filled the space between them, and Marcus stared down at Hal with a sad, expectant hatred. "Well? Don't hesitate now, Hal. You've already come this far. Bring an end to this little tragedy of ours the only way you know how."

"It doesn't need to end like this, Marcus. I don't want to shoot you." Hal grimaced. "Please, don't force me to do this."

"Then put the gun down, Hal, and get the bloody hell out of my way!" Marcus pointed the end of his cane at Hal like the tip of a lance aimed straight at his heart. "I'm going to free this city from oppression, even if it means tearing it down. And I promise you that anyone and everyone who has ever wronged me is going to burn, whether it's the troopers, the politicians, that asshole Jonny, or even you, Hal. And when you're all done burning, I'll brush aside the ashes, and I'll learn to live my life again as someone who is well and truly free!"

Marcus's passion was burning hotter than anyone could extinguish, and his men seemed to feed off of his energy. They wouldn't be held in check much longer. Hal was fighting a losing battle. "I won't let you kill more innocent people, Marcus."

"You won't let me?" Marcus grinned wickedly at Hal. "Then prove it, coward. Gun me down like you gunned down my lover. Embrace your destiny!" Marcus held his arms out to his sides, exposing himself for a clear shot.

Hal swallowed a silent sob of grief. He couldn't do it. Memories flashed through his mind of quieter times. Playing games in the streets, wrestling in the living room, a quiet boat ride on a canal filled with sunlight. How could those moments ever lead to here, of all places?

"Come on, Hal!" Marcus urged him on with a single-minded focus. "Shoot me already!" That crazed and desperate cry filled the echoing chamber, begging for release. "Do it!"

Hal blinked away more water, clearing his vision. Marcus rested somewhere beyond the brass sights of his weapon. Visions of a city lit by flame danced around the periphery of Hal's imagination. The barrel trembled nervously around its target, but found its purpose with the beginning of one slow exhale. That wasn't his future. Hal wouldn't let it be his future.

Hal watched the sights steady themselves with quiet calm and his finger brushed against the cold metal finish of the trigger. The exhale was over.

"I'm sorry, Marcus." Hal let his eyes rest upon the broken man that waited in the short distance beyond, and he pulled the trigger.

A rush of silence filled the room.

Everyone looked around at one another, expecting something dramatic to happen, but the moment failed to arrive. The bullet never fired. Hal's finger was paralyzed, halfway along the trigger pull, frozen firmly in place. He struggled to force the action through, but it was useless. Soon, Hal's entire body felt pinned despite the desperate will to move forward.

Marcus's laugh was the first sound to break the silence. It started slow, like scattered raindrops falling on a hollow roof, but soon grew in volume and frequency to flood the space around them. He stood at the edge of the platform, a dark halo shimmering over his head as he gestured towards Hal with one hand while the other firmly gripped the meteor that rested atop his cane.

"Hahaha!" Marcus's voice echoed with empty delight. "You were actually going to shoot me, weren't you? You cocky son of a bitch!"

Hal fought with every ounce of his willpower to move his arm, to move his finger, to even breathe, but Marcus held every vein of his body still with an iron-fisted telekinetic grip. He could only watch with growing terror as his brother continued to laugh in his face.

"Did you *really* think you could just walk in here and save the day?" His laugh bounced off of the columns of the grand chamber, reflecting even more hollow than before. "That's always been your problem, Hal. You never think things through. You're such a hopeless romantic that even when your entire world is on the line, you foolishly believe that somehow everything will turn out for the better." The laugh eventually fermented into something far more sour. "That's not how the world works."

"Stop this! Let him go!" Miri's cry for mercy went unanswered.

A deep thirst in Marcus's eyes seemed to finally awaken after being hidden for so long. "You can't escape the connection we share, Hal." He stepped down onto the main floor, pushing aside scattered fragments of glass with one foot. "If I can't have peace, then neither can you. If I can't have love, then neither can you. If I can't hold on to my happiness, then neither can you!"

Hal watched with helpless horror as his arm started to move on its own. The barrel of his weapon wavered away from Marcus and traversed slowly sideways, drifting over towards Miri and the two converts who held her in place. A panicked realization flashed across her face, and she desperately fought against the grip of her captors, but her body was too weak to have any chance of breaking their grasp.

"Don't despair, Hal! There's one thing we can each still salvage from all this carnage." Marcus guided Hal's arm into place, where the barrel of the pistol aimed steadily at Miri's center of mass. "That thing, that forgotten word, is *justice*."

Hal tried to cry out, to talk, to move, to do anything at all, but he was frozen. No amount of will could overcome the singular one that gripped him. Marcus stretched out his own arm, as if he were the one holding the pistol, and rested his finger on an invisible trigger. "You see, I will have my justice . . . and you will have yours."

Marcus's head tilted sideways, giving Hal a cruel, curious stare. "Do you know what emptiness feels like?"

The finger finished its motion, and the weapon jumped back to life.

The gunshot cracked the air like a thunderclap, striking Miri square in the gut. She screamed out in pain and collapsed onto the cold stone floor as her captors finally set her free.

Marcus eased his grip a little, allowing Hal's long-delayed cry of anguish to finally escape his lungs. It burned out his core until there was no air left, and the pistol fell free from his fingers with the last gasps of pain.

"There." Marcus closed his eyes and nodded, seeming to savor the moment. "That's it. That's it exactly. Finally, you understand."

Marcus opened his yellow eyes once more and refocused his attention on Hal's shattered soul. "I had hoped the meteor would unite us,

Hal. But I understand now that you were never worthy of the gift given to you. This false life of yours, you were never strong enough to live it."

An icy burn started to trickle through Hal's veins. He could feel tiny fragments of the meteor begin to move through him and drift towards the core of his chest. Marcus grinned wildly at Hal like a crazed puppeteer holding his beloved creation over an open flame. The shards collected and condensed into a small dense marble in the center of Hal's solar plexus, tugging towards the waiting reach of Marcus's outstretched palm.

"I'll take that life back, now."

As if yanked by an invisible thread, the meteor shard was pulled free from Hal's chest with a sudden jerk. The heavenly relic flew into Marcus's waiting grasp, and he clenched his fingers around the stone with a euphoric sigh. Hal's legs buckled and he collapsed onto the floor with a heaving cry, clutching ineffectively at the new hole just beneath his sternum.

"Now we're even." Marcus's words somehow made it into Hal's head over the volume of his pain. "You can rest now, Hal. Your role in this old world is over, and there is no place for you in the new one." Marcus's voice carried the burden of truth through the cold air. "You can finally disappear, just like you've always wanted."

This can't be happening. This can't be happening! Hal's thoughts tried to find traction, to urge his broken body onward, but his energy stores were depleted. Gravity pulled him onto the polished stone floor with an endless grip. He couldn't fight against it.

Hal lay there, alone, ignored now by the others in the room. If anyone was speaking, the words didn't register in his mind. Hal was dying. He knew it. He could feel it. All he could do was stare off to the side at one row of stained-glass windows, and wait for the end to come.

A subtle flash of light or shadow from beyond the window caught the attention of Hal's tired eye. Seconds later, a few panels of the window shattered inward, and a rounded object bounced through and spun lazily across the marble floor. He had just enough time to recognize what it was and close his eyes before the blast wave hit.

The concussion of a half-dozen sparkers erupted in asynchronous harmony and echoed throughout the room. A larger blast from behind threatened to collapse the entire building as shattered timbers passed through the air above Hal. The troopers were finally here, two minutes too late.

Armored soldiers surged through the doorway and the windows, filling the space around them all at once. The attack began in earnest with the sound of a hundred weapons finding purpose in unison. The inevitable battle was finally here, and it came with only one word fitting to describe it.

It was a massacre.

From all around, bullets flooded the air, met with the multicolored flashes of powers unleashed in full. Beams of energetic destruction, clouds of poison, walls of pure energy and more greeted the onslaught with an even greater volume. If chaos itself could be captured into a single moment, that moment was this.

Somehow, it felt like everyone was losing the battle. A grenade scattered a cluster of cultists into memories. A trooper spontaneously burst into flames with a quickly extinguished scream. Bullets sent bodies falling on both sides. Hal managed to turn his head and saw his brother, Marcus, standing in the center of it all, laughing. It was the laugh of a man brought face to face with his fate. A man who reveled in the purity of it all.

A trio of soldiers surged through one shattered window and charged him at close range. Marcus fired his pistol into the face of the point man, dropping him hard before he made it two steps. His companion tried to spear Marcus with a bayonet, but he barely missed as Marcus spun to the side, grabbing the barrel of the gun. A dark halo shimmered to life, and suddenly the soldier's helmet crumpled inward, crushing his skull before he could even react. That same telekinetic force flung the corpse into the lone survivor and sent him crashing back through the window.

Hal couldn't watch anymore. Keeping his eye open was nearly impossible, and unconsciousness beckoned for him with greater insistence. The din of the combat faded from his perception, and he was left alone with his thoughts and the echo of old memories. *I must really be dying,* Hal thought to himself. *That old cliché is true, after all.*

Voices in his mind sang a quiet lullaby, like forgotten ghosts, like the whispers of old friends.

"You may not think so now, but soon enough we'll be living in a different world."

"You carry a large burden, young man, but do not let it define who you are."

"We often don't have a choice when we discover who we must be."

"I just enjoy the journey. You'll undahstand someday."

"Someone has to have the courage to do what is necessary."

"I am grateful that you chose to share your story with us. I know that it is difficult to tell."

The memories were slowly fading into the dark, but one final question shined brighter than the rest.

"Hey Hal?"

"Yes, Miri?"

"Do you think we each have a destiny?"

Hal remembered the cold sunlight reflecting off of the mountains and Miri's confused face.

"Why do you ask?"

"Well, I don't know. I'm just thinking, do we have some sort of unique purpose for being here? For being alive?" Her beautiful eyes looked so lost that morning as they stared into the wind. *"Am I meant for something special, or am I just another snowflake among millions of snowflakes, blowing around in the wind without direction or control?"*

"What do you think, Miri?"

"I think I do have a destiny. We all do. I have to believe that." Her casual certainty rang true, even now. *"The world can feel like such a cold and terrible place sometimes, but I don't want to believe that it is. I guess, in the end, I just want to know that my life matters somehow."*

"It's not so cold when you stand in the sunlight." The words of Hal's response echoed louder now in his mind than they did back then. *"I think we can each make our own destinies, Miri. I have no idea where our paths will lead, but maybe someday we will discover if we are worthy of the time have in this world."*

"Do you think our lives will be worth it?" Miri's gentle face had looked up at him, searching his own for an answer.

"I don't know, Miri. But one day . . ." Hal remembered his calm smile as he held her close. *"One day, we will find out."*

Hal opened his eye once more, and drew in a final lungful of air. One arm pushed against the earth and moved it just enough to crawl onto his knees and raise his head. The battle had devolved from a focused assault into the raw unrestrained fury of hand-to-hand combat as pockets of survivors still struggled for victory. One trooper strangled a gasping cultist between two shattered pews, wringing the life out of her second by second. Hal reached forward and took hold of a long, sharp fragment of glass, gripping it tightly in his hands.

Some steps beyond, through the field of shattered glass, Marcus too was still on his feet. He was beating the already pulverized face of a trooper lieutenant with his bare fists, and his blade tails lashed out at the body, relentlessly slicing at it again and again. Marcus was beyond laughter now. Instead he was simply screaming: screaming lungfuls of hatred into the corpse of the man who had failed to kill him. Hal balanced his weight under one leg and pushed the earth again, rising unsteadily to his feet.

A glimpse of violet stole Hal's vision, and he saw that Miri was still alive, crawling forward on her arms but dragging a dark trail of blood in her wake. Marcus didn't notice her, and she inched her way towards him with desperate determination. Hal felt his body move, and he started to lurch forward.

Miri reached Marcus and stretched out one hand, grasping at his ankle. A bright halo of her own shimmered to life as fingers found their grip, and suddenly the screams of hatred were replaced with a single cry of pain. She shared her sensory link with Marcus, and it doubled him over and staggered him to his knees. He clutched his abdomen and tried to protect his phantom gunshot wound, crying deeply just as Miri cried behind him.

Hal shuffled forward into reach, braving the flurry of tail blades that thrashed without aim. With one broken cry of effort, Hal released the air from his lungs and stabbed his glass dagger down at Marcus, and felt the jagged edge sink deep into flesh. One errant tail flashed in the corner of Hal's vision and cut deep across his face in one last gasp of violence. He felt his body collapse onto the floor, finally spent of all it could give.

The world was so eager to fall away, Hal barely felt it leave him. The last sensation he remembered was Miri's fingers gently closing around his own, before the night finally claimed its prize.

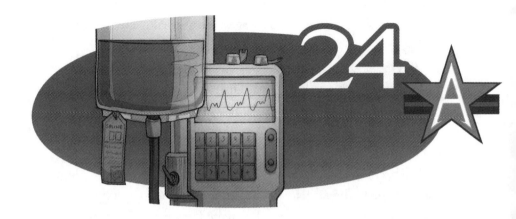

Is this what dying really feels like?

That question was the last thought to flow through Hal's mind, and it seemed stuck there in midstream, unable to move forward. There was never any pearly gate, no flash of light or sage old man to give a recitation of his sins. There was just the question. The single question that waited an eternity for an answer.

Beep.

A sound broke through the haze of timelessness.

Beep.

There it was again, and suddenly Hal realized he was having thoughts. Why was he thinking about having thoughts?

Beep.

Hal tried to open his eyes, to wake up, but he only partially succeeded. There was nothing to see, but he was clearly awake. He was thinking about being awake and how odd this felt.

Beep.

Something was covering his eyes, and yet even so they felt fused shut somehow.

His eyes were covered by bandages. He was lying down. He was alive.

Beep.

Why?

Hal wanted to cry, but he couldn't. Why was he alive? Was the universe playing some great cosmic game with him? He had given his world everything, and yet it demanded still more. The call of life always asked him for more.

The beeping accelerated as he felt his heartbeat speed up. He was in a hospital bed. The air felt still and cool to his half-working nerves. He tried shifting his weight a little, but halted when he felt the tug of tubes sticking into his body. There were tubes in his arm. There were tubes in his stomach. There were tubes in his nose.

He heard a sound like a gasp of surprise. Wherever he was, he wasn't the only person in the room. Hal heard footsteps shuffle from his right to his left and then further beyond, leaving the room entirely.

So much for pleasant introductions.

Hal felt his tail begin to stir, and it slowly opened its four sleepy eyes. It was a strange feeling. With his normal eyes blinded, Hal for the first time remembered that he still had these ones. Their sight didn't manifest in his mind with clear images, and it really couldn't be classified as the sensation of vision, but somehow they granted an intuitive feeling for his surroundings. He understood without seeing that this room was longer than it was wide, and he shared this space with other beds cradling other unconscious patients. This room felt dim. This room felt tired. But most of all, this room felt forgotten.

He lay there alone with his thoughts for some time before the sound of footsteps returned. These new ones were sharp, and each footfall echoed through the halls with a sense of purpose. Before long, the echo became a direct sound and the footsteps approached all the way to the front of his bed.

"Mister Adhil. You're awake."

The voice was terse, female, and confident in the way that only hard-won experience could provide. It seemed to be waiting for his response, and only after a fair amount of delay did Hal attempt to speak up himself, testing his vocal chords.

"Um, good . . . morning?"

"Good morning indeed. I'm surprised you can speak."

Hal heard the sound of metal brushing against plastic and the faint flutter of paper as charts and diagnostics were consulted. "I don't think we expected you to wake up today, if ever at all. Tell me, how do you feel?"

Right to business then.

"Tired. Like I'm trying to wake up from a dream that I can't remember." After a few moments without a response, he hazarded a question. "Are you my doctor? Am I really alive?"

"The answer is yes, to both." The clipboard clattered back into place at the end of the bed. "Forgive my abruptness, but it's not often that I get the opportunity to have these sorts of conversations. I'm Doctor Gretchen Kennedy, and this is room 13B of Bergmann Memorial Hospital. Long-term care."

The footsteps moved closer to him. Hal could sense the faint pressure of fingers poking at buttons on his monitors. "Your blood pressure is a little high for someone who's been in a coma, but everything else looks normal."

Hal's heart froze.

"Wait, I've been in a coma?" He dreaded the answer that was to come. "For how long?"

A minor sigh escaped the doctor's lips. "I'm afraid you've been asleep for quite some time. Let's see, a little over a year, it looks like." Her voice lowered a bit. "It's pretty rare to have anyone wake up like this. Most of the time, it's just a waiting game until the plug is pulled."

Hal tried to find more words, but they were slow in coming. So many thoughts were racing through his mind that it was difficult to settle on any

273

one, but eventually enough laps had been completed to allow the most pressing one to rise to the fore. "Why am I still alive?"

"Don't you mean 'how am I still alive'?"

"Sure." Hal shrugged, or tried to, at least. His nervous system felt like it had been rebuilt out of molasses. Arguing semantics could come later.

The doctor took a moment to formulate her explanation. "Statistically, you should have been dead on arrival. Every Dreamkeeper's physiology is different, but the brain can only survive without oxygen for so long before the damage is irreversible. That amount of time is usually measured in minutes, not hours. Survival rates as a function of time are very easily modeled." Dr. Kennedy's voice actually sounded annoyed. "You don't fit the model. Your life is an anomaly."

Anomaly. That word was an unwelcome one. A word the doctor hesitated to even speak. No one ever knew how to handle anomalies.

"I've been writing a paper on your condition, but even I don't really understand it. From all appearances, you have very late-stage cancer that's spread to every single part of your physiology. But, for some reason, it doesn't seem to be hurting anything." The doctor grumbled in dissatisfaction at her apparent lack of understanding. "It's the most widespread and comprehensive cellular mutation I've seen in a living body, and somehow it's benign. This collage of old cells and new cells—it's just what you are now."

"That's good, isn't it?" Hal didn't understand why she sounded so disappointed.

"I suppose."

Hal heard the sound of a pen clicking to life and the sharp scribble of notes on a clipboard.

"Your mutated cells appear to use a different respiration cycle than normal, allowing for greater anaerobic energy production. I've been trying to nail down the specific chemistry, but all the cell samples I take die quickly when removed from the host. It's remarkably infuriating."

Hal managed to tilt his head ever so slightly in a nod of understanding. It made some sense. He wouldn't have been able to wake up from being drowned if his cells couldn't somehow get by without oxygen, even if that meant going dormant for a long time. After his mind finished absorbing the information, he offered what he imagined to be a wry smile. "Sorry to be so inconvenient to you."

"It can't be helped." The pen clicked again and the clipboard clattered into place at the foot of his bed. The doctor sighed once more. "Now that you're awake, I have to make some calls and take care of some paperwork. I know it sounds cliché, but you should just take it easy. We have an awful lot of difficult physical therapy to look forward to." It sounded like the doctor was walking away.

"Wait." The footsteps halted in reaction to Hal's word. "What happened to Miri?"

"Miri?" The doctor sounded like she was thinking about who that name was attached to. "Oh. Yes. The purple-haired fox? She'll probably be dropping by soon." Hal heard the faintest of chuckles. "She visits you almost every weekend." Without another word, the footsteps faded into distant echoes down the hallway.

The news was such a shock to Hal that he simply lay there, stunned, for what felt like another year and a half.

Miri was alive?

No way.

This had to be a dream.

No person could ever get that lucky. No life could ever be so blessed. Could his?

Hal felt a familiar constricting sensation in his throat. He struggled against the inevitable pressure before finally giving way to a singular emotion that spilled out from his lungs.

The emotion wasn't relief. Relief is too transient. Relief is a cold glass of water on a hot summer day. When the heat fades, it fades as well.

The emotion wasn't happiness. Happiness is warm, soft, and intangible. This feeling was strong, massive, and overwhelming, like a cresting wave, reaching, peaking, and ready to crash onto shore.

The emotion Hal felt was joy.

Joy surged forth from his heart, flowed through his lips, and poured into the room, carried forward by the current of laughter. He laughed longer and harder than ever before, feeling the purity of those echoes reflect back and wash over him. For the first time in his life, Hal understood what laughter was always meant to be. Laughter is the celebration of joy.

Hal laughed until his body was exhausted. Even though he was blinded, the world felt brighter than it ever had before.

It wasn't long before his world became a lot busier as well. No Miri yet, but instead an army of medical assistants, perhaps drawn by his honest and vocal expressions of joy. There wouldn't be any of that here. This was a hospital.

Tests were run, samples were taken, interviews conducted. A lot of medical jargon and stern, disbelieving voices. What's two plus two? What year were you born? Do you feel dizzy? Nauseous? Is it difficult to think of words? Apparently he was supposed to be braindead, and the experts had a hard time accepting that he was not.

Amid the flurry, Hal learned more about his physical health. His muscles were atrophied from being in a bed for a long time. Between that and the old gunshot wounds, learning to walk was going to be difficult. Good thing he had some experience under his belt.

Both of his eyes were blinded. One had been smashed and one had been sliced, and neither one would be able to show him the world again. The bandages that covered them kept people from being shocked by his appearance.

The scarring on his body was extensive. Bullet wounds, lacerations, blunt trauma. Pristine and low mileage he was no longer. One young resident described it best when he remarked that Hal looked "pretty hard-core." It wasn't a description Hal was accustomed to, but it would do.

Somehow, none of these facts particularly worried Hal. What else could he do but laugh at it all? He was alive. It wasn't a perfect life, not even close, but it was something.

Maybe something was enough.

Eventually the nurses and doctors and residents finished their poking and prodding. They would be back, they promised, with more questions and more tests, but for now, Hal could relax in peace. His energy level was hardly up to the task of sustaining such attention. Simply laughing had drained him a good deal. The sound of the heart monitor was soothing, almost entrancing, and he flirted with unconsciousness as time passed without being measured.

Soon enough, the unmeasured future came to pass, and Hal felt the presence of someone else in the room. A warm hand gently placed itself on his own, and even without words, Hal knew who it belonged to.

"Hey, Hal."

Miri's soft voice crossed the space between them, sounding calm, but perhaps a bit sad. The quiet of the room told Hal that they were completely alone. It didn't seem like she knew that he was awake.

"Today's a special day for both of us, isn't it?"

Hal forced himself to remain still. He wanted to hear what she had to say without interrupting her. Hal honestly didn't even know what day it was.

"I finished my dissertation. If all goes well, I'll be 'Doctor Rodgers' soon." The great news was delivered with a wistful tone. "Heh. Doctor. I don't know if that title even means anything to me anymore."

Hal stopped himself from frowning at Miri's words. Her voice had a quality to it that he could feel but not quite place. The faintest trembling in her fingers telegraphed the subtle wavering that was soon to follow in her voice.

"You know, Hal, it's strange. I thought I'd be happy about this, but for some reason, the more things go back to normal, the more it feels like everything about my life is wrong."

Lost. That was the word Hal had been searching for. Miri's voice sounded lost.

"I always imagined that when I got to today, that Dr. Kincaid would be here to congratulate me. To tell me that I did a good job. He'd smile and say how I have a bright future ahead of me, and I think I would actually believe him."

She drew in a long, hesitant breath, taking a few precious seconds to gather more strength.

"And I thought that you would be there too. That we would cross this line together. I pictured Dr. Kincaid saying the same thing to you, but you'd just smirk and make some joke about how I did all the real work. We'd all laugh and smile and everything would feel right. Like I was actually meant to live that moment."

Miri sniffled. "But that's not what happened today, is it?" Her voice became more strained. "Spirits, Hal. How many times have we had this conversation? This is so stupid."

Hal almost spoke up to comfort Miri, to let her know that he was still here. But something stopped him before he could start. Why did he suddenly feel afraid?

"I know you can't hear me. But I just wish . . ." Hal felt the dull sensation of a droplet of water falling onto his forearm. "Sometimes I just wish that I could go back in time and remember that I was happy once. Back when we could just watch the stars together, and talk about the wind and mountains and snowflakes." Miri sniffled again, fighting against the strain in her throat. "Now that today has finally arrived, I honestly don't know what the hell I'm supposed to do with my life. Every day just feels like I'm going through the motions. Have you ever felt like that?"

Hal heard her laugh at her own words. "Of course you haven't. Every day you had a new sky to look up to. I always wanted to know what that would feel like, if only for a moment." Her hand squeezed his. "Everyone says that I need to accept it and move on. But they don't know what we've been through. The small moments we shared. What they meant to me. Not one person in the world understands who I am."

Hal finally broke his silence, and his tail bobbed to life, angling towards her. "I do."

"Holy!" Miri screamed in surprise and Hal heard the sound of a chair clattering to the floor. The faint tremor he felt through the ground meant that Miri fell too. Hal frowned, wondering if he was a little too cruel in surprising her like that.

"Miri? Are you ok?"

A fist responded with a firm punch to his side. "Hal? You asshole! You're awake? Were you listening this entire time?" Another fist landed home, even stronger than the last, followed by another.

"Ow. Sorry." One jab struck him in the gut, close to where some tubes were. "Ow! Hey! Don't mess up my happy tubes!"

"You're such a jerk!" She sobbed freely, striking with one last punch to his side. The attack soon turned into a hug, and Miri embraced Hal tightly, crying into his shoulder. Hal would have cried too if he was capable, but he settled for gently wrapping his free arm around his love. They stayed like that for a long time, allowing the gravity of their improbable reunion to fully sink in.

"Hal. Oh, Hal." She spoke his name over and over, as if repetition would prove that he wasn't an illusion. Her voice was muffled from being pressed so close. "I thought you were in a coma! The doctors told me every time that there wasn't much chance you would ever wake up!"

"Yeah, well, I'm an anomaly, apparently." Hal smirked. "I thought you were dead."

Miri pulled her head away, presumably to wipe at her eyes, as she struggled to compose herself. "I very nearly was."

"Then how?" Hal only got a few words into his question before her head was resting close again.

"You have terrible aim."

"I'm being serious."

"So am I!" Miri jabbed him much more gently this time. "The bullet hit me in the stomach, a few inches below my ribs. Right here." Her fingers guided his hand along her side to where a patch of her fur was missing. Hal's fingers felt the odd, soft flesh of raw scar tissue. "It missed my vital organs. That said, I nearly bled to death in that church, but the medics were on the scene super quick. A *lot* of medics."

Hal grimaced as he remembered the final minutes of that encounter. To him it had just happened yesterday, but Miri had a lot more time to recover from the traumatic events. Unpleasant as it was, this was his opportunity to learn about the aftermath. "So, what happened?"

Miri sighed, closing her fingers around his. "The troopers won, but I don't think even a dozen people made it out of that room alive. So many bodies that used to be people just . . . everywhere. All over." She tightened her grip. "Trooper ops always have paramedics on standby, and it felt like every single unit in the city was there to triage the casualties. It was all over the news for weeks."

Hal felt her face nuzzle into his shoulder. "All it took was a few emergency blood transfusions, two surgeries, and way too much time in the hospital to get me back on my feet again. You know. Easy stuff compared to what you're used to."

"Sounds like."

Miri's voice was harder to hear. "I thought I lost you forever, Hal. Are you sure this is real?"

Hal snorted. "Not at all. I'm probably hallucinating."

"Is that so?" A little edge of mischief worked its way into Miri's words. He felt her head shift, moving up to plant a kiss on his neck.

"Ehhh, still not convinced."

A finger poked the side of his face. "Hmph. Nice try, but that's all you get. We're hardly alone."

Hal pretended to be disappointed. "Hospital wards don't do it for you?"

"Sadly, no."

"Well, there's one date idea out the window."

The two of them laughed at the joke, still trying to come to grips with the new reality they had both earned. Hal didn't have enough energy to keep up the banter, which seemed to suit Miri just fine. They lay together in silence, enjoying each other's company all the same.

Unfortunately, they weren't able to savor the moment for too long before more footsteps came down the hall. These ones sounded heavy. Boots marching in lockstep. Hal didn't need to hear the word to understand who was coming.

"Troopers." Miri's voice sank low, and she pulled away from Hal to sit back down in the chair beside him.

The loud boots entered the room, breaking the calm silence they'd been enjoying. Some of the boots stopped there, but another pair continued approaching with a sharp sense of purpose. "Ah, Miss Rodgers. I didn't know you were here." The new voice sounded imperious and overbearing.

"Prosecutor Graham."

Apparently these two knew each other, and from the iciness of Miri's tone, it was not exactly a pleasant relationship.

"I need to speak to Mister Adhil."

"Go right on ahead, but I'm not leaving the room, so don't even try to make me."

The prosecutor sighed as if weighing whether to force the issue. He must have decided to let it be, because his next sentence addressed Hal directly.

"Halcyon Adhil, I am here to inform you that you are under arrest for crimes against the city of Anduruna. The list of charges is rather extensive, I'm afraid."

Hal grumbled. "Last I checked, I'm lying in this bed because I tried to help the city. What the hell am I being charged with?"

"Murder. Aiding and abetting a domestic terrorist. Power use. Illegal possession of a firearm. Many more items along that vein. Any one of them could put you away for a long time." The voice seemed to take immense satisfaction in reciting Hal's so-called crimes. "You're in an awful lot of trouble."

"Gee, I've never been in trouble with the cops before," Hal quipped dryly, unable to hold back the snark.

"You don't seem to be taking this very seriously."

"And you don't seem like a very pleasant person."

"Hal."

Miri chastised his tone, but it was difficult for Hal to keep the edge out of his voice. He smiled a false smile towards the sound of the prosecutor. "Thanks for the friendly notice. So, do I get to talk to a defense lawyer now?"

"Oh, no. Not at all." The prosecutor laughed, and Hal decided that this gloating sound wasn't what laughter was supposed to be. "Your guilt was determined by the courts many months ago. Sentencing simply hasn't been carried out because of your medical condition."

"What?" Despite his physical weakness, Hal felt a fire begin to burn inside of him. "That's not fair. A defendant is supposed to be able to confront his accusers. You can't just convict me while I'm in a coma."

"Terrorists like you don't get the same rights afforded to normal citizens."

"I'm not a terrorist!" Hal's exertion strained his weak lungs, causing him to cough violently. Miri's gentle but firm touch made sure he leaned back in bed, preventing him from overextending himself.

"It's true." Miri spoke up for Hal. "Hal was the one who helped stop Marcus! He should be thanked for what he did, not condemned!"

"That's quite enough from you, Miriel. The only reason we didn't banish you for power violations is because you agreed to cooperate with the investigation and prosecution. But you've played that card already, and it would only take one word from me to have you arrested as well."

Prosecutor Graham cleared his throat, clearly not afraid to throw his weight around as he pleased. "Just because the two of you may have done some admirable things does not erase the crimes committed. We are a city of law and order, and those who violate our laws will be punished accordingly."

Footsteps paced in front of Hal, and he pictured the prosecutor wearing a smug expression as he clasped his hands behind his back. "You have no idea how much of a shit-storm you created, Adhil. How many good men lost their lives because of everything that happened. Our finest company of shock troopers was obliterated in that confrontation, and we lost many more people in the weeks that followed as we hunted down the last remaining elements of your brother's little insurrection. Those soldiers will never be brought back to life, and someone has to answer for their deaths."

Hal was not pleased with the way they were being treated. It was only due to exhaustion that he failed to raise his voice. "So I'm the last loose end, huh?"

"Indeed." The prosecutor paused in his pacing. The volume of his voice seemed to address Hal directly, instead of reciting a monologue into the room. "Your brother is dead. Even if we had tried to save his life, it would have been too late. You stabbed him through the heart." Hal frowned. "Every known associate of Marcus is either dead or rotting in prison, and the meteor shards that we recovered are safely secured from the public and renegades like you. Rest assured, we won't allow more citizens to make the same mistakes you have."

Mistake? No. His life wasn't a mistake. The meteor wasn't a mistake. This petty man would never understand.

"So what are you going to do to him?" Miri asked.

"Lucky for you it's an election year, and the Viscount is trying to project a softer image. Instead of execution, it will be easier for everyone if you merely disappear. Leave Anduruna and never return."

"Banishment?" Hal struggled to untangle the knot of conflicting emotions that balled up inside his heart.

"Yes. It's the standard punishment for grade-one power violations. Trust me, you're getting off a lot easier than I think you should. As soon as you're discharged from the hospital, your citizenship profile will be deleted, and all of your assets will be seized by the state. You will cease to exist. You will leave the city and you will not be permitted to return. If you do, the consequences will be severe."

"You can't do this to him!" Miri argued. "After all he's sacrificed, you're just going to reject him?"

"Would you rather we shoot him instead?"

"This isn't right!"

"It doesn't matter. It's the law." The prosecutor's voice had a finality to it that indicated the issue was no longer up for debate. "Now silence yourself, unless you want to suffer the same fate."

"I won't!" Miri didn't relent. "If you're going to banish Hal, then you'll have to banish me too!"

"Calm yourself, Miss Rodgers." Graham's voice became intensely cold and serious. "This isn't the sort of choice to be made lightly in the heat of passion. There is no undoing it once it's been done."

"I told you my answer. I have nothing more to say to you, Mister Graham."

"Miri, you don't have to—" Hal started to protest, but he was quickly cut short.

"Hal, shush." Miri gave his hand a determined squeeze. "After all we went through to find each other, I'm not letting you disappear again."

"So be it," the prosecutor grumbled to himself. "We don't need a dissenter like you causing trouble, anyways."

"Wait." Hal got the impression that the man was preparing to leave. "Before you go, I have one last question."

"What?"

"What date is it today?"

"Excuse me?" The prosecutor sounded peeved by Hal's mundane question.

"The date. Today. What is it?"

Repeating the inquiry only seemed to irritate the man more. "It's April 15."

Hal felt the beginnings of another laugh stir in his soul, and he was unable to hold it back. Soon he was laughing in earnest, filling the room with the sound of joy.

"And why do you find Tax Day so funny?"

Hal managed to slow his laugh long enough to speak. "No, it's not that. I don't think you'd understand. I'm just happy to be alive."

"You awakened are all the same." Graham's voice sounded grim and spiteful. "You have no respect. This city is better off without you. You might be happy now, but when you're alone in the wilderness, cold, hungry, and lost, you'll wish you could come back."

A smile emerged on Hal's lips, undaunted by the warning. "You're welcome to believe whatever you like. It doesn't change the way I feel."

That seemed to bring an end to the conversation, and the footsteps of Prosecutor Graham stomped out of the room. As silence returned, Hal felt his body relax. The smile didn't go away. Happiness was not the normal reaction to a situation like this, but Hal decided that he just wasn't meant to be a normal person. He certainly was pretty bad at it.

Miri remained with Hal, letting her guard back down now that they were left alone. She laid her head next to his and snuggled close. For a long while, the two of them merely enjoyed the sensation of being together. Being alive. The beeping of his heart monitor reminded him every second that yes, he was here. Life was here. Love was here. He had everything he needed. Everything else, well, those were just minor details.

After a time, Hal finally recovered enough energy to speak. He almost didn't want to break the silence, but the words on his mind had to be spoken. "Thank you, Miri."

"Mmmm?" Her muffled voice sounded like she had fallen half-asleep. "For what?"

"You know. For staying with me. For everything. I don't know how I ever got so lucky."

Miri nodded sleepily, brushing her cheek against Hal's shoulder. "I think we're both lucky."

"I suppose that's true."

"Mmm." Miri placed a hand on his chest, lifting her head slightly. "Hey, Hal?"

"Yes, Miri?"

She gave him a light kiss on the cheek.

"Happy birthday."

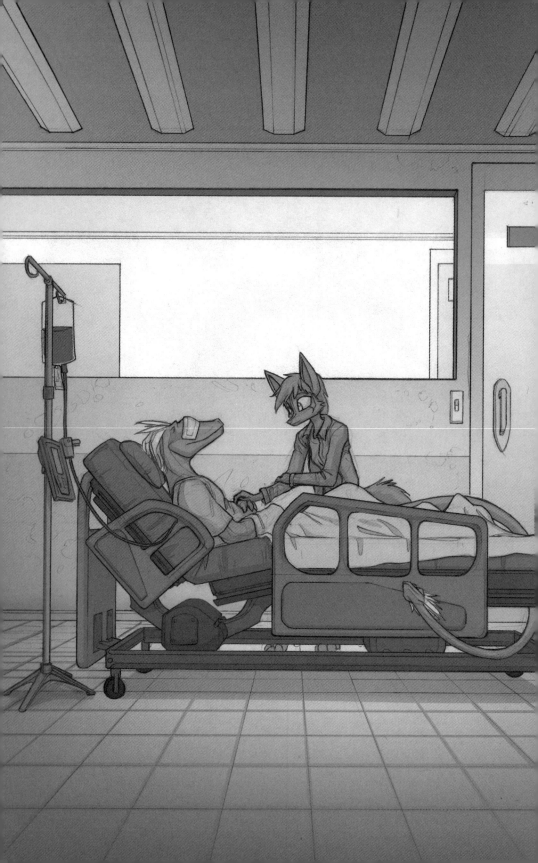

25

Hal balanced the chisel delicately between his fingers, sensing the subtle shifting of its weight as he adjusted to the perfect angle. With a patient but firm tap, he hammered the end with his mallet and chipped away the last few fragments of stone. A quick burst of air from his lips pushed aside the dust and laid bare the final cut of the "L". He used his fingers to trace out the letter and verify that all was as he'd imagined it.

After months stuck inside the hospital, getting outside was quite literally a breath of fresh air. The cool evening wind had a humid weight that lent a calm silence to his solemn task. Saying goodbye was never easy, but at least this time Hal could do it on his own terms.

He moved his hand over all the letters in turn, examining the sum total of his long efforts: MARCUS ANDREI ADHIL. His brother's tombstone was finally complete.

"Hey." Miri's voice emerged from behind his shoulder, and Hal instinctively looked up, even though he couldn't see her.

"Hey, Miri."

Hal allowed his fingers to dwell on the cold stone surface. Marcus's body was long since disposed of by the authorities, but after a great deal of argument, he won the time to craft a marker for Marcus and Vanir, here in the Calypsa cemetery. The new headstones rested near the older ones for the rest of Hal's family, and through supervised visits, Hal had been able to carve the new names into place himself. It seemed only fitting that he should be the one to memorialize the lives that ended by his hand.

"I think it's really nice of you to make these for them," Miri offered with a sober tone. A warm hand rested gently on his shoulder. "You did a good job, Hal."

"Thanks." Hal smiled wistfully, letting the bittersweet moment sink in now that his task was done. Miri must have sensed something in his tone.

"Are you sad about what happened?"

Hal chuckled lightly in response. "I don't know. A little, I guess, but . . ." He struggled to find the right words. "It's hard to explain. Despite all that happened, and all that he did, I think I finally realize that I still loved him, Miri." Hal let his fingers linger on the last letter. "Marcus may have been misguided in his methods, and he might have let too much hate spill into his heart over the years, but you know, he never stopped fighting. He never stopped fighting until the very end."

Miri's hand gripped Hal a bit tighter, giving him a soft gesture of comfort.

"He saw the city for everything that it denied us, and he raged against it. He wouldn't accept anything less than true freedom. I can't help but love him for that." Hal placed his hand on the earth beneath him, soaking in its cool and fortifying touch. "I only hope that now he has found the peace he so desperately craved his whole life."

"I think he did," Miri said confidently. From the way the sound shifted ever so slightly, Hal imagined she must have been nodding as she said so.

"Yeah," Hal agreed. "Maybe we all did." He stretched one hand out to the space at his side, and Miri was quick to grab it firmly and help Hal back up from his crouch. He grunted at the effort, but soon found his shaky balance beneath him with a few steady breaths.

From the pace the air had been dropping in temperature, it felt like it was nearly sundown. Most people would find it hard to see or work in the dark, but Hal was surprised how quickly he adjusted to using his other senses to navigate the world. In a way, the world had grown larger, not smaller, after his struggles and injuries. He could hear subtle sounds from across a large room. He could feel the slightest changes of texture with his touch. In fact, because he couldn't anticipate his surroundings beyond his direct experiences, every moment had a hidden delight that surprised him.

Right now, that pleasure was the sound of the first insect of the night chirping to life. It sat somewhere in the grass beyond, alone, calling out in the hopes that someone might find it. That tiny creature had no idea that Hal could hear its cries. Perhaps it felt like it was entirely alone. Perhaps it would never know that Hal was actually right here, keeping it company. Still, it continued to sing, and Hal continued to listen.

What a beautiful sound. What a delicate little moment they shared.

"It really is a nice night."

Miri slid closer to him, helping steady his body. "You're right. The stars are starting to come out. The sky is really clear now."

Hal laughed, letting the warmth of that emotion run its full course.

"What's so funny?" Miri didn't understand why Hal was laughing at the sky.

"I was just thinking." Hal pulled Miri closer and gave her an affectionate hug. "In spite of all the troubles in my life, all the terrible things that happened to my family, to Marcus, to us . . ." Hal shook his head. "All of it led here, to this place. This moment. This next fresh breath of air."

Hal inhaled deeply and held the air before slowly letting it leak back into the world. "It's not so bad, is it?"

"No." Miri rubbed her cheek against his shoulder. "I suppose it isn't that bad at all." She laughed a little herself, understanding what Hal meant. "It's definitely not what I expected, but I guess that's just how life goes sometimes."

A new voice interrupted them both from somewhere behind. "I'm sorry, Mister Adhil. Miss Rodgers." It was a familiar voice by now, after being under guard for so many months. "It's time to go. The lieutenant is waiting in the groundcar."

"Thank you, Nik. You have good timing. I think we're all done here." Miri helped turn Hal around and guide him back down the path.

The soldier's voice, still cracking slightly with the awkwardness of youth, sounded relieved. "Good. I hoped I wouldn't have to interrupt you before it arrived." Hal couldn't see the gesture, but he knew the green recruit was waving the two of them along. "This way."

With Miri's help, Hal was able to work his way down the shallow hill with only a slightly halting limp. It was likely that they would never set foot in that cemetery again, now that the day of their discharge had officially arrived. That was just fine though. Cemeteries weren't places one should linger for long.

"What took you so long?" Another new voice, this one sharp and commanding.

"Why so impatient, Lieutenant?" Hal smirked. "Did you get passed over for promotion again while I was limping out of the cemetery?"

"Screw you, Adhil."

"Good to see you too, Scott."

"You're hilarious." The tone in the officer's voice was anything but amused. "Just get in the damned groundcar. The sooner I can finally be rid of you, the sooner I can get back to doing real work." The leader of their guard detail was as cheerful as always. As much as some things always changed, other things stayed the same.

Miri stepped in first, before helping pull Hal up into the passenger compartment. He nearly hit his head on the ceiling, but her experienced and steady touch held him low enough to clear it with just a little room to spare. After they both took their seats, Hal felt the entire carriage shake from side to side as Nik clambered in to take a seat across from them. A heavy metallic thud told Hal that the trooper's rifle, a mere formality at this point, was laid to rest against the other wall of the carriage.

"It's going to be a long ride, sir." Nik's softer voice seemed ill-fitting for his large frame and the profession he chose. "You should probably get comfortable."

"Damn it, Private!" The lieutenant clambered into the front of the groundcar with a huff, clattering the reins of the manekale beast waiting to pull them onward. "How many times do I have to tell you? Stop talking to the prisoners! We pay you to be their guard, not their friend!"

"Sorry, sir."

A violent lurch spurred the groundcar into motion, and just like that, they were on their way. Nik dutifully fell silent, though not without indulging in a small sigh of frustration. Hal felt for the kid, but somehow he sensed that Private Hobbes here would get through life just fine.

The groundcar clattered and creaked as they trotted through the streets of Anduruna one last time. The sounds of the city were muffled and muted when heard through armored walls. Already the places Hal knew seemed like they were becoming memories, fading quietly into his past. The day didn't end with a climax or a dramatic finish. There was no bold underline marking the transition from citizen to banished wanderer. There was only the soothing rocking of the compartment where he rested.

The echo of hooves bounced back through the walls, telling Hal they must have been passing underneath one of the entrances of the perimeter aqueduct. He leaned his head against the side of the carriage and felt the small tremors pass through his body before the tunnel gave way once again to open ground. The sunset was probably behind the Starfall Mountains right now, giving them a sharp, dark outline in front of a golden sky. He couldn't look out a window and see the sight for himself, but Hal still had a clear picture in his mind.

Miri's fingers snaked around his own, sliding into place with a soft, affectionate touch. She didn't say anything, but Hal knew that this was just as big a moment for her as it was for him. Perhaps even more so. He returned her grasp with a firm squeeze of support, and she slid closer to rest her head against his shoulder. They each settled in for the long trip by resting together, sharing body heat and the cadence of breathing.

At some point, whether seconds or hours later, Hal drifted off to sleep. What his destination was, when they would reach it, and what he was going to do once they got there were mysteries to him. The soldiers never bothered to tell him, and in all honesty, it wouldn't make any difference. Hal slept soundly with Miri beside him, and the passage of time was lost.

The groundcar rocked a bit, waking Hal from his quickly forgotten slumber. He was unsure of the time until Lieutenant Fuentes banged his fist on the wall from the driver's compartment up front. "Private! Prisoners! Wake up!" The officer's voice echoed faintly through the steel. "We're here!"

Miri stirred, lifting her head. "Good morning to you too."

Nikolas's armor clattered as he shuffled to life; he'd likely been just as asleep as everyone else before the lieutenant interrupted things. Metal dragged across wood as the rifle ended up back in his hands. A cough failed to conceal the sleepy sound of the soldier's yawn. "Looks like we made it. This way, sirs."

The car lurched again as Nik stepped out, and Miri gently guided Hal up from his seat and through the door down onto the waiting earth beyond. His feet were standing on mixed clumps of dirt and grass, and the air felt invigorating with the weight of unevaporated dew.

"Where are we?" Miri asked.

"That's not for me to share." The lieutenant seemed to derive some cruel satisfaction from not filling them in. They could be anywhere, but Hal had to guess they were somewhere out near the Eridu delta, since he wasn't standing on a mountain or in a desert. There were worse places to end up.

"Halcyon Adhil. Miriel Rodgers." The voice took on an overly official bearing. "You are hereby discharged from your custody. If you ever return to Anduruna again, your lives will be forfeit." Hal pictured the lieutenant smiling as he gave the address. "Do you understand?"

Hal couldn't help but laugh at the whole affair. "Sure. Yeah. Go on home, Scott."

"Hmph." Hal heard the manekale attached to the groundcar shuffle a bit, clattering its harness. "Come on, Hobbes. We're outta here."

Nik stepped close, offering them a more sincere goodbye. "Take care of yourselves, sirs. I don't think we'll have the opportunity to meet again."

Hal stretched one hand out towards the sound of the voice, and he was pleased that the gesture was returned with a full handshake. "You might be right, Private. Take care of yourself as well. Don't let the jackal over there boss you around too much. He's all bark and no bite."

Miri laughed and offered her own warm words. "I appreciate all the company you gave us, Nikolas. I won't forget you."

"Thank you, ma'am."

"Private!" Nik's grunt of amusement was quickly drowned out by more orders. "How many times do I have to tell you! Get back in the groundcar before I personally kick your ass all the way back to Anduruna!"

"Coming, sir." The faintest twinges of disrespect slipped their way into the final word.

Heavy bootsteps crunched the grass behind them before clambering up into the vehicle and disappearing behind the heavy thud of a door being closed. It didn't take long for the groundcar to march away, towed by the powerful gait of the animal that pulled it. The sound of those wheels creaking and rolling faded to silence, and soon both Hal and Miri found themselves entirely alone.

They stood together, holding hands for a quiet moment before curiosity got the better of Hal. "So, where are we, Miri?"

"Um . . ." Miri's weight and sound shifted around, as if she was giving the area a full survey. "It looks like we're a long way from the city. I can't even see the tower from here. Lots of fallow pasture and gently rolling hills."

Hal nodded. "Is there a hill nearby we can walk to?"

"Yeah." Miri's hand started to pull Hal in one direction. "This way."

They marched through untrimmed grass for a few minutes, climbing a gentle slope to reach the nearest peak. As Hal reached the crest of the hill, he felt the air grow a little less cool. Warming rays of sunlight kissed the surroundings, and he could predict Miri's words before she even spoke them.

"Oh, spirits!" Miri was taken aback by the sight. "The sunrise!" Her fingers squeezed Hal's own. "We're close to the ocean. The light is reflecting off the water. Millions of sparkles. Just like the snow." Hal knew that she was smiling as bright as the morning. "It's so beautiful."

"I know."

Miri shifted her weight, turning towards him. "But, you can't even see . . ." Her words trailed off, too late to hide her disbelieving tone.

Hal laughed and let go of Miri's hand. Reaching up, he felt his fingers brush against the gauze bandages wrapped around his eyes. He took a few seconds to feel out the knot that held them in place, but it didn't take long before it was loosened by his careful work. Hal pulled the bandages away and felt the sunlight and the wind wash over his whole face for the first time. The air felt sharp and energizing as it touched his scarred flesh, but there was no pain. Hal's grip relaxed, allowing a short gust of wind to pull the gauze completely free from his possession. The fabric drifted away with the current, carried off to places unknown.

Miri didn't recoil or gasp in surprise at his appearance, but instead waited patiently for the answer he had yet to give her.

"Hey, Miri."

"Yes, Hal?" She chuckled at the reversal of the ordinary.

"Would you like to know what the sunrise really looks like?" Hal opened his hand again, waiting for her to take it.

Her fingers warmly wrapped back around his own. "Ok."

With the troopers gone, there was no one left to stop them from sharing the moment as it was meant to be shared. Miri awakened her power, and the image of the sunrise as she saw it was what Hal saw as well. Her heartbeat was superimposed upon his own. Indeed, the sun was just now cresting over the ocean that sat not far away, and orange flashes of light reflected gently across the shifting surface. Hal smiled at the sight.

"Are you ready?"

Miri nodded.

Hal allowed his own power to come to life. With their senses now linked, the orange sunrise that drifted gently above the horizon finally became what it always was.

An explosion of color poured forth, reflecting off of everything in creation. Prismatic hues that had no name scorched the morning itself, welcoming it with brilliance. Shades of red, orange, purple, and gold bounced off of the water and bent the air. The sky beyond the horizon became deeper, wider, and full of shimmering life. The weight of glory buckled Miri's knees, and suddenly it was Hal who supported her as she took in the true majesty of her world for the very first time.

"Oh, Hal." Her voice was breathless as water welled in her eyes. "Is this?" Her voice caught, and she swallowed, blinking away tears. "Is this what you see?"

"Every morning."

She sobbed happily, absorbing the warmth of that sunrise alongside him. "It's the most beautiful sight I've ever seen."

Hal laughed deeply, letting that celebration carry out into the wind. "Well, I think you're in luck, Miri. Tomorrow there will be another sunrise just like this one."

Miri laughed as well. Something was different about this one, though. It had a weight to it. A wholeness. It wasn't a "laugh at Hal's joke" type of laugh. It was more. It was the laugh that Miri always wanted to have, but could never unleash until now. The laugh that celebrated life itself. "I think I'd like to see that one too."

Hal saw himself through Miri's eyes as he angled his face towards her and grinned. "We can see the entire world together, Miri. That is, if you'll be my eyes."

Miri pretended to give the proposal serious consideration. "Hmmm." The hum turned into a wide smile. "I'll be yours if you'll be mine."

Hal nodded. "It's a deal."

Miri punched Hal playfully. "That's the best line you got? 'It's a deal'? You could have said something really romantic instead of really lame."

"Haha, sorry." Hal scratched at the edge of one eye. "I'll work on that."

"You better."

Miri leaned forward to give him a light kiss. They watched the sunrise together, sharing a warm embrace. Once the beautiful sphere of light cleared the horizon completely, Miri spoke up. "So, where do we go from here?"

Hal shook his head. "That's a great question. You know, I'm not really sure."

"Me either."

"Well, I'm glad we're in agreement."

They shared another laugh together before Miri held Hal tighter. "I've never been this far from the city before. I lived my whole life in the shadow of those walls, but now we're so far away, I can't see them at all." She ran one hand through her windswept hair. "It's exciting, but it's also a little scary, knowing we can never go back."

Hal returned the hug. "Truth be told, Miri, I'm a little scared too. So much about our lives has changed." He felt his lips curl into a joyous grin. "But you know what?"

Miri looked up, watching Hal smile with honest and unrestrained love.

"Somehow, I get the feeling that everything will turn out ok."

SPECIAL THANKS AND ACKNOWLEDGMENTS

This book was made possible by the generous contributions of hundreds of different people who believed in bringing *The Wayward Astronomer* to print. This first-edition printing would not be in your hands without the support of the following individuals:

Gretchen Kennedy
Scott Fuentes
Laura Licciardello and Alex Mitchell
Brettly S.
Blue M. Paws
Lloyd Issel
Trevor Rudd
Sinclair Silverfang
Marty z-c
Nick Capen
Nelson
Taridium
Jayce Rebel
Robert Mullins
Bagaveev Corp
Naquadrea
Brandon Litt

Brook B. Poppington
Patrick Gray
Ben Ericson
Erin D.
Tanara Kuranov
Jon HH
Adam Davis
Jeremy Banks
Chimera Dragonfang
Apah Chan
Achiah
Iselwyr
Alex Lanzendorf
Michael "M5" Valant
Amy and Greg Baskin
Jacqueline LeClair
Rutger van den Heuvel
Alexander "Red" Havermann
Matthew Hergott
Anita Solanki
Elizabeth Johnston
Karl Pierre Belanger
Erik Anderson
Trenton Arney
Matthias Berghöfer-Palmen
Daniel Hastings
David Hawes
Laura Collins and Randy Baker
Kari
McCrazy
Kourtney Harms
Umbre Rygone

Connor Davidson
Ganer
Nathanal Johnson
Eric Mandia
Nathan Hall
Lance Whalen
Equestrian Wyvern
Stephen Olberholtzer
Fallenaltair
D.Q. Chrissy
Sharyn Hinchcliffe
Darkspeeds
Alexander Snyder (GreySky—God of the Machine)
Garrett Simpson
Arno "DD" Smet
Chris (Faestre) Delzell
Joshua Plair (BoomerTheTiger)
Kelli Panthaky
Rikke and Thomas Plesner Skovby

In addition, I would like to thank David Lillie for the tremendous effort he has put into making The Wayward Astronomer what it is. Not only has he created fantastic illustrations to bring this story to life, but this tale would not exist had he not spent years developing the Dreamkeepers universe that serves as its setting. I would also like to thank my editor, Kate Ankofski, and all the good people at Mill City Press for helping me produce a beautiful book.

Lastly, I want to thank all of my beta readers who shared in the journey alongside me as we discovered this story together. Your feedback and encouragement made this book possible, and I don't think I could have come this far without you.

Never stop dreaming.

Would you like to explore more of Anduruna? *The Wayward Astronomer* is only one small part of the ever-expanding Dreamkeepers universe. Your next adventure is waiting for you at:

www.dreamkeeperscomic.com

Also, please feel free to explore the official site for The Wayward Astronomer for more artwork, merchandise, and updates on events that may be happening in your area:

www.thewaywardastronomer.com

Thanks for reading!

FERMENTAE

Hands down the most popular adult beverage in the Dreamworld, fermentae can be carefully crafted to retain almost any flavor. Caramels, fruits, vegetables, freshly tilled earth—any substance containing moisture can be sapped through the unique brewing process.

Derived from diony seeds, great care must be taken when raising the plant itself. Voraciously consuming every bead of wetness in their environments, the liquid is absorbed and stored in their root system, comprised of one hyper-porous seed. The diony plant never grows substantially larger; everything is stored, ever more pressurized, in the modestly proportioned seed. When the plant dies, the stem wilts and detaches from the seed, releasing all of the stored moisture in a spectacular spray.

The culminating spray of nectar, or fermentae, has a pleasurably intoxicating effect when ingested. The first hapless Dreamkeepers to learn this died horrible deaths, as the moisture was drained from their bodies over the weeks by the tiny seeds growing within them. However, some determined soul soon discovered a method for making the nectar safe to drink.

By either boiling or freezing fermentae, the microscopic seeds are destroyed. Each technique gives the fermentae a different flavor. Diony can grow in fruit juice, coffee, saltwater—anything that contains moisture. The nectar will derive flavor from the moisture it is grown in.

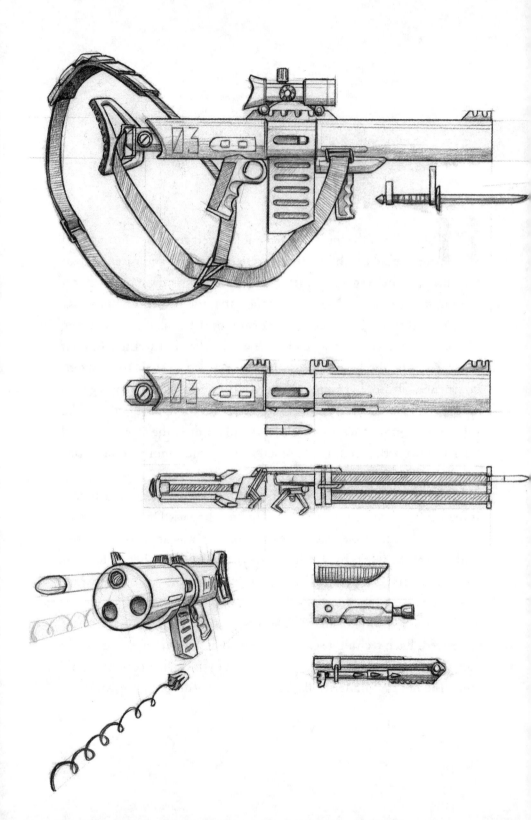

SPRINGERS

The earliest projectile weapons in Anduruna were variations on slings and slingshots, firing rounded ball-shaped projectiles. Eventual innovation led a crossbow-like design, where a flat horizontal piece of wood would be winched back, and then trigger-released to "slap" the projectile forward. A barrel was soon added for a modicum of accuracy. This wasn't a high-powered weapon, but eventually more advanced ways of propelling the ball through the barrel were developed, culminating in the springer cartridge.

The springer rifles of today use hyper-compressed springs stored in cartridges to propel projectiles at high velocity. When triggered, the cartridge is quickly knocked open. The spring rockets forward, propelling the round of ammunition towards its target. Side slats on the rifle barrel are designed to sling the spring out and down, clearing the weapon immediately for another cartridge. Ammunition cartridges are speed-loaded into the weapon through cylinder clips for an impressive rate of fire. Manufactured exclusively for use by the Anduruna City Guard, private citizens do not have access to spring weapons. Springers are capable of being extremely lethal, even after their heavy needle-shaped rounds penetrate walls or other barriers. Any contemporary citizen of Anduruna risking a powers infraction, or any major infraction against City Central Authority, will find themselves facing the full deadly power of an armed shock trooper squad.

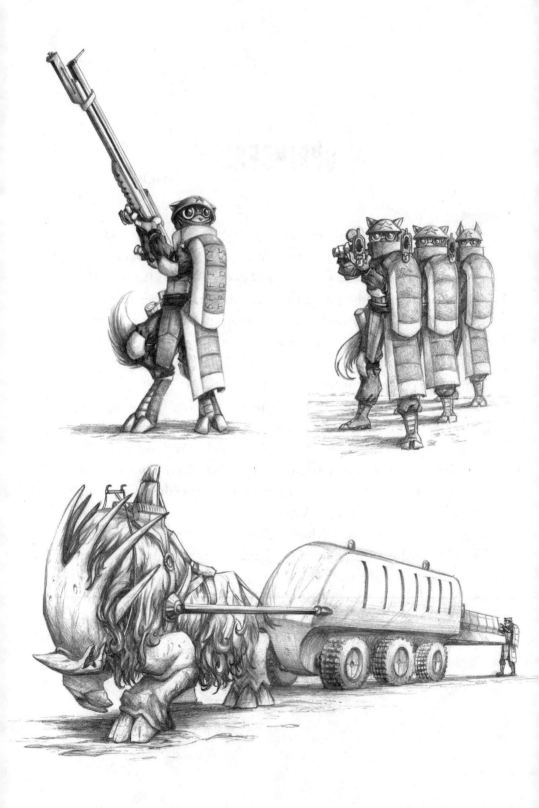

SAFETY TROOPERS

The seven districts of Anduruna usually rely on their own local police forces to investigate crimes and maintain day-to-day law and order. However, when it comes to enforcing the federal laws of Anduruna, especially the ban on power use, City Central Authority is not afraid to send the safety troopers to eliminate potential threats.

Lethally armed and heavily armored with the best military technology available, few Dreamkeepers on the wrong side of the law are able to stand toe to toe with a trooper squad and survive. Troopers are trained specifically for hunting down and neutralizing power-awakened Dreamkeepers, and their discipline under fire ensures that every raid is a successful raid.

One preferred tactic of trooper squads is to arrange groups of soldiers into a firing line, where the overlapping armor plates of each soldier create a nearly impervious wall. Concentrated volleys of springer fire are quick to eliminate most threats, even when they have the advantage of light or medium cover.

The debate rages on as to whether the safety troopers are noble heroes that protect the public from danger, or merely an oppressive and violent symbol of the force of City Central Authority. However, there is one fact that people from both sides can agree on: anyone who receives a visit from the troopers is not going to have a good day.